Howard Jacobson was born in Manchester in 1942. He was educated at Cambridge where he subsequently taught for a while, and has spent several years in Australia, lecturing at Sydney University and working in publishing. He has, of course, taught English at a polytechnic. He is co-author – with Wilbur Sanders – of *Shakespeare's Magnanimity*. *Coming From Behind* is his first novel.

He now lives with his Australian wife in Cornwall and London.

Coming From Behind

Howard Jacobson

BLACK SWAN

COMING FROM BEHIND

A BLACK SWAN BOOK 0 552 99063 9

Originally published in Great Britain by
Chatto & Windus/The Hogarth Press

PRINTING HISTORY

Chatto & Windus/The Hogarth Press edition
published 1983
Black Swan edition published 1984
Black Swan edition reprinted 1984
Black Swan edition reprinted 1985

Copyright © Howard Jacobson 1983

This book is set in 11/12 pt Century

Black Swan Books are published by Transworld Publishers Ltd.,
Century House, 61-63 Uxbridge Road, Ealing, London W5 5SA,
in Australia by Transworld Publishers (Aust.) Pty. Ltd.,
26 Harley Crescent, Condell Park, NSW 2200, and in New
Zealand by Transworld Publishers (N.Z.) Ltd., Cnr. Moselle
and Waipareira Avenues, Henderson, Auckland.

Made and printed in Great Britain by the
Guernsey Press Co. Ltd., Guernsey, Channel Islands.

for
ANITA & MAX
and for
ROSALIN

1

'That's eet, that's eet! Yo'm found eet, yo' bugger! Yis, that's eet!'

Lynne Shorthall, mature and by all accounts responsive student from Cradley Heath, on her way to collect the degree her husband never wanted her to study for, calls in at the Polytechnic in order to show off her ceremonial finery and say a last goodbye and thank you to her lecturers and tutors, and stays a little longer than expected in Sefton Goldberg's room.

Sefton Goldberg, on all fours above her, his knees and elbows glued with the perspiration of effort and anxiety to the polytechnic linoleum, as naked as Noah but for the academic gown and hood which Mrs Shorthall insists he wears, it being degree day, hopes to God he has remembered to lock his door. While Lynne Shorthall wrinkles up her nose and bites the air and gargles Black Country familiarities, Sefton Goldberg can think of nothing but the position of the little metal nipple on his Yale lock. Is it up or is it down? He thinks he can recall depressing it, but what if some fault in the mechanism, a loose fitting or some over-zealous spring is at this very moment urging and encouraging it up again? Is he imagining things or can he actually hear his door unlocking itself? What he would like is to get up and check, but such alarmism is inconsistent with his idea of manliness; and he is not well placed even to take the rudimentary precaution of stealing a glance. Now that his gown has ridden up his back and hangs over his face, he is as blind as a school photographer,

7

and it is his other end, anyway — hence the degree of his anxiety and vulnerability — which confronts the door. Simultaneously recalling what he has read of the Japanese girl who has the gift of sight in her nose and the joke about the patient who swallows a glass eye, Sefton wonders if by sheer effort of will he can make himself see through that part of himself which he has never seen — achieve, quite literally, tunnel vision. He does not, on this occasion at least, make medical history, but the amount of muscular flexing and stiffening required merely to *imagine* an anal squint makes Lynne Shorthall noisily, nasally happy, and causes her to prolong her last goodbye and thank you. Sefton's own happiness is kept within reasonable bounds by a sharp stabbing pain in his bowels, and the sudden recollection that he has experienced an identical discomfort in identical circumstances once before.

He was younger then, and in another country. And wet-eyed, smudgy-featured, orthopaedic-looking Helen Burns only resembled Lynne Shorthall in that she too was not someone Sefton Goldberg would willingly — supposing him to have had a choice in the matter — have invited on to the floor of his office.

How they got there, these women he did not really care for but who could by no means be said to have coerced him, was a mystery which Sefton, being of a fatalistic faith, did not trouble himself to solve. It was a bit odd, that was all. And Helen Burns's presence was if anything, considering the competition she faced, even odder than Lynne Shorthall's. At the Polytechnic, Wrottesley, you took pretty well whatever was thrown at you; whereas when Sefton was a young man teaching first at the Coryapundy Swamp Institute of Technology and then at the University of Woolloomoolloo, New South Wales, he could afford to be as pernickety as a sultan. With the exception of Helen Burns, who wore orphanage shoes and indeed looked as if she were on day-release from one of Dr Barnardo's poorer homes, the girls he taught were all tall and tanned and sociably athletic and had sand between their toes. They came to Sefton's lectures twirling parasols, their books and folders wrapped in floral towels, and were somehow able to give the impression that their studies were merely an amiable interruption of that perpetual holiday referred to in other parts of the world as life. Sefton loved them for the width of their shoulders and for the way their sentences invariably ended in an interrogative curl as if everything (including Sefton) was so wonderful and amazing to them that they could only ask questions about it. And because he was Jewish and short and knew all the answers they loved him in return. And yet it was on Helen Burns — blurred, white-skinned, academically ambitious orphan Annie — that Sefton forgot to lock his door.

Reluctantly recalling it all now, Sefton is thankful the Polytechnic, Wrottesley, does not run to a campus postman. If you ever get any mail at Wrottesley it waits for you, a month late, at the bottom of a tin drawer which you share with a hundred others. Well, so much the better right now, thinks Sefton, as he listens for sounds outside his door and hears, over the roar of years, the cheerful tread and the incessant whistling of Frank, spitting image of Ken Rosewall and the University of Woolloomoolloo's most popular, most reliable, most relaxed, and most ironical campus postman. Unflappable Frank! So untouched was he by what he saw of human hopes and passions as he did his rounds in his grey shorts and his matching short-sleeved grey shirt, whistling his way through the Italian operas as if they were all comedies, that he might have been of a different species altogether. But even Frank paused fractionally, on that hot afternoon, after he had pushed open Sefton Goldberg's unresisting door and found himself staring into the raised, white, unambiguously busy hindquarters of the visiting Pom. At that moment of supreme shame and exposure Sefton became cruelly alert to every accompanying sight and sound: he heard the blood rush from his body, listened to the icy echoing

9

plummet of his temperature, and he detected a quite un-Puccini — and un-Frank-like intake of breath in the final whistled bars of *e lucevan le stelle* . For a millionth of a second the stars had stopped their shining and unflappable Frank had flapped. But not for any longer than that. He was a postman. He had a job to do. He hadn't called on Sefton to check on his teaching methods — if he'd found the Pom in the attitude of a rat up a drainpipe, that was the Pom's affair — he had come with a letter. And so he did what he was paid to do and posted it, where it wouldn't go astray and where it somehow seemed to belong, between the now motionless, frozen cheeks of Sefton Goldberg's buttocks.

I only hope that isn't from my mother, was Sefton's first coherent thought. But it was only after Helen Burns had silently slipped from under him and slid back into her institutional shoes and stockings and crept from his room, that he could summon the courage to reach behind him and find out. It was all right. It wasn't from his mother. It was only a bill from Heffers for the latest book they had sent him — F.R. Leavis's *Nor Shall My Sword* .

Defenceless on the floor with Mrs Shorthall, the front of him still blacked out by the drape of his gown, the rear of him still raised as if in supplication to the genius of Linus Yale, Sefton Goldberg takes the measure, for the first time, of the exquistite Australian forbearance implicit in Frank's literal performance of his duty. Sefton is not taxed to imagine the consequences if there were campus postman at the Polytechnic, Wrottesley. 'I didn't want to disturb you like, when I could see you was busy, and I didn't, you know, want to leave it with the Head of Department in case there were any questions asked, so I kept the letter for you. I haven't held it up to the light or anything. Do you mind if I keep the stamps?' Followed by the damp expression of some dismal Midland vexation, followed by the circulation of malicious but dispirited rumour. Followed by anonymous notes and phone calls to every member of Sefton Goldberg's family. Followed by pictures of Sefton Goldberg on the paedophile page of the *News of the World* . Followed by Sefton Goldberg hanging himself from the Yale lock in his office; bound for that exclusively English circle of Hell where once respected public figures lash themselves for petty crimes.

Sefton finds himself missing everything he has ever known that isn't English. Specifically, in this context, he cherishes the memory of the mirth with which big Bob Rourke, senator and wine grower from South Australia, confessed on national television to his enthusiasm for opening his flies every time one of his secretaries entered his room. Resign? For what? For not being a poofter?

Not being a poofter himself, but being Jewish, which is worse, Sefton Goldberg considers that he is already guilty enough without the added *tsorris* of being found on the floor of a polytechnic, in Wrottesley, in the Midlands, in England, with a woman who, quite frankly, would not make him the envy of all his friends. And therefore, although he is tenderly and teacherly, although he is even momentarily transported, he is massively relieved when Lynne Shorthall finally departs to collect the degree her husband never wanted her to study for because he was frightened about who she might meet while she was studying for it.

Not that Norman Shorthall could ever have imagined, even in his blackest moments of fear and fantasy, what goatish Jew, initiate of secret rites and rituals, would at the eleventh hour do the deed of darkness with his wife. The thought that he has been demoniacally lecherous and done a disservice, into the bargain, to a gentile from the Midlands, is Sefton's only consolation on this unexceptionally wretched Wrottesley afternoon.

And enables him to return, with a brief spurt of energy, to the application forms which spill out of his In tray and into his Out tray and over the sides of his desk.

He has spent the morning filling them in and posting them off, but there were more waiting for him, after lunch, at the bottom of the communal tin drawer. His colleagues were astounded by the number of positions he found, in these austere times, to apply for.

'I'm desperate,' he told them. 'And I'm flexible.'

Accordingly he didn't confine his attentions to advertisements which stipulated a specialism in the Long Novel — that area which he had made all his own and which guaranteed him a near-perfect freedom from the bother of student interest and enquiry. He applied as well for Curatorships and Wardenships, for Extra-Mural Tutor Tutorships and Intra-Mural Research-Assistant Superintendentships. He tried for Deanships and Rectorships and, when there were any going, Vice-Chancellorships. He put himself forward as Keeper of rare collections of books and as Caretaker of significant buildings with literary associations. He let it be known that he was prepared to consider being a Community Poet, although he had never written a poem, and a Playwright in Residence, although he couldn't abide plays. He offered himself in an administrative capacity and an entrepreneurial, in an advisory and a managerial, and even, in reply to a vacancy in *The Lady*, in a companionable. He recognised no limit to his choice except a geographical one; he would do anything (academic, of course; or at least academic*ish*) provided it wasn't in Sheffield or Leeds or Leicester or Newcastle or — obviously! — Wrottesley; anything provided it *was* in Cirencester or Windsor or Cheltenham or Winchester. London, or more specifically Hampstead, was no doubt where he belonged, but it would have to wait until Sefton could enter it in triumph. In the meantime what mattered was to get away from the perplexed nasal querulousness of working-class Wrottesley. The defeated and the defeating poor. Other people's poverty depressed him far more than his own. What he wanted now, simply as a background to himself, was other people's wealth. O,

12

for a beaker full of the warm south! The inane ululations of the indiscreetly well-to-do? — music, sweet music to Sefton Goldberg's ears, after the mutterings of the Midlands! Their unshakeable complacency and prejudice? — bliss, bliss, like the warm sun on his back, after the wrung-out despondency of Wrottesley!

Of course, he was perfectly aware, with a name like Sefton Goldberg, the sun might not turn out to be the only hot thing he would feel on his back in these demi-paradises. He had picked up from an Oxfam shop a *Jewish Year Book* which gave the Jewish population of every town in Britain which had a Jewish population, and by Jewish population they sometimes meant no more than seven families, and a synagogue in a tent — but Winchester did not even make the list. So it wasn't going to be home-from-home exactly, and the residents were not likely to be hanging the Israeli flag or their daughters from their bedroom windows to welcome Sefton. But the warfare would be fairly open. You knew where you were with the middle classes; they never pretended to be anything but rude. Very well. Sefton didn't mind that. It was infinitely preferable to the urban guerilla tactics of the Midlands: complain and run. He liked a clean fight. And you could always get them to admire cleverness in the end. One way or another he would squeeze a bit of regard out of Winchester. Whereas five years in the unpretentious working town of Wrottesley had him huddled into his overcoat, shrunk into himself, his head grown beneath his shoulders like one of those Othello beguiled the innocent Desdemona with traveller's stories of, in deference to the raw susceptibilities of the natives. Who, after all, in local parlance, did he think he was?

He should by now have known. His name, his address, his marital status had gone down as requested many times today. He paused on the seventh line of an application for the position of Head of Pastoral Care at a Church of England College of Agriculture in Bath and wrote against RELIGION — having toyed with 'tenta-

13

tively agnostic' and 'aggressively Jewish' — 'none'. He told again the story of his life, lying a little about his qualifications and a lot about his interest in students and their welfare. From a sheet of what was once a hundred identical photographs of himself trying to look earnest and gentile he cut out an example, deciding this time against shading in the bridge and bottom of his nose with black biro. He pasted the back of the photograph and punched it into place on the form. He had reached that stage of an afternoon's applying where he didn't care if he got the job or not; so there was a touch of recklessness in some of his answers, a suggestion of unconcern in the illegible flourish of his signature. And behind the recklessness and the unconcern there was a faint, mad hope that those might be the very qualities that were being sought.

He had been trying to get out of the Polytechnic, Wrottesley, from the day he had got in it. Even as he had shaken hands with his new colleagues and collected his allowance of paper clips and drawing pins from the stationery office his pockets had been stuffed with prospectuses from other institutions. But just recently his efforts to escape had become more urgent and determined. There were two minor reasons and one major reason for this. The two minor reasons were the coming on of old age, signalled by his thirty-fifth birthday, and the coming through of his divorce at a time when he was enjoying none of the things he had originally wanted a divorce for. The one major reason was the coming out of Godfrey Jelley's second book — just when Sefton Goldberg had reconciled himself bravely to the coming out of his first.

Godfrey Jelley had been Sefton Goldberg's best friend and closest rival at school. The rivalry had been mainly literary — each attempting to have heard of more books than the other or to have run up bigger fines at more local libraries — but they also kept a watchful eye on one another's style of dress, debating technique, and success with girls. They were the only

14

two Jewish boys in the school who were planning to go to university to study something other than dentistry or law. As befitted his strenuous intelligence Sefton Goldberg went off to fret and worry over literature at Cambridge, while his friend and rival went to Oxford to read a bit of philosophy, a bit of politics, and a bit of economics, as befitted his instability and flashy brilliance.

It didn't take Sefton Goldberg long to perceive that Godfrey Jelley was enjoying Oxford a lot more than he was enjoying Cambridge, was getting a lot more out of his irresponsibility and frivolity than Sefton was getting out of his seriousness. When they met during vacations back in Manchester Godfrey was blooming, full of gaiety and assurance and laughter. Whereas Sefton was prim and tight, practising those disapprovals which as far as he could see were indispensable to a formed critical intelligence.

'I had afternoon tea with Richard Burton and Elizabeth Taylor,' Godfrey Jelley announced. 'They often come back up for the theatre.'

'Did you really,' Sefton replied, trying to control the bottom part of his face. 'That must have been a bore.'

'It wasn't. They were very sweet.'

'Sweet? Is that an Oxford word?'

Oxford sounded an altogether brighter place than Cambridge, and when Godfrey referred familiarly to the High and the Broad, as if they were his, Sefton was unable to find any Cambridge equivalent to which he could refer familiarly in return, and he was forced to switch the conversation around to Dickens and D.H. Lawrence instead. In town at night, chatting up the girls they both frankly missed at their respective universities, Godfrey succeeded effortlessly in making his Oxford experience a part of his charm, whereas the more Sefton enlarged upon his interest in Fanny Price and Little Dorrit and the young Ursula Brangwen the less likelihood there seemed of the evening resolving itself in the way it was supposed to.

'They're just scrubbers,' Sefton would whisper to

Godfrey, the minute the girls tripped off to the toilets.

'Isn't that the point?' Godfrey would reply.

Later on, fortunately, Fanny Price didn't stand in his way. When Sefton Goldberg took his degree there was still only one *Educational Supplement* and a Jewish boy from Cambridge could still count himself somebody. Temporary lecturing jobs in the giant holiday campuses of Australia came easily and he found himself enjoying offering his disapprovals (and even developing some new ones) to a couple of thousand smiling surfies and Olympic swimmers at a time. He worked up a line in lecture patter that had more to do with the night club than the academy. He grew his hair, wore a leather tie, smoked cheroots, and from time to time tore up famous books in public. Despite taking advantage of his female students (or being taken advantage of, by them — he never really worked it out) on a scale that no one who wasn't Jewish or Welsh could ever possibly understand the need for, he still rooted critically for Little Dorrit and the burgeoning Ursula; but his audiences supposed he was being ironic and his reputation for cruel dry wit soared. He even began to wonder himself if he hadn't been practising irony all along. So it didn't matter in the least that stories and examples of Godfrey Jelley's journalistic successes back home in England floated across the waters to him every now and then. Godfrey was now making his living having afternoon tea with sweet and famous people and writing about it afterwards for the Sunday papers. 'Poor Godfrey,' Sefton was even sometimes able to find it in him to lament, 'having to spend his afternoons with that lot. He deserves to get on, God knows.' They had carved things up neatly between them; Godfrey belonged unequivocally to middlebrow showbiz and he belonged — yes, Sefton belonged to serious scholarship enlivened by cruel dry wit and not too encumbered with knowledge. Strictly speaking, they were not in competition at all.

But when Sefton decided that he had outgrown the

naive and too readily responsive cultures of the new world and returned, unremarked, to the old; when he discovered that England wasn't inclined to take him up and that Australia was not able, because of some foolish new policy of favouring nationals to take him back; when he found himself having to turn his thoughts from the idea of a personal Chair somewhere elegant to that of a junior job in a polytechnic somewhere vile — if he was lucky; and when he finally understood that no journalist anywhere had any intention of enjoying afternoon tea with *him* : then Godfrey Jelley's fame became a problem for him. After a couple of years in Wrottesley it became an obsession.

It wasn't though that he was jealous.

He had had a long naked stare at that possibility, and he wasn't.

However he hadn't read what he had read (which was a damn sight more than Godfrey Jelley had read!) without learning that these things can creep up on you if you are not careful; so he decided it was probably best all round if he kept well away from any magazine or newspaper in which the latest of Godfrey's afternoons with the famous was likely to appear. They unsettled him, and he didn't derive any pleasure either from observing how servile his old friend's prose had become. He really didn't.

But then came the book. It was no more, in fact, than an anthology of pieces already published describing afternoons long since spent. But Sefton Goldberg was incapable of taking the idea of a book lightly. For him a book had magical properties. In a book the word was made holy. Why else did he disapprove of so many so vehemently or make such a ritual out of tearing them up in lectures? In a world where reputation was evanescent and human passions were transient, only the book was stable and permanent. Even to be remaindered was to be remembered.

In the main Wrottesley was a pretty good place to live if you wanted to keep away from books. Most of the shops in the new precincts — and there wasn't much of Wrottesley that wasn't new precinct — sold baggy jeans and built-up shoes. It was hard enough to find a jacket that wasn't made of leather with a death's head on the back, let alone a book. But there was something about Godfrey Jelley's book which Sefton was sure would recommend it even to Wrottesley taste. He knew it was out there somewhere, and he knew that the only way to arm himself against the shock of coming up against it suddenly and unexpectedly was to go and find it. See it before it saw him. Embrace it as a saint might embrace a leper. With this intention he hovered about W.H. Smith's for days, his coat collars turned up, his fists plunged deep into his pockets. He was used to temptation and, being Jewish, he was used to a quick capitulation to it, but he couldn't work out on this occasion which the temptation was: going in or staying out.

On the morning of the third day, having decided it would be best for him to stay out, he went in. He wondered which course of action would guarantee him most misery — asking an assistant if she had a copy (and thereby forcing himself to pronounce the title and the author), or going looking for it on his own. In the event he did not have to make a decision; two steps into the shop and there it was, or rather, there *they* were — an immodest pyramid of them, stacked high like the most popular soap-powders on special offer by the entrance to a supermarket. And clearly discernible on the cover of each was a collage of photographs of his old school-friend and rival, Godfrey Jelley, clowning with Morecambe and Wise, exchanging punches with Mohammad Ali, smiling beneficently at the Pope, chucking Germaine Greer under the chin. Sefton Goldberg, sick at heart, took a couple of turns about the pyramid and relived the whole of his life. He reached out his hand to one of the thick shiny blue volumes tentatively, as if it might go off or bite. He held it finally in his right hand and tried to coax his left to turn a page.

18

It wouldn't. It couldn't. All feeling and power had fled from his fingers. He twisted it in his hand and stared at the blurb on the back of the jacket. Through a mist he read the words EMINENT RICH POPULAR SUCCESSFUL CHARM INSIGHT BEST MOST.

He returned the book unopened to its pile, went home and put himself to bed.

Sefton Goldberg would not have thought very highly of himself if he had not been able to arrive at some rather more generous acceptance of his friend's triumph. Especially as it was no less true than previously that they were not competitors. They were doing different things and just because Godfrey had done his and Sefton was still musing and mulling it didn't mean that the battle — supposing there to have been a battle — was over. Oho no! For many years now he had been planning a sort of history and vindication of the will to failure in art. He had always hated the determination that makes men finish things and deemed it a fanatical and esentially gentile quality. His book was to be a defence of spoiled canvasses and unfinished symphonies and abandoned novels. It occurred to him that the highest tribute his book might pay to failure was not to get itself written at all. This notion had much to recommend it, but its subtlety might well be lost on Godfrey Jelley, and Sefton was keen not to disappear from his friend's recollection altogether. I've a shock or two in store for him yet, he said to himself, and although this pronouncement didn't lead to any resumption of his book on failure it did help to take his mind off his friend's book on success.

He was further helped by that same friend's sudden disappearance from public view. For a good year Sefton heard nothing of him, read nothing by him, came across no references to his afternoon conversations with the famous, concluded or to come. It was becoming safe to read the newspapers again.

'So much for fame in that sort of world,' said Sefton to himself with still cautious satisfaction. He was always gloomily superstitious and he knew that if he showed too much complacency Godfrey Jelley would suddenly show up as President of the United States. In which eventuality Sefton was not certain that he would be able to resist the one surefire way of writing himself into the history books. So he made a point of thinking clean and open thoughts, and not pushing his luck.

It was only on the publication of Godfrey's second book that Sefton gained any knowledge of where he'd been or what he had become. How it had happened was still not clear, but Godfrey Jelly had tired of the tinsel and the tea-cakes and the talk. He had torn away the veil and ripped off the mask and lifted the scales and washed off the motley and stared into the heart of things. Not content with that, he had also peered into the abyss. But not on his own. It had been a group activity. A certain well-known intellectual guru had, in a fit of more than usually obstinate hagiological fidgets, collected together as many spiritually jumpy actors and actresses as he could find in order that they might discover the truth that was both of them and beyond them in one of the driest and most unaccommodating stretches of desert known to man — that is if anything can be known to man. Godfrey Jelley had gone off with them, but only secondarily as a journalist. Primarily he went as a fellow questing human being. Tents were pitched, cameras were mounted, texts were thrown away, all inhibition (that curse of the moderns) was abandoned, a bedouin tribe trouped by on cue (on divine cue, that is), and the search for the silence on the other side of language and the language on the other side of silence began in earnest. Godfrey Jelley, newborn, pink and tender as an unhealed scar, watched in wonderment and as he watched he wrote — or rather, the he on the other side of he wrote.

It seemed to Sefton Goldberg, who bought the book immediately this time, in order to familiarise himself with its appearance and so not be shocked by suddenly seeing it somewhere else, that his friend's style and vocabulary had not changed all that much. Incredibly, he still began sentences with adverbs like incredibly, followed by a comma. He still found people sweet even if this time they were nomadic lepers. And he still dropped names, though here again there was a slight shift of emphasis and he now referred familiarly to the Japanese Noh Plays and the Persian Passions as he had once referred to André Previn and the Promenade Concerts, and Jimmy Connors and Flushing Meadow. Myth, legend, and ritual were, however, newish in Godfrey; as were the blind mendicants who saw more without eyes than we saw with them, and the crazed herdsmen who were more sane in their insanity, and the deaf mute camel drivers who drove a greater distance and spoke a deeper language.

Sefton was in no way surprised when the newspapers frothed about the book's great diffidence and wisdom. He was not shocked when the *Observer* admitted that it had found the book so readable that it had not been able to put it down; and he was not saddened when the *Sunday Times* confessed that it had found the book so disturbing that it had not been able to pick it up. He even kept his head when the reviewer from the *Yorkshire Post* vowed that after reading Godfrey Jelley his life would never be the same again. What did for Sefton was the enthusiasm with which the serious academic world took up 'this journey through the desert wastes of self. Even the Drama boys at Sefton's own Polytechnic went mad about it and stuffed copies on the library shelves and on their courses. They insisted that they knew no better work on the religious nature of drama and the duplicity of meaning.

The old tacit working agreement which had apportioned the garish to Godfrey and the serious to Sefton was now broken. Godfrey had turned his back on popular journalism and frivolity and had overnight become a notable literary figure. Overnight! Without having studied English Literature! That's what really nettled

21

Sefton. Godfrey hadn't even suffered the deprivations of being at Cambridge!

No bed was now large enough for Sefton Goldberg and his shame. He made the terrible mistake of being honest with himself. 'Bitter? Of course I'm bitter!' he repeated to himself each morning as he made his way across the ring-road which separated the Polytechnic car park from the Polytechnic. The wind was always especially sharp and bleak here and the lights were always against him. The students coming to and from lectures were dowdily dressed and looked slow-witted. At the bus-stop long queues of Wrottesley working people muttered and complained through running noses, and the Jamaican bus-drivers had mad glints in their eyes, as if they were thinking of ploughing their vehicles into the lines of waiting passengers.

'Poor bastards!' thought Sefton Goldberg, meaning the drivers. 'Bitter? I'll say!' meaning himself.

And he made the even more serious mistake of welcoming envy into his heart, instead of going on pretending, as is sensible and usual, that he hadn't noticed it was there. It was a demanding and a time-consuming guest. Once he admitted that he envied Godfrey Jelley it became a kind of terrible duty to admit that he also envied everybody else. And not just successful writers and critics. He envied television announcers, disc-jockeys, sprinters and politicians. He envied Mick Jagger and Herbert von Karajan and Andrew Lloyd Webber and Stockhausen and the panel of *Any Questions* . He envied Bruce Forsyth, Henry Cooper, Chairman Hua, and even Virginia Wade for winning Wimbledon. He didn't have a clue who Barry Sheene was, but he envied him. His envy was rapacious and did not discriminate on the grounds of race, colour, creed, age or sex. It simply hurt more if the object were his age, male, and Jewish. If he also knew him personally it was agony.

Envy on this scale made it impossible for him to find any refreshment or relaxation outside of himself. All of those activities whose very virtue is that they enable you to think about what isn't you were denied him. He didn't dare pick up a newspaper for fear of what it would tell him of the success of some old *shmuck* of a friend. He couldn't become absorbed in a good book because he resented the author his talent if he had any, and envied him his fame either way. He couldn't go to a concert because he envied Harry Blech and the London Mozart Players their skill and their life-style and their applause. If he went to the theatre he would sit sullen in the stalls, pondering the good fortune of the actors, the happy chance that had made the director the director (while something quite different had made Sefton Goldberg Sefton Goldberg), and imagining what a terrific time *they* were going to have when the curtain fell. Films, naturally, were out; so were cricket, horseracing, darts championships, snooker exhibitions and, surprisingly even to him, ballet.

His only consolations during these terrible days came in the form of the unexpected demise or humiliation of someone famous. An idolized pop star ate himself to death. A beautiful film actress took an overdose of sleeping pills. A yiddish rock opera called *Shiksa* written by Pinchas Finklestein who had been in Sefton's class at primary school flopped on its first night in the West End. All these things helped. Slowly his confidence began to trickle back. He was still alive and he hadn't flopped. A tragic aeroplane crash killing twenty of the world's most popular and successful novelists, travelling back from a convention in Hawaii on the future of the novel, came just at the right time.

'Fame!' he reflected. 'So who wants it?'

He began to feel almost jaunty again. Not strong, but up and about.

But it had been a narrow escape and the lesson was clear. He had to get out of the Poly and he had to get out of the town it was in. As long as he spent his afternoons on the floor with the likes of Lynne Shorthall he was not proof against the news, say, that Godfrey Jelley had

23

been seen dancing the night away at Annabel's with Valerie Perrine. His idea, when he had taken the job, that he might make something, for a while, out of being a big fish in a small pond, had proved misguided. Big fish need big ponds. Being Jewish, Sefton didn't know much about the names or breeds or needs of fish. But he knew a bit about himself. He should never have gone among the gentiles — at least he should never have gone among the poor ones.

'Trouble with your eyes?' asked Peter Potter, popping his head around the door and picking his words as if they were ripe strawberries.

Sefton Goldberg, having completed his application to St Michael's Agricultural College, Bath, had stretched himself far back in his office chair from which position he could focus the window of his room so that it perfectly framed the nearest of the football club's floodlights. Over the years he had become intimate with it but every afternoon he still counted the individual lamps on the pylon, checking and rechecking his addition in order to satisfy the meticulousness of vacancy. He could also make them dance and disappear by closing first his left eye and then his right. In which occupation Peter Potter found him as he popped his head around the door.

'Yes, there is,' said Sefton. 'They are too old and they have seen too much.'

Peter Potter's head was still the only part of Peter Potter in the room. Even to Sefton's old and experienced eyes this ability to send out the head so far in advance of everything else was remarkable. There was no sign of a body, not even a hint of one. Only a pair of pale eyes, themselves not all that fresh, but twinkling with exaggerated vivacity, and a mouth moving rapidly about the corners in anticipation of all the amusing things it had to say. The impression he gave of being a wonderful marionette expertly worked was if anything augmented when the rest of him finally arrived. He was very slender and very fine. Beneath the loose clothing the limbs seemed as if fashioned in porcelain and strung with silk. He was in the habit of arranging himself, as if he were careful of his own value and fragility, on sills and ledges — out of harm's way but prominent. Students observed him with fascination when he lectured to them from atop a table or a cupboard, his knees drawn up to his chin or his ankles tied in a little bow. When he was dejected he would crumple, like a cast-off doll; but when he was bright the strings were all drawn taut. He was bright now.

'I didn't expect to find you here,' he said. 'I thought you would have been over the road cheering them on.'

'Cheering them on?' Sefton looked perplexed.

Peter Potter eased an attenuated wrist out of his sleeve and whimsically consulted a watch. 'Aren't they all becoming B.A.s about now? With honours?'

'Oh! Cheering *them* on. No I couldn't bear to. Especially as I told most of them they were going to fail. If they saw me they'd gloat and smirk.'

'You could be magnanimous. Show them that your apparent discouragement was in fact a spur.'

'Magnanimous?' Sefton spoke in the tones of a child-murderer well-versed in his own nature. He hunched himself, round-shouldered, in his chair. He had a gift of droll lugubriousness which he employed to damp his Jewishness so that it shouldn't be too much of a trial for Peter Potter. He knew that he was the first Jew Peter had ever struck up a friendship with and he wanted to make the experience easy for him. As long as he remained hunched and dejected he was fairly sure that Peter could cope. 'Magnanimous?' he repeated. 'Never. Besides I've decided I can no longer be a party to degrees. We give too many. It's time we started to take some back.'

'Well, you are welcome to mine,' said Peter, shining.

'Liar!' thought Sefton, as he watched his companion conjure himself onto the metal filing cabinet in the corner of the office. Up there with his legs folded he looked crazily out of place, like something from the out-side which had flown in by mistake. He often struck Sefton as resembling a little English garden bird, though which garden bird Sefton Goldberg, being Jewish, couldn't be expected to know. In the same way, although he had never been to church in Berkshire he always heard in Peter Potter's intonations the music of a Berkshire choirboy. Born in England, citizen of England, teacher of its language and its history and its literature (the long novel), Sefton was still alarmingly naive about the English. He was shaken when he dis-covered that Peter Potter — the mellifluous Peter Potter — had been born in Nottingham, the son of a miner, like D.H.Lawrence; and that he still had living an old poor mother to whom, like a Dickensian villain, he was careful never to refer. The discovery didn't anger him. He didn't share the belief held by many at the Polytechnic that the only reliable guarantee of intellectual good faith was the retention of regional vowels and sympathies if you had ever had them or their prompt acquirement if you hadn't. He was simply surprised by the completeness of the transformation of himself that Peter Potter had effected.

How was it managed? What had he done to himself to remind one of the silvery winter sunlight of a southern seaside town? To smell of rectory gardens and hedge-rows and late pale flowers of which Sefton Goldberg didn't know the names? Had he, D.H.Lawrence-like, rolled himself in something? He hadn't, at any rate, rolled himself in a Frieda. Large, domineering, ebullient women might not have nightly peopled his nightmares but they were regular objects of his humour, familiar characters in his daily fictions. He was at his ease only with boyish women. Hips and breasts belonged for him to comedy and not to passion. And passion itself belonged to propriety and principle. In this regard Sefton was able to distinguish the Nottinghamshire miner's son. Peter Potter had found himself his own boyish woman; in best Nottinghamshire miner's son

26

fashion he had said 'That's her!' the moment he had seen her pushing her bicycle, and he had married her quickly before the white fires of his intensity had proved too much for his principle. He was uxorious rather than happy, and spoke of his marriage in the strangest way as if it were, impersonally, a sort of public boon like Oxfam or the Salvation Army — a thing of inestimable good to the society it existed to serve but of only incidental profit to its officers. A marriage for the race, as it were.

Marriage reverence wasn't entirely new to Sefton. Many of his friends at Cambridge had believed in marriage, imparting to the word a flat artisan unambiguousness of tone which made him think of Richard Hoggart and Raymond Williams, and they had looked forward to the state as if that was what, primarily, their study of English Literature had been preparing them for. But they were all gentiles. Jewish men, as a rule, weren't hot on reverence. They went in, of course, for unashamedly public wife worship, but that was another thing entirely. Sefton Goldberg had been a Jewish husband once and although he hadn't gone quite as far as public wife worship himself he could see how he might have. It was a necessary act of contrition and atonement. For never finally being able to renounce the world for the woman who had renounced the world for you. Being Jewish, you simply couldn't give up your collusion with other men. Your heart was in the marketplace. A Peter Potter conspired with his wife; a Sefton Goldberg conspired against her. For which, if you were any kind of *mensh*, you knew you owed her something. Expiation on a scale. On the night before his barmitzvah Sefton had lost a doughty battle with his nature and had not kept his hands off himself — not even that once. He did not believe then that he would ever experience a profounder guilt. But marriage acquainted him with unimaginable self-reproach. He accused himself even more energetically married than he had abused himself single. In the matrimonial life of

27

the Jewish male every day is Yom Kippur.

Sefton Goldberg's super-Jewish squeamishness about intimate marriage talk and Peter Potter's Nottinghamshire squeamishness about intimate talk of any other kind ensured that their conversation was distant, chaste, and ironic. What they had in common was the Polytechnic, and they were not hard pressed to people it, in their talk, with villains and grotesques: with fat ladies for Peter Potter's delectation and with Marxists and Trotskyites for Sefton Goldberg's. What they also had in common — else they would not have had the Polytechnic — was failure. But they did not acknowledge this to one another. Sefton insisted on the official version of his professional life: he was simply passing through and would soon be somebody again in Bournemouth or in Harrogate. While Peter Potter, for his part, could deem no man a failure who was a good and happy husband. Nevertheless they were engaged in a deadly silent rivalry which would never have come about had they not been idle, frustrated and disappointed. But then if they had not been those things their friendship would not have come about either.

Their friendship consisted primarily in their trying to beat one another, during their lunch breaks, at darts, pool, snooker, space-invaders, table-football, dominoes, and even the fruit-machine, which is not normally regarded as a competitive game for two. Their rivalry consisted in their trying to beat one another, at all other times, at everything else.

Once, Peter showed Sefton a signed first edition of some poems by T.S.Eliot which he had picked up at a jumble sale for ten pence. Sefton took one look at the inscription to Ezra and went out immediately and consoled himself by opening a massive credit account at Austin Reed's. When he heard about it, Peter let it drop that Barclaycard had just raised his borrowing limit to four figures and that American Express was wooing him personally. Sefton took himself for a week's break in the Auvergne. Peter moved his marriage for a fortnight to the Dordogne, and brought back better wine. Recently Peter had re-renovated his country cottage and exchanged his Mini for a new family Escort. On top of that he caught the train to Oxford one afternoon and came back with every novel on the Booker Prize short-list, in order that he should have something firmer than mere intuition to go on for not liking them. So all in all he believed, with reason, that he had Sefton on the run. On the other hand, Sefton did just mention that he had sent off to a publisher a quick sketch of his rough draft of his vague plan for his book on failure. For a month after that Peter would pop his head round Sefton's door each morning and ask:

'Any word?'

'No. Nothing yet.'

'Ah, well,' Peter would say sympathetically, scarcely able to conceal his relief. But the not knowing made him tense. And the strain of having to prepare his face day after day for the expression of congratulation, should the worst come to the worst, told on him.

But today, balanced effortlessly on the filing cabinet, he struck Sefton as being more than usually pleased with himself. He twinkled comically: quaint and merry as a pixie, witty and dangerous as a goblin. Sefton searched his brain to recall what, if anything, he especially wanted at this moment, because it was clear from Peter's look that he believed *he* had it. It was the same expression he wore when the fruit machine rattled out its jackpot into his waiting hands while Sefton was at the bar changing another note.

Hunched in his chair and wondering what he was being beaten at, Sefton listened cautiously as Peter Potter delivered himself of familiar verdicts on the depressed state of learning in the Polytechnic. The glint of triumph had still not left his eyes when he conjured himself off his perch and appeared, for his final trick, at Sefton's door.

'No Nick?' he asked, nodding towards the second desk in Sefton's room.

29

Nick — Nick Lee — shared Sefton's office but hadn't been seen for months. He kept a briefcase permanently on his desk and one of his jackets permanently over his chair so that by re-arranging them three or four times a day Sefton was able to make it appear that Nick was around somewhere but had just popped out — in all probability to the library. Nick and Sefton had not come to any formal agreement about this — and indeed, if Nick could have been found to be asked, he would have been as insistent to Sefton as to anyone that he had been in the Polytechnic all day and had just popped out momentarily to the library — but Sefton acted out of some automatic loyalty to him. And he was not the only one. Somehow or other essays were collected from Nick's desk and returned marked; notes and messages from Nick to his students were pinned to the door; and every week or so a new jacket appeared on the back of his chair. Without ever being there Nick Lee was much more up to date with his work than Sefton was.

'No, no Nick.'

'Pity,' said Peter. 'I wanted to remind him about dinner on Friday. I hope you haven't forgotten?'

'Forgotten? I've scarcely thought about anything else,' said Sefton.

His reply was only a little extravagant. Peter was an excellent cook, specialising in traditional English country dishes which most Nottinghamshire miners' sons would not have known about, and serving them up in far greater abundance than either his own or his boyish wife's meagre appetite justified. Sefton knew that Peter enjoyed having him as a guest partly to impress him and partly to watch him make a pig of himself. After a couple of mouthfuls Peter and Miranda Potter would lay down their cutlery and stare across the table as Sefton chewed and raved and sighed and allowed the juices to run down his chin onto his shirt. It was the least he could do. It was his way of saying thank you for the meal and of making his Jewishness harmless to those who had been brave enough to let it in to their home. And besides, he was so obviously not ambitious as a cook himself, and his own superiority when it came to big eating was so unlikely to be challenged by anyone in the Potter household, that generosity of appreciation was possible all round.

'Well, don't expect too much,' said Peter, and Sefton knew that he could look forward to unicorn *en croûte* , at the very least.

Peter appeared to be on the point of leaving, but with his long clean fingers on the knob of Sefton's door he hesitated and made, to Sefton's sense, a very poor job of pretending suddenly to remember something.

'Oh!' he exclaimed. 'I almost forgot. Do you think you could give Cora a lift when you come?'

'Cora?'

'If it's not too much trouble.'

'I'm to give Cora a lift?'

'If you don't mind.'

'To your place?'

'If that's all right with you.'

'Cora *Peck* ?'

'Cora Peck.' Peter Potter tried for an urbane smile, a passing gallantry to all the other Coras in the world who were not being offered lifts to his place, but there was much untoward and far from courteous activity around the small area between his lower lip and jaw.

Sefton Goldberg's features were not composed either. He had risen from his chair in alarm. There were things here he didn't like or understand. For Cora and Peter were not on speaking or visiting terms. They were not even on mumbling terms. Strictly speaking they were on no terms whatsoever. For his part Peter could not bring himself to talk *of* her let alone *to* her. His hatred of Cora reminded Sefton most of his own hatred of spiders and reptiles — he bore towards her a total and unstinting metaphysical grudge. Even when he wasn't thinking of her some corner of his soul must have been willing her not to be. It affected his conception of the

31

universe that she should be in it, just as it affected his conception of the Polytechnic. He winced involuntarily when she came near him, drawing his head far back from his shoulders; and when she spoke within his hearing the blood drained clean away from his face and black rings appeared suddenly round his eyes. His antipathy dated from the day she first arrived at Wrottesley in her silver lurex boots and her gypsy earrings and her silky blue zip-down jacket with an enormous appliqué mouth, parted, on the back of it. There was altogether too much of her for Peter's taste or comfort. Not too much flesh — she wasn't buxom; but too much decoration and appurtenance and vociferousness; and beneath the din too much female anxiety and pallor. Sefton once observed to Peter that as one got close to Cora Peck one could actually hear the hormonal battle raging, and Peter so enjoyed the remark that Sefton regretted having made it. Remembering Peter's preference for boyish women he felt he had served an undeserving cause.

Cora Peck taught creative writing at the Polytechnic and this endlessly irritated and for some reason even galled the two men. She duplicated and circulated her own pieces which were mainly concerned with excrement, introspection, and physical decay as a metaphor for spiritual disablement, though it was always her contention that subject matter should be subservient to innovatory form and that fiction should truly affirm its fictionality by expanding and fracturing conventional genre. She knew writers who were just obscure enough to be interested in fracturing the genre and just famous enough to be worth knowing, and she talked openly about how she soon expected to be joining their ranks. She hated Peter Potter for hating her and she hated Sefton Goldberg because he goaded her, because he knew how to make her scream, because he closed his mind to innovatory structures, and because — although she did not know that this was why she hated him — he was Jewish.

So it was pretty difficult to understand how it had come about that Peter had invited Cora to his home, that Cora had accepted, that Cora had wanted a lift from Sefton, that Peter had offered to get her one, and that Peter and Sefton were now discussing it. Pretty difficult to understand and pretty worrying.

'I thought you two weren't speaking,' Sefton said at last.

'I didn't think we were either,' Peter conceded. 'But I ran into her outside my room, and instead of looking the other way, as she can normally be relied upon to do, she smiled warmly, said she was in high spirits, loved everybody, and wanted a party to celebrate her success.'

Peter Potter looked hard at Sefton Goldberg, and that earlier glint of triumph showed again in at least one of his grey eyes.

A cold hand clutched at Sefton's heart. 'What success?' he enquired, with a kind of operatic casualness.

Peter's reply belonged to the same convention. 'Oh,' he said, as if searching his memory for some quite trivial item of information, while Cherubino was shinning down the drainpipe, 'she's being published or something.'

Sefton tried to remember how one's face behaved when one was pleased for somebody. 'Oh, that's nice,' he said. 'What is it, a story? An article?'

'I think rather more than that.'

'Not her prose poems? Not her verse novellas, surely?'

'Everything, it seems,' said Peter, allowing a few more absolutely irrelevant details to come back to him. 'All of it. The lot. The collected works.'

Sefton Goldberg called upon all the experience he had gained over the years of confronting disappointment. 'All of it?' he was able manfully to repeat. But the cold hand at his heart clutched a little more frantically and a hoarse derisive rattle escaped him. 'So who's the publisher? Slut Press?'

'No,' laughed Peter, brightly. 'It's all highly reputable, actually. She's been chosen to open a new series featuring the best modern young writers.' And he went on to mouth the initials, as if to keep something very adult from the children, of the distinguished publishing house which had taken up Cora Peck — introspection, metaphorical disfigurement, innovatory form, excrement and all.

Centuries of bitterness etched their lines about Sefton's drooping mouth and echoed in his words as he tried to deny Peter Potter his vicarious triumph. 'How are they going to keep her down on the farm now, eh?'

'They aren't,' said Peter promptly. 'Apparently there's some kind of writing fellowship attached to the deal, too — five years, I think.'

'So she'll be off?'

'I should say so.'

'To Rome, Paris, Hollywood?' Sefton looked sadly, as he spoke, at the application forms piled high on his desk for situations vacant in Chichester and Canterbury and Poole.

'I supose she'll go to London,' Peter guessed.

'And write reviews of other modern young experimental writers for the Sunday papers?'

'I expect so,' said Peter. He was in the best of spirits. Sefton was taking it every bit as badly as he could have hoped.

'And appear on television with Melvyn Bragg?' Wanting to be deadly, Sefton only made himself more miserable. The thought occurred to him that Cora Peck would go to London and straightaway meet up with Godfrey Jelley. He had an idea that somewhere in Hampstead stood a house (to which he fancifully gave the name Bradbury Lodge) where all the famous literary and academic figures the English-speaking world came together to discuss eros and thanatos and have a good laugh at his expense. 'Anybody heard anything of that *shmuck* Sefton Goldberg? He's *where* ?' Cora Peck, as the latest to have refreshed herself at this source of amusement, would be a much sought-after companion.

Preoccupied with the realisation that bookshops and libraries and newsagents were once again not places he could safely visit, Sefton thought he heard, in the remote distance, Peter Potter confess his ignorance of Melvyn Bragg. He didn't watch book programmes on television. He didn't interest himself in the trappings of literature, the personalities and the publicity and the gossip. Consequently, that busy glamorous life which Sefton was already vividly prefiguring for Cora, he, Peter Potter, would neither know nothing of nor care anything for. When you have a marriage like mine, Peter seemed to be implying, you do not need to envy Cora Peck.

Because he only *seemed* to be implying this, Sefton Goldberg could only seem to imply, in return, 'You lying little turd! You'll watch her on television with Melvyn and you'll be every bit as sick as I will. You'll watch her in a darkened room, when your wife has gone to bed, and you'll wrinkle up your little face and gnaw your knuckles and tie your ankles into a dozen indissoluble knots. The very thought of it would be destroying you now if it wasn't for the pleasure you are getting from watching it destroying me. Win your own battles, you miserable little prick!'

And indeed, it would have to be admitted that the miserable and lying little prick, even as he rejoiced in someone else's proudest moment, could only partially exult. His jaw too was far more mobile than he would have wanted it. And the misery lines about his mouth appeared to be only a couple of thousand years younger than Sefton Goldberg's.

'So, it's celebration at your place?' Sefton was just able to say.

'Yes. Yes, it is. It seemed only fair to offer it, as there was already a dinner planned,' Peter Potter barely managed to reply. 'That's if you don't mind giving her a lift?'

'No. No, not at all. Now I know what it's for I don't mind at all,' Sefton Goldberg could not quite find it in him to conclude.

2

Up until the day on which Cora Peck accosted Peter Potter in the corridors of the Polytechnic with a joy so spontaneous as to overcome all his instinctive revulsions — a day on which, it seemed to Sefton Goldberg (the more he brooded on it), the sheeted dead should, at the very least, have gibbered and squeaked — up until that day it had been perfectly easy for Cora and Peter to enjoy an absence of all relation without any of that embarrassment in public places which is a characteristic feature of the social life of educational institutions. They had not had to avoid one another because they had not had to pass one another. This was one of the unplanned advantages of belonging to a department which had no definite physical location but was scattered randomly over what was sometimes cruelly called the campus, and housed wherever there was a broom-cupboard or locker-room which could definitely be spared. The Department of Twentieth-Century Studies, so called in order to meet the Polytechnic's stringent requirements of relevant contemporaneity, fooled nobody, least of all Dr Gerald Sidewinder, whom it was necessary, if you wanted anything, either to fool or to please. He recognised it to be, despite its busy new name, the same tired collection of sentimental grammar school boys with indifferent degrees and a hostility towards advertising; the same old champions of forgotten causes such as marriage, vitality, even chastity (as an idea, and when it wasn't inimical to marriage and vitality); enthusiastic readers of contemporary Irish poetry and David Holbrook, who lamented the passing of open-air markets and T.F. Powys, and who, when they first arrived in Wrottesley, consulted the appropriate volume of Pevsner — in short, the same weary campaigners that had once been Humanities and before that Arts and before that Liberal Studies and before that English and History. It seemed there was no getting rid of them. Deprivation, derision, bribery, had all failed. Back they always came, scorched, flattened, and featherless, like the indefatigable victim in the sort of Walt Disney cartoon of which they didn't approve. They had nowhere else to go. So they were kept on, kept busy, and kept apart.

Dr Gerald Sidewinder, bored as a snake, eyed them with a replete and indolent malevolence. He was said by some to have a degree in chemistry, and by others a diploma in accountancy, and by others again a doctorate in surveying. The mystery which attached to his past clung still to his present. No one knew what precisely or even what approximately he was employed by the Polytechnic to do. No one knew who had appointed him. No one knew in which part of the building he had his room or what his secretary was called or what his internal telephone number was. No one knew how, officially, to address him, or in what place and on what matters. Such confusion was not unusual in the Polytechnic and arose, in part, because of the system of nomenclature it had adopted. Mindful of its obligations to a technological society and anxious not to be confused with Oxford or Cambridge, the Polytechnic aspired to that ideal system of relations which obtained in the best engineering factories and machine shops. It would have been pleasing had all the staff consented to wear overalls but in the meantime it helped that things were kept in smooth running order by a Director rather than a Vice-Chancellor and that the various indispensable skills were superintended by Heads of Sections and not Professors. Or it would have helped if only the staff had accustomed themselves more quickly to these new identifications. The members of the Department of Twentieth-Century Studies were particularly tardy. The word might even be dreamy. They could not get used to querying their superannuation contribution with the Finance Officer instead of the Bursar. They hankered after idiomatic conversation with the College Porter and were disquieted by the suspicious demeanour of the Chief Security Officer. And they continued to submit cantankerous items for inclusion on agendas to Faculty Chairmen instead of to Deputy Assistant Sub-Directors with Special Responsibilities For . . .

Even without the aid of such uncertainties Dr Gerald Sidewinder's presence in the Polytechnic would have been vexatious. He was long and thin and dusty, and had the air of being always parched. His eyes were inattentive to anything further than six inches from his face, but within that range they were busy and troubled, as if on the look out for flies. When he was spoken to — which was not often because of that doubt as to what he should be spoken to about — he would flick out his tongue as if he were taking moisture to the dry corners of his Mexican moustaches and he would rub at the folds of his cheeks in a manner which suggested they contained fine deposits of sand which irritated him. These immediate physical requirements engrossed all his attention. He found listening to anybody difficult but he found listening to academics impossible. He cut short their sentences, ignored their proposals, sent out his tongue on its laborious errand, and reminded them, at the first suggestion of anything remotely like complaint, of redeployment, retirement, resignation, and redundancy. In private he must have been still more terrible; but there were few reports in circulation of what intimate conversation with Sidewinder was like. There were, however, those who went about strangely distant and dazed as though they had once fallen overboard the *Pequod* or dined, late and at his place, with Mr Kurtz; and it was assumed that

39

such were they who had got within six inches of Dr Gerald Sidewinder's indifferent gaze and felt his carelessness warm and dry upon their face.

Naturally, such disdain was upsetting to a profession accustomed to deference. But to the Department of Twentieth-Century Studies Sidewinder's contempt for pedagogy seemed especially menacing. For here the teaching was inspirational and evangelistic. Here the arid wastes of mere information were flooded and made to bloom. Here the sap ascended audibly — whoosh! — in the tree of knowledge, and lilacs were bred out of the dead ground. It was a damp, pluvious department. Its lovers of rural poetry drove in from streaming country cottages and glistened through their lectures; its urban homosexuals, unable yet in Wrottesley to proclaim their crimson joy, were susceptible and lachrymose; the foaming tide of Ms Peck's obstinate femininity swelled daily and daily washed her pale; and even Sefton Goldberg, who was merely passing through, had trouble with his sinuses and sought fresh employment in English spas and watering holes. Gerald Sidewinder had only to roll his dead eye in the direction of any member of this department for the courage to ooze clean away from the poor object of his regard.

Sefton Goldberg was as fearful as anyone, but he felt that he shared, in a sneaky sort of way, Sidewinder's low estimate of teachers. And in an even sneakier sort of way (and because he was Jewish) he felt that he also shared Sidewinder's low estimate of himself. Actually, Gerald Sidewinder had never once in five years done anything to suggest that he had even noticed Sefton Goldberg, let alone bothered to form an estimate of him. But the very presence or proximity of Sidewinder made Sefton feel so miserable, abject and incompetent that he was sure a low estimate attached itself to him as inevitably as an odour attached itself to a rose. It wasn't a question of noticing. And the fact that Sidewinder didn't bother to notice him rather confirmed his idea than otherwise. He didn't *need* to!

He was used to gentiles making him uncomfortable. One way or another they all did. At school they had made him feel over-developed, furtive and hairy. Wandering about the school yard, his head teeming with thoughts of patricide and incest, and watching the Ormerod twins exchanging marbles with the Haydock brothers or flicking cigaratte cards against a wall, their short trousers hitched in hardy healthy Protestant fashion high up their blameless thighs, Sefton felt that from his own body, notwithstanding the concealment of his heavier jacket and longer trousers, things were visibly sprouting and multiplying and dropping, moment by moment. Fresh breezes winnowed the innocent down on Alan Ormerod's exposed limbs and fanned Derek Haydock's secret place cool; but Sefton Goldberg burned like a forest fire and sweated like a jungle. Colour blazed in his cheeks. The wax in his ears melted and popped. At a rate that would have shamed Mr Hyde black hairs sprung from his nostrils and his knuckles and his wrists. His moustache and sideburns he could hear grow. And all day long a fine hot trickle of perspiration traced the length of his spine and glued his shirt to his back. In the state he was in, he was well aware, loved by his family though he might be, even incest would be hard to come by.

Cambridge had not been much different. Dr Geoffrey Tolcarne, the occasionally post — but mainly pre-Chaucerian — Sefton's first teacher at Cambridge — didn't save cigarette cards or wear short trousers; but he did collect mediaeval stringed instruments and Sefton had once caught him shopping in King's Parade in a sort of yeoman's smock and twice swimming in the Cam in nothing. And he was white and clean and faintly mottled by wholesome regimen, as were the Ormerod twins, and he seemed equally free in his person of any crease or fold or crevice that might have harboured heat. His room, too, in which he thought and wrote of knights, pilgrims, troubadors, was open and austere. Here, where light streamed through grated windows upon stone floors, monastic stools, a faded tapestry, harps, lutes, and gyternes, a man could feel both sensuous and incorporeal, untroubled by those antinomies between matter and spirit which were to fret and finally dissociate the sensibilities of post-mediaeval mankind. Sefton Goldberg — a case in point — his head still teeming with unspeakable thoughts and unrealisable desires, even though by now the idea of patricide had palled and passed, arrived at Dr Tolcarne's for his first class on the importance of chastity in *Gawain and the Green Knight*, took one look about the room, saw objects whose names he did not know but which made him think of words like psaltery and triptych and sacristy, and broke into a sweat. Geoffrey Tolcarne, for his part, took one look at Sefton Goldberg and broke into whatever is the opposite.

Even as he dripped on the ancient stones Sefton was able to understand that Dr Tolcarne had selected the objects in his room with great discrimination and refinement, and that Dr Tolcarne would never have selected him. Sefton saw no reason to question Dr Tolcarne's taste. So he put up no resistance to the eminent scholar's suave transitions from the question of courtliness to the question of honour, from honour to hospitality, from hospitality to liberality, from liberality to money-lending, from money-lending to usury, and from usury to the murder by Jews of young Hugh of Lincoln — to which, had he been there and then accused, Sefton would have readily confessed. At the end of the hour, during which every item of his clothing had stuck itself to every other, he gathered up his books, rounded his shoulders and backed out of the mediaevalist's presence, wringing his hands. By mutual, tacit agreement never to return. For his part he would have understood if Dr Tolcarne had hosed down his room the moment he left it. And for all he knew Dr Tolcarne had.

So he was used to gentiles making him uncomfortable.

But with Sidewinder it was different. Sidewinder did not merely aggravate his physical clumsiness; Sidewinder made him feel naive, unaccustomed, boyish — morally and philosophically and practically callow. This was a new humiliation. Sefton had always prided himself on being, in so far as a proper worldliness demanded it, something of a cynic; and even in his Fanny Price days he had known how to say the sorts of unexpectedly harsh and heartless things which win attention and pass for cynicism. But Sidewinder taught him that he knew nothing at all of that perfect carelessness of the feelings and the opinions of men, that pure indifference to their regard or their execration, which is cynicism proper. Watching the slow movement of Sidewinder's tongue; listening to the flat vowels of his Chorley accent, Sefton realised that all along he had only been dabbling in misanthropy, which is a passion.

What other solution was there to the little moral conundrum which had often troubled Sefton — why it was, if he was so disenchanted with the human race, that he still wanted its applause? And by applause, the applause Sidewinder didn't need or crave or seek and he, Sefton Goldberg, did, he meant not simply the general idea — recognition, approval, appreciation, perhaps even reward — no, he meant the vulgar, literal thing: the hum of a packed auditorium, the sound of hand against hand, cheers, roars, whistles, encores. This was not mere vanity or fantasy; as other men fulfilled and understood themselves only through work or physical love or religious faith, so Sefton was perfected only when his ears rang like sea-shells with the tumultuous swell of acclamation.

Why then hadn't he joined a rock group or a political party? What possible promise was held out to him by those application forms which arrived at the Polytechnic by the sackful, twice a day, and for whose completion he tinkered with his biography repeatedly, like some sinless Jewish Ancient Mariner, still waiting for the bird? What, in short, was he doing at his age looking to academic life for the rewards and satisfactions of show business? That last question, which presented itself to him on most afternoons as the light in his room began to darken and there was not the faintest echo of a plaudit to be discerned, always prompted another: what would he have thought of himself, at his age, if he had looked to academic life for anything else?

One's teaching — 'my teaching', as Peter Potter called it, in tones almost as ceremonious as those in which he spoke of 'my marriage' and expressive of intimacies of relationship almost as unfathomable — one's teaching was not when one was thirty-five what it had been when one was twenty-three. Peter Potter insisted that his was, but Sefton wasn't taken in. It didn't seem to him that there was much that was strictly pedagogic, for example, about Peter's commitment to the ideal of personalized teaching. 'I prefer small groups,' he had said on more than one occasion, after Sefton perchance had voiced his preference for something approaching a Nuremberg rally. Sefton was prepared to allow that his own predilections were not everybody's, but he knew never to trust a man who preferred small groups. He had come across too many. He had explained to Peter that small group teaching was rife in Australia. 'It's the lapsed but nostalgic Catholics who are especially keen on it. They huddle their hand-picked students close around the text and together they probe and finger it as if it has a sex.'

'There's no sex in my seminars,' Peter reassured him.

But of course there was. You could tell that from the flush of excitement and guilt which had still not left Peter's cheek an hour after it was all over, just as you could tell it from the little heaving chests of Peter's whittled-down group, the four or five unassertive, serious women before whom Peter had arranged himself on tables and cupboards and tied his ankles in a bow. Like all small groups they had met in the late

44

afternoon when the light was fading and spirits were wan and the words on the page were scarcely distinguishable from the barely-shaped hopes and the half-formed possibilities and the intimations and the maybes and the almosts that faintly brushed one another in the gathering shadows. Sefton sometimes wondered whether Miranda had any inkling of what her husband got up to on his busiest teaching afternoons.

Arthur Twinbarrow, who specialised in all the twentieth-century poets whose first or second names were Tom or Thomas, was not a small group man, but he too was able to use words like teaching and education without embarrassment and had even been heard to speak of enriching the sensibilities of his students. He was a man of bafflingly indeterminate middle-age who gave the most conscientiously tortured tutorials and spent every penny he earnt thereby on his four children, sending them to the sorts of public schools and private schools and special schools which alone could be relied upon to put into practice his high ideals. Consequently he was poor in the way Sefton remembered his grammar school teachers being poor in the fifties, and he went about in shiny trousers and a threadbare jacket and ate his lunch from a plastic box and rationed himself to one coffee and one biscuit or two coffees and no biscuits per day. His belief in the ameliorative properties of education had caused his shoulders to stoop like an old man's and his hair to turn pure white. But even Sefton Goldberg had to admit that it had also caused his eyes to burn and flash with that sort of inappropriately optimistic vitality which is sometimes seen in invalids.

Sefton once carelessly asked Arthur if he had watched a particular play on television the night before.

'Television? We can't afford one of those.'

'Arthur, everyone can afford a television. Don't tell me you're opposed on principle?'

'No, not principle. Poverty.'

'Arthur, you're not *still* paying those exorbitant fees, are you?'

'Yes, oh yes. Will be for years.'

'Arthur, I know it's none of my business, but is it worth it? They'll still ignore you when you're old —'

'They ignore me now.'

'— or drink themselves to death, or chase loose women, or end up in a job like ours.'

'I believe they must be given a good start.'

'But Arthur, *we* had a good start. We even had a good middle. And look at us! And we are the lucky ones — they say.'

'They're right,' said Arthur, his eyes, despite the rest of him, shining with faith. 'We *are* the lucky ones.'

Sefton didn't envy Arthur his fervour, but he did sometimes look back, in a melancholy sort of way, to the days before the demise of his own. It had been fun, all that ferocity and acrimony, all that murderousness and contumely with which he had once fallen, like the Mongol hordes, upon whoever failed to grasp the significance of *Persuasion* or *Villette*. But age had damped his fire and the students at the Polytechnic, Wrottesley, had extinguished it completely. From the very first day of his arrival they had regarded him in corridors with such shrinking distrust, had raised to him in lectures such woebegone countenances on which was written, in a primitive hand, such deprivation, incomprehension and suspicion, that he knew before he had even opened his mouth that he had said too much and been too clever by half. If he had turned up at a home for the disabled and done handstands in a spangled leotard on the arms of their wheelchairs he would not have felt more indiscreet. 'Who did he think he was?' He gave them a full fortnight to find out. He treated them to his funniest stories and his most surprising comparisons. He loosened his tie and smoked cheroots and tore up any number of Penguin Classics, throwing the offending pages high in the air so that they would fall like confetti onto the hair and

46

shoulders of the assembled students. They sat throughout in silence, passive and suspicious in orderly rows, their pens held uncertainly in tattooed fingers, their necks an autumnal yellow and brown where they'd been biting one another to repetitive music the night before — waiting for knowledge. Sefton decided then and there that he was damned if he was going to give them any. At first he went no further than to keep things from them — his freshest insights, his most startling judgements, a trenchant phrase that had come to him in his sleep. He didn't tell them any more jokes either, and he didn't rip up any more Penguin Classics. But deprivation on this scale soon struck him as being rather tame, especially as his students lacked the wherewithal to comprehend the magnitude of their loss, and so he stepped up his campaign to include deliberately leading them astray — confusing chronology, moving without their noticing it scenes and characters from one long novel to another, misattributing authorship, and finally, in order that they should remain for ever in ignorance of the greatness of the great tradition, informing them that the major English novelists were Bulwer Lytton, Charles Lever, Harrison Ainsworth, Mrs Henry Wood, and Angela Carter. He also told them that the greatest English poets were Francis Quarles and Namby-Pamby Philips, and that the greatest living critic was Bernard Levin. At last his conviction that his students should be given precisely what they deserved led him to teaching them what he hadn't read and in some cases hadn't heard of. There was even some charity in that — it reduced the distance between their ignorance and his and ensured that they would not be overwhelmed by his scholarship or overawed by his brilliance or intimidated by his authority.

The only occasions on which he failed to honour his pledge to himself never to say anything he meant came when his need to abuse other academic disciplines grew too strong for him. Although he couldn't remember why he had once liked his own subject he hadn't in the least forgotten what he hated about other peoples'. The Historians who were reluctant to discuss great men because great men were never typical; the Linguisticians who were at present cock-a-hoop because every other department wanted them to come along and explain what diachronic meant; the Geographers — the Human Geographers, that is — who dressed like Alan Bates dressing like Michael Henchard and who said fuck in lectures; all these provided Sefton with opportunities he found it hard to resist. There were few things he loved more than to rat publicly on his colleagues. But the sight of his audience conscientiously writing down everything he said always brought him to his senses. Lowering his own head, he would return to the long novel, quietly misleading his pupils below the din of the turning buses outside on the subject of *Put Yourself In His Place*, by Charles Reade. A novel which he told them ranked with E. Lynn Linton's *Grasp Your Nettle*, and for which they subsequently searched the shelves of W.H. Smith's and Zodiac — Wrottesley's adult soft-back bookshop.

Whether they were retributive or ultimately philanthropic, Sefton's efforts to deprive his students of knowledge had not resulted in any significant drop in the numbers of degrees and diplomas that were handed out by some trade union official in the Wrottesley Civic Hall each year. This very afternoon they were being distributed again, and many over whom despairing parents and learned child psychiatrists and indefatigable remedial teachers had shaken their heads were now B.A. The sounds of doors opening around the building and of group laughter disturbed Sefton in his reveries and told him that the ceremony was over. Through his window he could see familiar heavy faces, perplexed but happy under their mortar boards. A noise at his door, not so much a knock as an exhausted dying lunge, was followed, as it invariably was, by the appearance of Charles Wenlock, Head of the Department of Twentieth-Century Studies. He was wearing his raincoat and carried his academic robes over his arm. He had the air of a bringer of bad news, and the further air of never having been the bringer of anything else. He gave a long wailing sigh and collapsed, without crushing his coat, in a chair.

This was a perfectly standard entrance and caused Sefton no alarm. Charles Wenlock appeared to be in his customary state of agitation, somewhere between dudgeon and umbrage — occasioned, as likely as not, by the weather, or a sleepless night, or an imagined slight from a colleague, or too tight a collar. The long wailing sigh, giving way to more minor, supporting groans, was to Charles Wenlock what a belch is to a hedonist: a gesture of defiance and contentment, an acknowledgement that one has been getting what one wants. In Charles Wenlock's case this was usually indigestion, lumbago, dispute, and a profound philosophic sensation of impotence.

So there was nothing obviously untoward about this collapse. But Sefton did notice that his visitor was a little redder and a little hotter than usual. And there was about his dudgeon something a trifle abashed, and about his umbrage something a mite culpable. After a few more minutes groaning he came up with a smile which seemed to ask for both forgiveness and appreciation. Had it not been for Charles Wenlock's seniority Sefton might easily have asked, after such an entreaty, 'All right then Charles, what have you gone and done this time?' And his head of department would have lowered his eyes and flushed deeper and loosened his scarf and sighed and looked oddly pleased with himself. He had that arch and archaic air of enjoying his incorrigibility which in the English popular farcical tradition belongs to an elderly country bachelor caught out with one of the kitchen girls.

'You've heard?' he asked at last.

'Heard what? You mean about Cora?'

Charles Wenlock waved his hand dismissively, as if

to imply that he wasn't prepared to waste good wailing and complaining time on trifles.

Sefton felt ashamed of the smallness of his own pre-occupations. 'Then I haven't heard. What's happened?'

Charles Wenlock made his lips very thin and nodded his head in the direction of the Civic Hall, from which the newly-graduated were still reluctantly straggling. 'That b****** Sidewinder!'

He mouthed his innocent profanities quaintly, putting in his own asterisks. Sefton liked this old-fashionedness in him. It went with his being something of a provincial, mildly bohemian toff of earlier days, some country versifier of merit who had a small private income and the easy left-wing affiliations that belonged to poetry rather than to politics. He might have known Auden and Spender and shared their aspirations. But instead he was here, in a polytechnic, in Wrottesley, running a department notoriously vulnerable in the matter of relevance — and still managing not to swear.

But only just.

'The rude, ignorant b******,' he went on, red with anger, his mouth full of asterisks.

'What's he done?'

'Said!'

'What's he said?'

Sefton remembered that as Assistant Sub-Director with Special Responsibilities for Prospective Development, Sidewinder would today have been addressing the crowds in the Civic Hall — reassuring even those who would never return as to the rosy future of the Polytechnic, promising ambiguous developments, hinting at unambiguous redeployments, keeping them guessing still what his job actually was, before handing them over to the guest of honour, Alf or was it Bill of the Boilermakers. It wasn't difficult to imagine Charles Wenlock, done up in his academic robes, sighing and moaning in his seat as Sidewinder brutalised his finer senses. He was a most fastidious man.

'He said the Polytechnic had been struggling for

50

some time to overcome the problems caused by shortage of adequate teaching accommodation. He said he had not been deaf to the sometimes bitter complaints of several departments. He said he had come up with a plan of wholesale reorganization which he was sure would be in every way satisfactory to all but the most difficult to please.'

'And?'

'Computer Sciences will go from B Block to C Block. Biology for Physiotherapists will go from C Block to A Block. Languages for Secretaries will go from A Block to D Block. Business Studies will go to the Bus Station Annexe. Social Sciences will go from E Block and F Block to G Block, H Block, J Block, K Block and L Block.'

'And we stay where we are, I take it,' Sefton interjected, having caught the drift.

'Oh no,' said Charles, demoniacally. 'We too, despite our sometimes bitter protestations in the past, are to be rehoused. Together. As *a* Department.'

'Well that's a good thing,' said Sefton. 'Isn't it?' he added a moment later, as Charles Wenlock only squinted at him as if he were a fool.

'You haven't yet heard where the b****** intends to rehouse us.'

'M Block?'

'There is no M Block.'

Sefton shrugged. But he was compelled by the wildness of Charles Wenlock's squint to spell out his ignorance and his curiosity. This was the price one paid for ever letting Charles Wenlock know that one thought good anything that emanated from Gerald Sidewinder. 'Where does he intend to rehouse us?' he asked, penitentially.

'There,' said Charles, pointing his arm towards the window.

Sefton looked out. Buses were loading up their passengers. Circling and reversing and shuddering. Beyond the queues of pinched bad-tempered workers

Sefton saw the last gowned graduates disappearing with their still stunned families into the town.

'In the Civic Hall?'

Charles Wenlock shook his head.

'Worse than that?'

Charles Wenlock nodded.

'In a bus?'

Charles rose and joined Sefton at the window. He pointed with his finger. 'To the right of the Civic Hall.'

Sefton peered. To the right of the Civic Hall the ring road ploughed its way through the middle of the town. To the right of that was Wrottesley Ramblers football stadium watched over by its four gaunt pylons. To the right of that, mysteriously, was the ring road again.

'You did say to the right?' Sefton was conscious of being a bit obtuse.

Charles Wenlock made a precise, stabbing movement with his finger. 'What's that?'

'The football ground.'

'What else is it?'

'I don't know.'

'Have a guess.'

Sefton swung around and stared with disbelief into Charles Wenlock's smiling eyes. 'Oh no, not there?'

'Yes.'

'We are to teach there?' Suddenly Sefton's teaching seemed to be very dear to him.

'We are to do everything there.'

'What happens when it rains?'

'They aren't giving us the pitch. We'll be in the South Stand. That's to be your room there, just above where it says Schoolboys £1.'

'Does that mean I'll be able to see the game for nothing?' Sefton had not the faintest desire to see the game, but he was trying to look on the bright side.

'No. We don't get windows. Anyway, you wouldn't want to watch. They're awful these days. Nobody wants to watch. That's why they need the rent.'

'So we're helping them through a bad patch.'

'Why else? Sidewinder has connections with the club, of course. It's his ruling passion.'

'Sidewinder has a passion?'

'He used to be a player himself. He had a trial with the club.' Despite himself Charles Wenlock allowed a little awe to show.

Sefton wasn't impressed by Sidewinder's having once had a trial. What thug hadn't? 'In that case,' he said, 'given Sidewinder's attitude to us, I'm surprised he wants us there. Doesn't he think we'll be lowering the tone? Does he know I'll be teaching Proust there?'

'He does,' said Charles Wenlock, suddenly becoming red again. 'He does think we'll lower the tone.'

Sefton laughed. Sidewinder's scheme seemed to him too preposterous for genuine anger. It was an act of pantomime devilry calling for pantomime rage. 'You're sure it's not a joke?' he asked.

'It's no joke. And I do know he thinks we'll be lowering the tone' — Charles was insistent and ominously repetitive — 'because he said so.'

'He actually said so?'

'He actually said so.'

'You mean he said it to you afterwards.'

'No, I mean he said it to me at the time.'

'From the platform?'

'Yes.'

The continuing rise in Charles Wenlock's temperature and the return of his earlier air of culpability filled Sefton Goldberg with forebodings and gave him the right, he felt, to a little pedantry. 'In what sense did he address *you* in his speech from the platform?'

'In the same sense,' said Charles Wenlock, with curiously compromised dignity, 'that I addressed *him* in mine.'

'But, Charles, you weren't making a speech.'

'No, but I made one all the same. Impromptu.'

'You didn't heckle him did you?' asked Sefton gratuitously, for he knew the answer. It was now certain that the afternoon had seen another of Charles Wenlock's famous acts of self-immolation. He could smell the flames.

'I interjected. I interposed. I rose and told him I deplored both the decision he had made about the rehousing of my department and the place and manner of its publication.' Charles Wenlock was heroic, but his enunciation was precise and thin, an exact replica, Sefton was convinced, of what it had been in the Civic Hall where students and parents and scholars and dignitaries and Bill the Boilermaker had gathered for a joyous academic occasion. Deplored. It was his favourite word. It offered to do battle but it sounded instead a glorious retreat. It was one of his wailing sighs made articulate. 'I told him I took the strongest possible exception to his not consulting the members of the department, and deplored the insult implicit in the notion that we might satisfactorily teach in a football stadium.'

'What did Sidewinder say to that?' asked Sefton, humbled into a minor role.

'He said good teachers could teach anywhere. But that if it was to be a question of insult, the football club might well consider itself the aggrieved party. It did, after all, boast an international reputation, whereas the department — he begged to be corrected if he was wrong — my department enjoyed a more modest fame.'

Listening, Sefton Goldberg died a thousand deaths. Even in report Sidewinder's words had the power to make him feel five years old. He could see the slow movement of his dry lips as vividly as if they were in the room. And he could hear the nervous perfidious laughter which Sidewinder knew how to provoke in an audience relieved that someone else was victim. 'I suppose that sparked off some merriment?'

'Oh, yes.' Charles Wenlock had learnt to be philosophical about other people's laughter. 'I should have sat down, but it seemed that if the football club didn't want us that was the more reason for our not going there.'

'Did you say that?'

'Oh, yes. In that case, I replied, after they had finished clapping him, the football club will be relieved if the Department of English Literature takes its obscurity elsewhere.'

'You mean the Department of Twentieth-Century Studies,' Sefton corrected him.

'Yes. I forgot.'

'Charles, you didn't — did you? — call us the Department of English Literature?'

Charles Wenlock gave a series of little moans and with a burning face he nodded the assent his mouth had become too dry to utter.

Charles Wenlock's absent-mindedness as to the name of the department of which he was head had not gone unnoticed in the Polytechnic; nor had it been allowed to pass as harmless eccentricity. Ever since the Polytechnic, in an attempt to give the impression of upward thrust and forward exploration, had adopted the language of space-travel and gone for modularity — offering primary units rather than major subjects and ancillary back-up units rather than minor subjects, and seeking from the students feedback rather than opinion — Charles Wenlock's fidelity to English Literature had been an embarrassment and an anomaly. In anyone it would have been regarded as tactless, but in the head of a department whose disciplines were now so multi- and inter- as to require a full-time navigational expert to explain to the stranded the complex system of inputs and through-routes, such an antiquated single subject bias was considered dangerously regressive. Especially when the single subject was English Literature. Or rather English Lit. Everyone had an imitation of Charles Wenlock's pronunciation of 'English Lit.' But no one could ever come close to the reedy quality of the original; no one could ever get it to evoke as he could such pinched refinement of sensibility. It made one think of Bloomsbury ruralized; of E.M. Forster leaning lightly on the arm of one of Virginia's cousins —

perhaps a soldier — in a Gloucestershire garden, and whispering sibilantly about the Sitwells. Every time Charles Wenlock forgot the name of his department and referred to English Lit. he brought the bland luxury of that garden into the Polytechnic; and even those who were only part-time union men and superficial socialists experienced the ignominy of exclusion and felt the need to loot and pillage.

Sefton Goldberg knew how Charles' mistake would have sounded in the Civic Hall. He could see, as the assembled guests would have seen, Charles Wenlock going redder and redder, enraged and abashed, and making a virtue of his embarrassment; fastidiously thinning and purifying his vocabulary; driving himself, victim of his own integrity, to the wall. And taking English Lit. with him.

'I take it that Sidewinder made something of that,' Sefton said bleakly, after a long silence.

'What do you think?' Charles Wenlock replied with some aggression. 'He said that if he had known there was a Department of English Literature anywhere in the Polytechnic he would have consulted it. Which just about brought the house down. There wasn't much point in going on. I wasn't going to achieve anything. I suppose I shouldn't have started in the first place.' He seemed to want Sefton to say, yes, he should have.

But all that came back to him was, 'And what do you think will happen now?'

'We go to the football ground,' Charles Wenlock replied with incorrigibly urbane resignedness.

'I wasn't thinking of that. I meant, do you think there will be any repercussions? Do you think Sidewinder will let the matter of your interjection drop?'

'Your guess is as good as mine,' said Charles Wenlock, surprised but not perturbed. Clearly he had not been thinking of consequences; but a new light appeared in his eyes, and it struck Sefton as being the gleam of anticipated persecution. 'What do you think?' he went on. 'Do you think he'll pursue it?'

'I don't know,' said Sefton Goldberg, austerely. But he was Jewish and wantonly indulgent and he could not deny the head of his department, whom he liked, a final twinge of pleasure. Especially as it was, for such a thoroughly gentile man, such a thoroughly Jewish pleasure. 'He might,' he conceded. And then, more alluringly, 'He well might.'

Charles Wenlock sighed and did up the buttons of his coat. Beneath the extravagant colours of his humiliations and furies there was still visible the deep tan of his last long Continental holiday. He always wore well-cut coats and fine woollen scarves. Inside his clothes he looked pampered and content. Well-satisfied with another hard-earned defeat.

'Are you coming to collect your car?' he asked.

'No,' said Sefton, consulting his watch, 'I've a few things to do before I leave.'

Charles Wenlock cast his eye over Sefton's application forms. 'You're still trying to get out?' It rang rather like an accusation.

'Half-heartedly,' Sefton lied.

'Well, if you come across anything suitable for me, let me know.'

'But Charles, I thought you loved it here?'

'I don't, you know,' he snapped, in one of his characteristic returns to literalness and touchiness. He was red-faced again, and tight lipped. He strangled a sigh in his throat, turned up his collar, and left.

Sefton Goldberg allowed his final words, 'I don't, you know,' to echo in his mind. And after a few moments he would not have been able to say for certain whether or not Charles Wenlock had added, 'I deplore it.'

3

In the highly improbable event of his being asked to nominate the one most un-Jewish thing he could think of, Sefton Goldberg would have been hard pressed to decide between Nature — that's to say birds, trees, flowers, and country walks — and football — that's to say beer, bikies, mud, and physical pain. But he would almost certainly have come down finally on the side of football. Nature, which had been such a mystery to him and caused him so much discomfort when he was a young student of literature at Cambridge, had lost over the years a little of its alien, para-Christian menace. But only after a hard struggle.

Sefton could still remember the first time he encountered Paul Morel absently putting berries into Clara Dawes's coat. 'You often find the berries going rotten in springtime,' Paul explained, while Clara stood patiently for him, watching his quick hands, so full of life.

'Shit!' Sefton had thought.

Finding his mother in her rocking-chair, wearing her black silk blouse, Paul Morel felt his heart contract with pain. 'It's such a pretty day, mother!' he said. 'And we saw a jay.'

'So fucking what!' Sefton had expostulated, throwing the volume from him.

It was a problem. What was he doing reading stuff like this? He, who didn't know a jay from a jemmy and who wouldn't have bothered to tell his mother if he'd seen either. 'And we saw a jay.' It was like a foreign language. If all English literature was about country walks — and that was beginning to look suspiciously like the case — then what the fuck did it have to do with Sefton Goldberg who was Jewish and who had therefore never taken a country walk in his life?

That was a question to which Sefton had not got around to finding an answer, even now. What happened in the country was as impenetrable as it had ever been. He still couldn't, today, tell a brake from a bosk or a rill from a beck; he still didn't know whether one ripped one's clothes on a tor or tumbled headlong down a coppice; and he was no more certain than he had ever been that one didn't swim in an osprey or feed crumbs to a runnel. But he was a bit more relaxed about it. He gave up trying to make head or tail of pastoral poetry. He kept a sharp lookout, when he was reading novels, for passages of description and learnt to skip them without damage to the plot. And of course he stayed away from any social occasion which might have ended in a ramble or a picnic or a hike. Once he gave up all hope of familiarising Nature in its details (they were not and they never would be Jewish), and came to think of it in a general way as simply that which was outside, he even found that he could very nearly enjoy it. He could punt in the outside, and he could drink wine and watch tennis in it. Women, before being led inside, liked to be taken outside. And although in Sefton's sensual imagination it was always 7.00 pm and his companion was forever formally attired as for an intimate candle-lit dinner, there was still time — if one hurried — for a walk onto a balcony or a promenade upon a terrace, beneath a wheeling sky. If at that happy moment the clouds were to scud and the stars were to flash and the ewes just happened to be in labour, so much the better. For his part Sefton, who was not given to looking heavenwards and didn't know a ewe from a sow, would in all probability not notice; but if the fortunate conjunction of these things was pointed out to him he would stand for a moment and attend and stroke his companion's shivering arm before leading her inside again to her table. This was a measure of how far he had travelled. He had still not arrived at a submission to the greater ordering, nor did he yet know — *know* in that Nottinghamshire way — that he did not belong to himself; but at least he no longer maintained that Nature belonged exclusively to the gentiles.

Football, however — he continued to maintain — did.

And he was not merely thinking of the obvious ways in which the game was not Jewish: that it owed its origins to a working-class culture that was shaped when the Jews were elsewhere: that it was played on Saturdays — the day of rest; that it was a violent game, demanding of its players sinew and brawn, whereas Jewish men had soft skin and bruised easily. This last was no small consideration. The whole art of existence, for many a Jew of Sefton's acquaintance, was to avoid sedulously, in one lifetime, the brutality of conflict and collision that the average footballer enjoyed in an hour and a half. Sefton was able to recall with some fondness the fights that never quite broke out between Jewish boys at school. They swore and gesticulated at one another; they mocked one another's disabilities and betrayed one another's confidences; they destroyed one another's families with calumny and vilification; satirized one another's girlfriends, blighted one another's hopes, desecrated one another's dreams. But they never raised a mark on one another's skin. Christian boys left their fathers' bankruptcy and their sisters' pregnancy out of it and got on with the business of nutting and butting and kneeing one another until one of them dropped.

Sefton himself had come to the conclusion early on in his school life that football was not for him. And once he had been forced to understand that he had no means of legal redress against the school for causing him to hurt his knees on frost-hard playing fields, he relied upon his mother's prolific pen and extensive knowledge of minor ailments to get him off. Every Wednesday afternoon he and Godfrey Jelley, who was too fat to play, and Aubrey Kershaw, who was too blind, sat on the platform in the hall and polished the trophies which the healthy boys were out there in the blizzard competing for.

Sefton's father was not altogether convinced that this was the best preparation for his son's approaching manhood. Every morning, before he went off to school, Sefton had to submit to an exhaustive interrogation from his mother on the subject of what he needed for the day — did he have his bus pass, dinner money, clean handkerchief, some form of identification, pens, ruler, and a little wad of toilet paper (just in case)? When he remembered, Sefton's father would add, 'And a note from your mother explaining that you're bilious?'

Sefton remained bilious until he went to university where sport was not compulsory. But that had been because of his dislike of the physical demands of football; what he had in mind, now, when he maintained that there was nothing more un-Jewish, was its spectacle — its occasion, and the idea of it — the metaphysic behind the ritual. To the spectacle he was far from unresponsive. He went to his first professional match on a Tuesday evening, late in life, grudgingly. But he was excited at once by the theatricality and the suggestion of fantasy which the floodlights lent to the ground. Beneath their glare the turf was an impossible technicolour green like the new baize of a billiard table, and the boy players, when they ran out, shone like polished idols. The cheering and the singing and the chanting from a crowd big enough to fill several hundred lecture theatres could not fail to have a profound effect upon him. He was as sentimental as Hitler about applause and crowds. As the stand rumbled and thundered around him his flesh thrilled and the spirit within was elevated and chastened. He felt the pain of his own isolated individuality. He caught himself longing for that mystical connection between himself and the rest of the populous universe which always

61

seemed fleetingly feasible to him at a Beethoven concert or during the singing of a national anthem. It did not matter a jot that there was unlikely to be a single member of that populous universe here today in the crowd with whom he could have managed even the most cursory connection. Ironic perception faded in the fervour of the occasion. He saw into the heart of things. Saw the sadness. 'Shit! shit! shit!' sang ten thousand voices and twice as many V-signs pointed heavenwards as Sefton Goldberg shivered and shuddered with emotion, and was sorry for all the lies he had told and the people he had hurt and the family he had disappointed and the humanity whose suffering he could not alleviate and himself from whom one day he would be separated for ever.

Predictably, he missed the first goal.

The crowd rose in exultation or in protest, leaving seated only Sefton Goldberg and, in front of him, a couple of orthodox-looking Jewish boys — perhaps *yeshiva* boys. They sat, self-conscious and uneasy, close to one another. Their embroidered skull-caps were fastened to the backs of their heads with women's clips; their hair sprouted from all parts of them, not quite as Sefton's once had, because of the body's inherent tropical zeal, but more as in fealty to a demanding ancient God; and bits of holy garments were visible from above their collars. Around and between all this they also wore, to Sefton's amazement, football scarves. The sight of Gandhi in a beany or an Ayatollah with a rattle would have been no more surprising. But it was only when Sefton realised that they were supporters of the team which had just scored; it was only when he heard one mutter to the other, 'I don't like it, Myer — they've scored too soon', and the other reply, 'I know, I know'; that he understood the significance of their sitting hunched and quiet amid the tumult. And only then did he understand how great a gulf divided them from the other spectators and from the game itself. They were doom-laden. They had highly developed imaginations of disaster. They feared pride and presumption. Quite frankly, if the goal couldn't go uncelebrated they would rather it had gone unscored. Success was liability enough without the added perils of publicity. A Jewish team unfortunate enough to take an early lead would have kept it quiet and hoped that no one noticed.

But such fears were alien to football. Above all else, the game gloried in the passing, delirious moment; gave the illusory promise, to players and spectators, of irreversible triumph and permanent reward. The scorer of the goal taunted the opposition, jeered at detractors in the crowd, lifted his fists to the heavens, unable to prefigure, though it happened every week, that a moment later his team would be the object of identical mockery and he would have to show his dejection as shamelessly as he had shown his delight. It was the unimaginativeness of irreligion; the optimism of impiety. Sefton could tell from just looking at the players that they were superstitious: clearly this one would not shave before an away match and that one always wore borrowed laces in his boots at home; but these were mere blank, primitive stirrings. On the field they knew nothing of retribution, learnt nothing from experience, feared nothing from providence. In the strictest sense the game they played was heathen. For the *goyim*.

Sefton stood dispiritedly at the window of his room and looked out across the flattened town to the sloping, rusting, corrugated roof of Wrottesley Ramblers Football Club. His new academic home! He did not want to go there. He had always supposed that in so far as his life had been moving in any direction it had been moving up and away. One aspired. One put things behind one. If he was going to spend the rest of his days in a football stand he might as well have played rough games in the school playground, all those years ago, with the Haydock brothers and the Ormerod twins. And acquired some skills more appropriate to his future style of life: how to squirm under a turnstile, which part of the forehead to use when nutting a policeman.

It had been a bad day for Sefton. First Cora and now this. By comparison with everything around it, the half hour on the floor with Mrs Shorthall seemed in retrospect like a little Golden Age. Sefton addressed and sealed a dozen envelopes and added them to another dozen already prepared for posting. Then he rose, put on his coat, readjusted the position of Nick Lee's jacket, turned out his light, and braced himself for the arduous journey to his car.

Only the phrase 'laid waste', with its strange conjunction of the ideas of savage devastation and methodical arrangement, could do justice to the formal dereliction of the Polytechnic car park. For it was waste in no merely fortuituous way, but appeared as if demolished freshly each day by one whose responsibility it was to move about the bricks and the rubble and the old bicycle tyres and the twists of newspaper, and even to add to them, according to some undisclosed official design for a polytechnic car park. Sefton noticed that the more this unseen presence perfected its art, the more the traffic which braved it sparkled and shone. Night after night the debris was shuffled and dealt, and day after day every car but Sefton's drove in vacuumed and waxed and smelling of shampoo. Wild growths of vegetation appeared, gorging themselves on masonry and petrol fumes; wickedly white fungi, as big as fists and more menacing, grew instantaneously from stagnant pools of oil and rain-water; and living things that slid and hissed took up permanent abode and brought up families in the junk and litter. Undeterred, the drivers washed their wheels and imposed an order of their own upon the rotting terrain, parcelling it out strictly, with a foot or two more for this department and a foot or two less for that, according to the number of doctorates in each. It was as if there were some silent, unacknowledged but deadly battle in the air, joined without hesitation by combatants who did not know and would not have recognized one another, and for no better reason than a native liking for hostilities. Sefton Goldberg saw in this conflict nothing that was essentially different from the usual not-quite-covert aggression of English social life; in the same spirit did the English compose anonymous letters and draw up secret petitions and bang on hotel walls and mumble their remonstrances in bus queues; out of the same frustrated fretfulness did waiters not catch your eye, porters not carry your bag, directory enquiries not give you a telephone number. England might or might not have been ripe for revolution, but it was clear to Sefton that it was already undergoing a sort of subdued civil war, the more disruptive and confusing for being between factions whose loyalties kept changing according to whether they were, at any particular moment, desirous of receiving a service or required to perform one. In a working town such as Wrottesley the war was particularly furtive, for the local working population entertained the fancy that it was animated by the salty, unpretentious good-naturedness, an easy friendly Midland warmth which guaranteed an endearment with every refusal; but the surreptitiousness of the fighting only increased its bitterness. In the main, and regardless of how they lined up, the middle classes fought more cleanly because they showed you their weapons. They weren't hampered by ideas of salty, unpretentious good-naturedness. This was the nearest Sefton Goldberg came to taking sides; for the most part he remained aloof like most foreigners from a battle that was not, except when he wanted something, his. But he was still naive enough to be surprised, every time he parked or collected his car, by the progress this national belligerence had made in the hearts of men of intellect and cultivation.

As he picked his way this evening towards where he normally kept his car he remembered that the degree ceremony had put more than usual pressure on parking space and that when he had driven in that morning his assigned and regular strip had been taken. He looked about to recall where he had parked. There it was, his old Avenger, scarcely distinguishable from the rubble on which it stood; but there too, nearby, was a small huddle of men in urgent conference, huddling and conferring as men never did in such a place of tacit enmity and quiet attrition. For these were members of the Department of Modern Languages for Business and this was their parking area and Sefton Goldberg was decidedly not a member of the Department of Modern Languages for Business and yet here, in their space, and still here at this hour, was of all people's and of all cars, his car!

He did not register the enormity of his crime, nor indeed of his punishment, all at once; but he pieced it together fairly quickly, noticing first that Bob Floss, Head of the outraged Department of Modern Languages for Business, was there; and then that his deputy or foreman, Dr Alan Haslemere, was there; and then that there had been attempts to stencil onto the unreliable surface of the car park the warning DEPARTMENT OF MODERN LANGUAGES FOR BUSINESS STRICTLY NO UNAUTHORISED PARKING — but the ground had refused to stay still, there was white paint everywhere, and already the words were curving and bending as if they were signalling the start of a memory sequence in an English film about lost illusions. It was only after Sefton had made all this out that he saw that the windscreen of his car was plastered over with gummed labels upon which was scrawled the same message which the shifting rubbish underfoot had not accepted. The primitive malevolence of this deface-ment incited him to anger.

'Which one of you did this?'

He stood close to his car as if it were in need of his pro-tection, and addressed the silent group of men.

It was Bob Floss, naturally, who undertook to speak

for his department. He separated himself just a little from his group, as a leader should. He was soft and corpulent, the fat-boy victim of every school bully, who now bullied a whole department of his own. He was that poeticully just but dreaded thing: the worm turned.

'So this *is* your car,' he said, in mock, jeering surprise. 'We weren't sure whether it was or not. I thought you'd have got about in something sportier.'

'You would have preferred something sportier to vandalise, would you?'

Bob Floss rubbed the area of his face where a chin should have been, and offered to weigh Sefton's words judiciously. 'Hardly vandalise. We just wanted you to know how we feel.'

Looking at Bob Floss's new white skin reminded Sefton that although the Head of Languages for Business wore the clothes and had the air of a man of fifty, he had only recently turned twenty-five. Sefton thought bitterly of Pitt and Nietzsche. Like all failed men he was morbidly conscious of his own and other people's age, and on the passing of every birthday he had raked history for examples of great literary or political or military figures who at the same stage in their lives had made similar or slower progress. Now that even the famous late-starters were beginning to look precocious, he couldn't find it in him to be generous to prodigies.

'How you feel?' he repeated, incensed, 'I think I understand how you feel. Let me see if I can express how *I* feel.' And in what seemed to him like one movement he had found himself an appropriately shaped brick and advanced upon the nearest of the gleaming Citroens.

Behind him Bob Floss was saying something about his duty to protect the rights and property of his department, and a voice faint with the pain of ownership pleaded, 'Don't'.

But it was Dr Haslemere — Alan — who interposed himself between the Citroen and the brick. 'There's no

67

need for this,' he said reasonably. 'There are other ways of sorting out our differences.' He spoke softly, with the mock-fraternal regional benevolence of a trade-union negotiator; as confidential and as harmless as an old family grocer, cutting your cheese with a length of wire.

But it wasn't Haslemere who persuaded Sefton to lower his brick. All the while he had held it aloft more like a pen than a weapon, and if he could have thought of something nimble or cruel or even merely apposite he was convinced that no one would have been able to prevent his inscribing it. But so debilitating had been his literary education that his mind was suddenly emptied of everything but quotations from Shakespeare, and of those the most insistent were eulogiums for dead or valedictions to dying heroines. Too much of water hast thou, poor Ophelia, there would have been a time for such a word, and pud out de light and den pud out de light, would all have fitted comfortably on the bonnet of the Citroen — Ah soldier! would have fitted twice — but they were all at once both more and less than Sefton wanted to say. He dropped his brick unused at last not because of the intervention of the friendly grocer but because he had discovered yet again that he had nothing original to write.

But Alan Haslemere could not be expected to know that.

'You see, you've got it all wrong son,' he went on, as if he had just been vindicated by ACAS. 'We're the ones who should be stroppy. You're in our spot. We're not in yours.'

'No, but somebody else was,' said Sefton, 'and I didn't find it necessary to smash his car up or let his tyres down.'

'Now'oo's done that to you, son? Oo's let your tyres down?'

'You might as well have. You willed as much.'

'Willed?' Haslemere held up Sefton's word by one corner and showed it to his colleagues. It might have been an item of fine silk underwear handed around a bar room.

'Not a word you know?' enquired Sefton, in the vain hope that it might be given back.

'Oh, I know the word. I'm just careful how I use it.'

'We use words, too, in our department,' added Bob Floss.

'Of course not with the same freedom,' said Haslemere.

'Or the same flair,' said Bob Floss.

'Or the same aplomb,' said Dr Haslemere.

'Or the same fucking arrogance,' said a voice to which Sefton could neither put a name nor attach the idea of liguistic virtuosity.

Actually, Sefton had not found it easy to attach any idea of Continental flair to the teachers of European languages at the Polytechnic, Wrottesley.

The linguists and philologists of his previous acquaintance had easily succeeded in backing him into a false position of patriotic insularity; with that temporary, alien look in their eyes and their coffee filters and their French wives in constant need of whispered idiomatic bolstering, they soon had him forgetting his wandering Jewishness and rising in stout but shrill support of English motorways and cakes. But Bob Floss's staff drank tap water and stayed at home — impossibly municipal — in an obdurate state of urban rusticity, like gypsies in a layby. Thus enabling Sefton to enjoy once more the Cosmopolitan scorn which was his birthright.

It was this, presumably, which prompted the charge of arrogance. Well, he was glad they had noticed. He didn't at all mind being accused of arrogance, and fucking arrogance was, if anything, even better. Snivelling subservience might have stung him but fucking arrogance never.

So it was altogether equably that he asked whoever cared to answer, 'Is that another of the words you use in your department?'

'That and plenty more you wouldn't understand,' replied Dr Haslemere, his friendly grocer's patience very short now, his cheese wire almost gone. 'Why don't you clean your windscreen and go home now, eh? And remember not to park here again. If your car is here, one of ours can't be. That's logical isn't it? I know your department is strong on logic.'

'Feeling,' Bob Floss corrected, with what might just have been a deliberate thinning of his vowels in imitation of Charles Wenlock. 'It's feeling they're strong on.'

'It's neither,' a third voice, unsteady with emotion, chimed in. 'It's superiority!'

The degree of hurt in the voice appeared to surprise Bob Floss and Alan Haslemere. It astounded Sefton Goldberg. He recognised the speaker, who had emerged suddenly from the shadows within which there was still some proprietorial stencilling going on, to be Walter Sickert Fledwhite, but other than his being the most recent recruit to Bob Floss's department, a film man, a rumoured structuralist and a great wearer of badges, Sefton knew nothing of him. He had looked him over a couple of times, the way one does when a new face appears in a stale institution, and had casually noticed that he had that air of rather anxious modernism which even when it did turn up north of the University of Sussex did not usually make it as far as Wrottesley. He was therefore a sign of the times, Sefton thought, a grim reminder of how difficult it was becoming for the right man to find the right job. Without giving the subject much thought, Sefton had even felt some sympathy for Fledwhite for having been driven, like Sefton himself, so far from his natural habitat. But he had never exchanged a word or a glance with the fellow, never met him over coffee or in the print room, never written him a memorandum, never even made him the subject of a joke with Peter Potter, despite the temptation offered by those badges. He was such an unknown quantity still that even Charles Wenlock had not yet felt slighted by him. What then, or who then, had wounded Walter Sickert Fledwhite so?

'Superiority,' he repeated, 'and contempt for people and ideas.'

'I think that's fair,' said Sefton. 'I think our contempt for people does precede our contempt for ideas — just. I suppose that's because we understand them better — people, that is — in our department. But if it's all right with you I'd prefer to discuss this some other —'

'I'm not talking about your department,' interrupted Fledwhite, advancing behind his outstretched finger as if it had a motor of its own and were dragging him after it. 'I'm not talking about anyone else. I'm talking about *you*!'

Sefton had never before heard the little pronoun sound so shockingly personal. It seemed to come up from somewhere deep and most unpleasant in Fledwhite's body. Sefton felt as if he had been spat at by a consumptive.

Suddenly the sky above the car park lit up. The floodlights in the football stadium across the ring-road had been switched on for an evening match and in their melodramatic penumbra Sefton could see more clearly the ashen features of his unsuspected enemy, his frail form, and the long finger pointing towards Sefton's chest like a pistol in the hands of a ballet dancer.

'No,' said Sefton. 'No. This is too ridiculous. I come to collect my car, all innocence. I find bits of paper stuck all over it. I discover this to be the act of grown men who instruct the young. I am abused and sworn at in rustic dialect. And now a person to whom and about whom I have never said a word calls me *you*, pokes his finger in my heart, and tells me I am contemptuous of ideas. If there is one sane amongst you, tell me: do I wake or dream?'

'Not just contemptuous of ideas,' continued Fledwhite, 'contemptuous of thought itself. You try to make a virtue of your pragmatism, your thissing and your thatting —'

'No,' said Sefton, holding up his hand. 'I won't hear any more of this — or that. Not here. I'm flattered that you take so lively an interest in my intellectual life. But that gives you an unfair advantage over me. You see I don't have a clue who you are.'

'Since when did that stop you?' Alan Haslemere interposed.

'From forming an opinion?' Bob Floss added.

'Or from passing a judgement?' Haslemere continued.

'Or from sending people up?'

'Or from putting them down?'

'Or from taking the piss?'

'Or from being a fucking clever cunt?' That unknown voice which had come to Sefton's aid with the charge of arrogance helped him out again. Floss and Haslemere really oughtn't to have him along.

'Me?' asked Sefton Goldberg, his back against his mutilated Avenger, hopelessly outnumbered and wondering if it were here at last then, the bliss of persecution. He would have loved them to say something about Jews. In his present responsive and vibrating state he could have picked up an anti-semitic remark delivered in a guilty whisper a hundred miles away. In an attempt to elicit one a little closer to hand he shrugged his shoulders in an exaggerated manner like Topol, fiddled with his nose like Jonathan Miller, squinted like Menachem Begin, mopped the sweat from his neck like Itzhak Perlman, and in that voice which ancient money-lenders employed to deny they had just devoured a pair of Protestant babies in their soup he repeated, smacking his rubbery lips, 'Me?'

Behind his long finger Walter Sickert Fledwhite was advancing again. He seemed to want to get very close to Sefton Goldberg. He seemed to want to exclude Floss and Haslemere completely. And he didn't seem to like Jewish jokes. Watching him advance, Sefton could understand why. He was ungenerously formed. He had small ears and bad eyesight. He was a young man, younger even than Bob Floss, but his hair was sparse, not so much thinning as innately thin in each particular strand. His nose was pinched and piqued and raw as with perpetual colds; and below it undulated one of those unfortunately curly mouths that inevitably excites speculation as to its role in its owner's sexual life.

For a thousandth of a second Sefton speculated, emboldened by Walter Sickert Fledwhite's badges. People who wear badges are not out to protect their privacy. Nor are they out to like Jewish jokes. Sefton knew not to take false comfort from his adversary's sporting, on the left lapel of his duffle coat, a brightly coloured piece of tin announcing his membership of an anti-Nazi organisation. There was a time when that would have implied at least a passing friendliness to Jews in the same way that membership of the RSPCA signified some concern for the welfare of animals; but now that what had once been simple had become complex and the new Jew could be shown to be the new Nazi, the badge had a distinctly unneighbourly look to Sefton's eye. It frightened him, even on Walter Sickert Fledwhite's little chest.

Sefton could not have said at what moment Fledwhite started to scream at him. All he knew was that there had once been quiet and stillness in the world and now there was only unbroken shrieking and a frail form trembling in front of him, stabbing holes in the night with its fingers. There wasn't much of what was being said to him that Sefton was able to make out. The most passionate outbursts are never heard. They are only observed. But the word superiority, returned to again and again, was distinct, as was the accusation that Sefton had asserted that superiority in his manner, in his look, in his bearing, in the way he drank his coffee, combed his hair and parked his car, and in what he said to students. Students seemed to be the key to all this. He had apparently said things to them. Improper things about his colleagues. He had abused

73

his position and his privilege. Made light up there in lectures of Walter Sickert Fledwhite when he should have been making heavy of Mrs Wood and Mrs Oliphant. Slander had out. As a rule guilt came easily to Sefton Goldberg — there weren't many crimes he couldn't have been convinced he had committed — but on this occasion he had no recollection of anything remotely resembling the attack he had the feeling he was being accused of having delivered. He was fairly sure that he had not said, 'Oh, by the way, when you come to consider the decline of the episodic form of the long late-Victorian Novel and its relation to the growth of popular education in the period, don't forget that inferior turd Walter Sickert Fledwhite.' And if he hadn't said it his students couldn't have written it down, and if they didn't write it down they couldn't have remembered it. Distortion they were capable of, but not invention.

Once, when he had started to turn green on a cross-Channel ferry, Sefton had been advised that the only way to avoid sea-sickness was to fix one's eye on something that was relatively stable; Sefton now recalled that advice and, in order to avoid madness, stared hard at Fledwhite's battery of badges and attempted to stay his gaze from every other working part of him. The badges told a stirring story of compassion and commitment. Fledwhite supported the rights of women as fervently as he opposed the rights of Nazis. He supported the Catholics in Ireland. He wanted crèches and clean air. He didn't want nuclear power or new airports or new motorways or new missile sites. He wanted to preserve seals and badgers. He wanted to encourage strikers and to restrain the police. He wanted the Special Branch investigated. The Tories execrated. Gays liberated. Sefton looked at that one again. And then he looked at it once more. It was possible that Walter Sickert Fledwhite was no more a gay because he wanted gays to be liberated than he was a badger because he wanted badgers to be spared. But it was unlikely. He should have known. Being Jewish this was, of course, the last thing he ever thought about. In the main Jews didn't go in for it. And he should have known from the name. Walter Sickert Something! He had met a Holman Hunt Something once, and a Dante Gabriel; they were both emotional. Mothers who gave their sons names like that wanted them to end up in Gay Liberation. This was one area where parental ambition had a good percentage chance of success, where desire was mother to the deed.

Sefton felt a lot clearer in his mind. He still didn't know what he had done, but at least he could understand a little better the person he had done it to. He wasn't fool enough to suppose that Fledwhite was staging an unconventional come-on, that Fledwhite desired him. They had never desired Sefton in the past. In the days when he and his friends hitch-hiked round the Continent there were many warnings about amorous truck-drivers, tales of propositions in cabs, struggles in sleeping-bags, expressions of admiration delivered in broken English in far-flung lavatories. But no hairy fist had slid from a gear-stick and inched itself crab-like to Sefton Goldberg, no invitations to a swim or a wrestle had come his way, and he had peed without notice or remark from Calais to Casablanca. So he had no reason to believe that Walter Sickert Fledwhite had seen something in him that half the signatories to the Treaty of Rome plus North Africa hadn't. On the other hand, if they didn't go for him in a big way he was prepared to accept that Fledwhite might just have noticed that he, Sefton, didn't go for them. He was reminded of how limited his tolerance was as he looked again at the now breathless, spent and almost silent person before him. He was all but dead from his outburst. His hair looked as if it might have been blown off his head by a sigh; his lips flopped in a triple cupid's bow; he was drained of all colour. He reminded Sefton of one of those school yard softies for whom every event was an agony and even the Jewish boys could push around. Sefton had not been tough himself but he could remember with what repugnance he had regarded the vulnerability of those young Fledwhites. He had wondered then what would ever become of them. Now he knew. It would be easy, Sefton thought, now that the screaming had stopped, to twist his arm behind his back and demand a bar of chocolate. Fledwhite probably had one ready in the pocket of his duffle coat. In the inside pocket where it was warm, above the heart and behind the Gay Liberation badge.

And then he remembered. Gay Liberation! The phrase popped up in the rear of his memory like a small comic face in the back row of a group photograph. He *had* been talking to his students about that. The word gay had arisen in some context, its old context, and Sefton Goldberg, erstwhile purist and protector of the language, had recaptured some of his vanished zeal and armed himself in the all-but-beaten monosyllable's defence, ranting for the space of a whole lecture hour against the new rigidities and pieties. 'My own mother,' he had concluded, 'my own dear mother, who has grey hairs, who at one time admitted to so little knowledge even of marital sex that I supposed I had been conceived in her sleep, now refers with familiarity and deference to gays. Around and around the little word she goes, picking her way as if she were in a mine-field; her eyes narrowed, her breath heavy, her ears cocked for some sound of disquiet from the graves of her innocent forbears. "Of course," she says, referring to the new proprietors of the off-licence down the road, the two young men with gold chains around their necks, "Of course, they're both gay." Of course! She not only knows what they do, to whom they do it and what it is called, she knows how much it hurts! Is this an example for a son?'

Yes, he had said these things, happily haranguing his students who had written it all down, not seeing its immediate relevance to their exams but expecting it would come clear in the end. And it had got back to

Fledwhite. That was the only explanation of what had occurred. 'Mr Goldberg thinks all homosexuals are freaks and should be lined up against the wall and shot,' some student had doubtless reported, trying to remember the gist of his notes. Or else Fledwhite had sneaked a look at some other student's folder and found the damning evidence. If Sefton was right about the pleasures of suffering then Fledwhite would do a lot of that sort of thing. He would be a dangerous man to leave alone with your mail or your manuscripts.

He stood quietly now, getting his breath back. His face was ashen and his narrow chest was heaving. But he looked, in some remote part of himself, satisfied. He'd set himself a test and he'd passed it. He had acquitted himself in the world of men. He had told somebody off. He was sufficiently pleased with himself, Sefton thought, to be considering the possibility of a friendship even.

So how am I to feel about this? Sefton wondered. Am I to feel guilty? Bob Floss and his cronies were still hanging about with their mouths open. From the football stadium that was soon to house Sefton Goldberg and his dreams came the strangled nasal sound, more of a bleat than a roar, of the Wrottesley supporters bewailing their team's latest ineptitude. Cora Peck would soon be off to be interviewed every night on television. Somewhere exotic Sefton's oldest rival Godfrey Jelley was lying in the sun grappling with major philosophical problems and God knows what else. In an hour or two Peter Potter would be enjoying the best sleep of his life. The long dying day seemed to be providing pleasures for everyone.

Something furry, bigger than a mouse but smaller than a man, knocked a few cans over and ran across Sefton's feet. To hell with it, he thought. He extended his hand to the lifeless Fledwhite. 'I owe you an apology,' he said warmly. 'I really am very sorry. I've only just worked out who in fact you are. You're the little poofter from languages.'

77

4

After which, because it would have been altogether
feeble to begin scraping the sticky labels from his windscreen and altogether dangerous to drive away with
them still on it, Sefton had no option but to leave the car
park the way he had entered it, on foot. He wasn't in
any hurry to get home, but he didn't like walking
through Wrottesley, especially at night, for fear of
being caught up in racial violence. Not once in the
time he had lived there had Sefton seen anything
approaching racial violence, despite a famous article
Godfrey Jelley had written years before describing
Wrottesley as a seething cauldron on a short-fuse soon
to give a new meaning to the word holocaust; but there
was so much ill-temper around the town in the day time
and so little to ease it at night, that Sefton didn't
see how one could be absolutely certain that people
wouldn't start hurling stones at one another just to
relieve their feelings let alone to give a new meaning to
the word holocaust.

Gingerly he made his way through the back streets
with his collar up, trying to shuffle like a Pakistani
when it seemed tactful to do so and to lope like a West
Indian when it seemed expedient. He did not attempt
to imitate the dejected slouch and bounce, slouch and
bounce, of the white inhabitants of Wrottesley — he
knew his limits and he had his pride.

He had to skirt around the football ground. There
was a smell of hamburgers and fried onions and
warmed alcohol in the air; the smell of the English at

play. Bleats of frustration and pain followed by whistle-blows were still issuing from the ground. A passer-by who didn't know better might have supposed there was a party on at the abattoirs. On street corners prostitutes who must have fallen below any standards of dress or appearance set by the EEC stood in their oldest clothes and scratched themselves, peering half-heartedly into passing cars and nodding meaningfully so that the drivers shouldn't suppose they were just ordinary housewives out doing the shopping when the shops were closed. No cars bothered to stop or even slow down. The oldest claim of the oldest profession, that it helped to minimize vice and hold marriages together, seemed thoroughly vindicated.

Sefton wasn't approached or nodded at. Like the European truck-drivers of earlier days, the prostitutes of Wrottesley gave him a miss.

As he walked he thought of Cora Peck; more particularly, he thought of Cora Peck's breasts, which were the only part of her he liked. As a rule he didn't believe one should enjoy a part when one didn't approve the whole — he was, it must be remembered, Cambridge-educated — and how could Cora Peck's breasts be admired separately from Cora Peck? He didn't know and he certainly wasn't going to get into any arguments over them. They weren't that important and they weren't even, as breasts go, all that full or all that round or all that high. Beneath her clothes — which was the only place Sefton had ever seen them — they swayed, if anything, rather too freely, moved in independence and in ignorance of one another and pointed, when they were still, in one direction too many. They were the sorts of breasts whose presence and activity one was always aware of even when their owner's back was turned. They were visible whatever she wore; through five cardigans and an overcoat at least one of her nipples would force its impression and stare out of her chest like a Cyclopean eye. Peter Potter was at a loss to understand why they should not, like all other deformities, be covered or cured. But it was precisely the blatancy and ineptitude of their carriage that touched Sefton. Knowingness was the word for what Cora Peck carried in front of her, and a girl had to be well brought-up and well educated and not too good-looking and a bit on the tense side to be as knowing as that. Sefton Goldberg had always found that combination irresistible.

Cora Peck was so clearly doing all that she had been brought up not to do when she first arrived at the Polytechnic in her silver lurex boots and her gypsy earrings and her silky blue zip-down jacket with an appliqué mouth, parted, on the back of it, and she was so clearly not doing it well, that Sefton was prepared to overlook the pale little face peering out aggressively through frameless spectacles and to welcome her as warmly as if she had really been the thing she was trying to be, in which event, anyway, he would not have welcomed her half as much. His excitement was put to the test on the second day when she turned up as if she were offering a drag impersonation of Marlene Dietrich: her thin legs not quite filling out black stockings and not entirely certain in high stilettos, her breasts pushed to her sides by a tight black jacket, her head topped by a beret and her face covered by a black veil beneath which, in the approximate area of her mouth, bled a red gash. Sefton only just prevented himself from enquiring whether anyone close had died. For a while he wasn't sure what he thought. But when he remembered that hidden away inside all this was a surgeon's daughter with six 'A' Levels and a B.Litt. from Oxford, a respectable Christian girl, a writer and an academic, when, that is to say, he could attach to those separated but unflattenable breasts the idea of their owner's mental life, then was he able to envisage the pleasures of lifting the veil.

For her part Cora Peck was glad to have someone to talk to in her new job. She wasn't sure what she made of Sefton Goldberg's suits and ties, but he had a foreign face and lots of hair and she supposed his dressing was of the higher bohemianism.

Sefton was looking forward to some involvement with Cora Peck but he wasn't, in the parlance of the people, over the moon about it. So it didn't cost him too much to sympathise, over lunch, with Peter Potter's horror of her.

'She looks like the madam of a cheap brothel.'

'Yes,' said Sefton with a lying little laugh. He had never been to a cheap brothel and he had never seen a madam. He was dead certain that Peter Potter hadn't either. But why be pedantic? He sort of knew what Peter meant. And Peter definitely knew what Peter meant. Poor Cora had breasts; that was enough for Peter Potter. 'Yes,' Sefton repeated, as if he had been thinking over the justice of his friend's description; 'but a brothel that no one goes to any more. I'd say she's lost track of customer requirements.'

'She's certainly lost track of mine,' laughed Peter Potter.

'Well, somebody will take her up.'

'I wonder. They'd be taking on quite a lot.'

'How do you mean?' Sefton often deferred to Peter in these matters. It seemed to him an act of kindness and it was no skin off his nose. On this occasion he was even curious to hear what Peter thought.

'Well it all looks pretty hysterical to me.'

'She'd be a screamer, you think?'

'I don't know about that. But she looks very tense and nervy.'

Sefton suddenly felt very sorry for Miranda Potter. He wondered how hard it was for her to keep up her husband's cherished image of contented, imperturbable womanhood.

'Maybe she's still a bit shy.'

'Shy?' Peter couldn't associate the idea of shyness with Cora's get-ups. 'She's rapacious.'

'But nervy?'

'And nervy.'

81

'Sex in the head?' Sefton helped out.

'I can't think where else you'd want it with her,' Peter joked. 'It would all be pretty mental, certainly.'

'Mental eh? I suppose you're right.'

Sefton stared into his lager. Mental eh? Well he had no objections to that. The young and even the slightly older Ursula were one thing, but Sefton had always secretly hankered after those women in Lawrence you weren't supposed to. If the truth were told (and if it were left to him it never would be) he would sacrifice a lifetime of Ursula's whispering 'It is my love, isn't it?' — she could throw back her rings until the cows came home — for a fortnight's ski-ing with Gudrun. And if anyone had pumped him when he was drunk he might have even half-confessed to relishing the idea of a country walk with Hermione, collecting catkins. The catkins themselves wouldn't have meant a lot to him but he was pretty sure he would have found much to excite him in the conversation. Poor Lawrence, of course, had been sick unto death with them, but Sefton Goldberg had almost forgotten the stimulation of being with a knowing woman, of communicating with a mind which was, in a cultivated way, unclean. Oh, for an obscene knower or two! Wrottesley had afforded nothing of that kind. What lady academics there had been at the Polytechnic up until Cora Peck's sensational arrival were of the sensible and conscientious variety, active members of the local Labour Party who looked like head-librarians and said 'Cheers' when they met you, and called butterflies flutterbies when they wanted to be feminine, and drank unusual beers in their own pint pots when they wanted to get on with men. Even the students, who at most teaching institutions, provided the pleasures and the consolations for men of Sefton's age and status, were nearly all of them working-class girls, and working-class girls were nothing if not not-knowing. There were no mental thrills for Sefton there. Poverty and Protestantism had done their stuff with them all right. They reminded

Sefton of the girls he used to meet at fair-grounds or pick up off the streets of Manchester from the Bedford Dormobile in which he and his sixth-form school-friends toured, day and night, for that sole purpose. Those were heady days in Manchester when Jewish boys were in demand for their foreign appearance and generous pocket money, before the Beatles changed the fashion and swung things back for clean-cut Christians. The Bedford Dormobile, screaming around the streets of Rusholme and Droylsden with its cargo of prematurely deep-voiced swarthy strangers from the south was too much for the working-girls of Manchester — there were no polytechnics then — and they leapt in through its ever-open sliding doors like mackerel rising to unbaited hooks on sunny days. Once in they were uniformly disappointing. They had dry lips and bad teeth and chests as hard as walnuts. Despite their readiness to swear and call things by their coarsest names they were prudish. If they could be persuaded to overcome the suspicious artisan puritanism of their upbringing it was only under the pretence of their not noticing and on the condition of your not acknowledging that they had overcome it; so that there could be no talk or discussion — Sefton Goldberg really wanted to talk to girls then — because that would be an admission of what, just below the line of vision and far below the propriety of remark, was actually happening. You had, in those days, to be very deft, very still, very quick, and very quiet.

It was only when he went to Cambridge and met properly behaved girls from substantial backgrounds that Sefton got any really disreputable thrills out of sex. There would always be a soft spot in his heart for the first well-accoutred daughter of the middle classes he ever crawled in and out of Girton for. Impeccably connected, educated to the highest level, she would urge Sefton to describe as graphically as he could all that he was doing to her at the precise moment he was doing it. What he didn't describe might as well not have

83

been happening. Sefton had no trouble understanding her requirements. It was bliss to him to meet someone as verbal as himself.

'This is bliss to me,' he had told her.

'What kind of bliss? Where do you feel it?'

'Here, right here,' said Sefton, putting himself rapturously into words.

It wasn't going to be as good as that with Cora. He wasn't such an avid talker any more and Cora would clearly be nothing like as good a listener — it was a parted mouth she had appliquéed on the back of her jacket, not a cocked ear. But she did seem capable of fulfilling most of the conditions necessary for Sefton's arousal. There was nothing artisan or industrial about her; there was no question of her being either actually or sentimentally Jewish (it was surprising how many people would dredge up from their past some exotic Jewish ancestor for Sefton's behoof); she had a further degree, a foreign language, and a dash of self-disgust; she wasn't fresh, she wasn't spontaneous, and she wasn't easy-going. All he had to do, for his part, was to resist ingenuity and not find anything in her to like. He felt pretty confident that he would never, under any circumstances or at any time, find anything to like in Cora Peck.

He was, therefore, after his lunchtime conversation with Peter Potter on Cora Peck's second day at the Polytechnic, really quite optimistic. For him.

On her third day Cora wore a white simulated leather boiler-suit with zips behind the knees and up the thighs and under the arm-pits and across the buttocks. The biggest zip of all (it was not only longer than the others but it had fiercer, bluer teeth) went diagonally from her shoulder to her waist, like Diana's bow. This she had half open over an insubstantial, clinging singlet, the colour of flesh. Her hair was pushed up inside a cream trilby. She made her way to where Sefton was drinking coffee in a hopelessly uncomfortable easy chair. All the

84

chairs in the staff common-room were low and pushed close to one another, so that it was impossible to reach your coffee unless you rocked to and fro as in semitic prayer. Sefton should have been good at that but his legs were short and squat and he regularly spilt coffee down his shirt. He was mopping himself when he saw Cora. It was only just after ten but already the biologists were playing bridge at round tables. Cora's entrance had interfered seriously with their bidding. As she moved her breasts swung heavily and from inside her half-unzipped boiler-suit now one, now another Cyclopean eye winked at Sefton Goldberg. Higher up, from Cora's other, lesser eyes Cora herself peered out apprehensively, as if in a state of vertiginous alarm at the foreignness and magnitude of her own superstructure. She was pale and strained with all those difficulties which Sefton comprehended by the adjective feminine. What a mess, he thought, and as soon as she joined him he asked her out.

Seated that night in the one pub in Wrottesley where there was a fighting chance of his not being knocked unconscious and her not being sold into slavery, Sefton nodded with cheerful traitorousness at Cora's perception that Peter Potter had a problem in regard to women.

'I'm sure he has,' Sefton agreed.

Cora had been trying out some first impressions of the staff at the Polytechnic. She knew she was making snap judgements but she would make them all the same and Sefton could correct her if she had been too hasty. This seemed to Sefton to be a natural and even a promising way of beginning things.

'I might be wrong, but he seems distinctly frightened of me,' she said with a kind of snort of harmlessness.

'It could be that he's a bit shy,' Sefton suggested feebly. Moderating didn't come easily to him; but it was a bit soon to tell her that Peter was distinctly frightened because she was distinctly frightening.

He'd need a few more drinks in him for that.

'Shy? I wouldn't have thought so — though of course you know him better than I do. He seems perfectly competent socially. Too competent, if anything. I thought he was frightened in another way. I don't know,' Cora hesitated and puffed inexpertly at a cigarette which she smoked through a shaking holder. 'Sexually or something.'

'Psychically?' Sefton ventured.

Cora moved something that Sefton wanted inside her boiler-suit and looked at him hard. He noticed that her eyes blinked frequently. She hadn't changed to come out. She had merely unzipped a few zips and slashed her face with lipstick. 'Well you'd know,' she said. 'He's your friend.'

Sefton ditched Peter on the spot. 'Oh, friend,' he said with dismissive wave of his hand. The first few hours Sefton spent with a woman were always precarious for Sefton's friends and principles. He would drop anyone and anything if he thought it would help.

'I'm told you have lunch together every day.'

'Yes, we do, but I suspect that's only because we haven't got anything else to do or anybody else to do it with.'

'So you sit and drink beer and gossip about your students?'

'That we don't do. In the main we play games.'

'Games?'

'Pub games. You know, darts and pool and any electronic gadget that you can put money in.'

'In other words you compete with one another?'

'To the death.'

'It sounds neurotic.'

Sefton sipped his lager and counted to twenty thousand.

'You're not a games player yourself then?' he finally asked.

Cora shook her head. 'I think games are a pretty dishonest way of dealing with your aggressions.' She

86

paused, as if she had a lot more to say on the subject should Sefton wish to hear it.

Sefton himself, meanwhile, was weighing his alternatives. He decided that he didn't care that much for games, at least not this evening. 'I'm sure you're right,' he said. 'But it's probably for the best that Peter and I act out our aggressions over the pool table. It has to be preferable to some of the other things we might otherwise do to one another.'

Cora seemed to go over some of those other things in her mind and even to find one or two of them to her liking. But she only said, 'So you play games and drink beer and gossip about your students?'

'When you have been here longer,' said Sefton with what he considered to be remarkably good temper, 'you will discover that our students are not interesting enough to gossip about. They slip miraculously from the memory.'

'You don't like your students?'

'I didn't say that. I said I have trouble remembering them.'

'Doesn't it come to the same thing?'

Sefton shrugged. It was part of his idea of the evening that he should appear unfeeling — not about Cora but about everything else. This would make his ultimate softness, his unexpected pliancy, the more stimulating for her. Provided she knew about knowingness. But Sefton was beginning to worry a little about that. He thought that he had detected, in the voice with which she had framed her last couple of questions, the old familiar female clang, that broken sound as of a thin cracked bell which all women emitted when they felt threatened but wanted to appear confident. He had been able to see the noises Cora would make from the moment he first saw *her*, but he had, he thought, been very careful so far not to ring her. It seemed you could never be careful enough.

'Then you shouldn't teach them,' she said, responding to his shrug. And when Sefton only looked surprised, 'If you don't like them or find them interesting you shouldn't teach them.'

It was the clang all right. Well, if he rang her early it might mean sweet music late.

'I know,' he said, leaning far back in his chair in an attitude (he hoped) suggestive of perfect, even oriental, male composure. 'I know. But what's a chap to do? A chap has to eat. You can't expect him to give up his meagre crust just because he isn't interested in the means by which it reaches him. And anyway, they can't *tell* that I find them boring. They merely think that *I* look the way *they* feel. They suppose it's in the nature of the subject.'

The small spots of colour which had appeared on Cora's normally white cheeks became large blotches of red. Her voice rose and broke. She wasn't, as a matter of fact, all that certain that a chap did have to eat. And if she allowed that he did she couldn't see why it had to be at the expense of young people who were curious and eager to learn. She had only been here a few days but students found her easy to talk to and to confide in; already, despite what Sefton said, she had met some extremely interesting and exceedingly . . .

It was worse even than he had expected. He didn't mind tension. What else, after all, had he asked her out for? But it was tension of the let us tear our pleasures with rough strife variety that he had been banking on. It had been one thing to find her excitingly objection-able, but even Sefton could discover nothing piquant in shrill highmindedness. And he knew that once aca-demic sanctimoniousness had forced its way into the room political pietism was sure to follow; in another moment she'd be telling him what was really happening in Chile. He was very disappointed. He might as well have been out with someone he liked.

As Cora's voice swung and cracked, Sefton felt that he was being brought to a significant trial of his courage and his probity. How much more was he prepared to sacrifice for that which might yet be denied him and which, even if it wasn't, he couldn't any longer be sure he would enjoy? He didn't like to catch himself stooping to calculation in this manner, but he had already betrayed a friend and put some cherished opinions at risk and he really was going to have to decide whether there was anything in nature, let alone on Cora Peck, for the brief possession of which it would be worth agreeing that his students were eagerly inquisitive, extremely interesting, and exceedingly God-knows-what else. There was a thing called integrity and a state of mind called living with oneself. Sefton had all but cemented these two firmly together when Cora unexpectedly rounded off a paragraph, rose from the table, and took both their glasses to be refilled at the bar. It wasn't difficult for a woman to cause a stir in a Wrottesley pub: the short young men, dazed and tubular in coloured sweaters, followed the smallest movements of anyone who wasn't a man as automatically as they poured beer at regular intervals through the space below their moustaches. But Cora Peck's unzipped boiler-suit created more than usual interest. 'Jus' yo' look at the fookin' teets on tha',' was only one expression of admiration which Sefton overheard, but it was enough to rekindle his ardour. He was shockingly vulnerable, when it came to women, to the opinions of other men. And he was, also, as a teacher of literature, a sucker for a succinct phrase. He couldn't, on the spot, come up with anything half so pithy on the subject of integrity. He let that pretty well determine which boats he would burn.

'You mustn't pay too much attention to my affected cynicism,' he therefore said, on Cora's return. 'It's merely a tedious social tic of mine and you were quite right to be irritated by it. I too think our students often get a raw deal from us — God knows it's not their fault that Wrottesley isn't Oxford or Cambridge. In fact it's precisely because it isn't that we should do more for them. I know I should, anyway.' He delivered his words with a kind of melancholy conscientiousness to the triangle of flesh-coloured singlet visible beneath Cora Peck's boiler-suit top. And then, out of politeness, he raised his eyes to Cora herself and smiled, seriously. That should do it, he thought; but he gave her a moment or two to see how, for her, his fleet smoked.

So he wasn't at all prepared for the ingratitude of her response.

'Doing more for them isn't going to help,' she said with an ironic, pitying catch in her voice. He just hadn't understood. 'The whole problem is that you already *do* too much.'

Sefton could hardly believe his ears. Not only was she treating what he had just said as a contribution to the world of ideas, she was going to the length of disagreeing with it. He had given her a bouquet and she was arguing with the scent.

'Don't you see,' she went on, 'that they are so smothered by your paternalism that they lose all faith in the natural soundness of their own judgements.' Her small face was as aggressive and as unappreciative as a schoolgirl's.

Sefton experienced all the loneliness of a man who had drowned his wife and strangled his children for a mistress who had turned out to be faithless. There was a sharp pain between his eyes. He took a little time to rub the spot. He needed a little time. If he could have believed that Cora's graceless refusals to accept his offerings were part of some furtive perverseness on her part, some dark, thrilling, mental challenge to his uncompromising male otherness, then he might have gone on offering. Might? For such hostility he would have put a match to anything! But her opposition to him seemed to be made up of a quite literal-minded attachment to her ideas which were different to his ideas (as if he'd been anywhere near expressing an idea at any time this evening), and an antagonism to him personally in which he could not detect a trace of obscene knowledge or abhorrent mystery. She was not initiate. They were not initiate together. She either wasn't an obscene knower at all or she simply wasn't one with him. That latter idea, implying that she might be one with someone else, left Sefton feeling too peeved for him to entertain it long. She wasn't one. Despite all the signs and against all the odds, she wasn't one. And the breasts, the left one of which was even now, it seemed, winking him over? Well, he had misread the message. He had always known that there was no possible way, in the second half of the twentieth century, that breasts on a woman like Cora Peck could be anything but aggressive weapons, at the very least and best a show of strength in an uneasy peace; but he had supposed that they knew something of the joys of fraternizing with the enemy and that they had whispered to him, even as they had bobbed and weaved, 'We'll betray our side if you betray yours.' Upon receipt of which intimation he had acted, he could now see, with the most foolish promptitude. He had given and got nothing back. In a word, he'd been hoodwinked.

So it was for Peter Potter and all who had gone down with him that Sefton left off rubbing the pain between his eyes and returned to Cora Peck's contribution to the great debate on education.

'Now help me out if I go wrong,' he said, with the most terrific concentration, 'but what I think you're driving at is this: we as teachers, no, no, *I* as a teacher, am inclined to be too paternalistic in my relations to my students, and this — I think I'm getting it — this makes them feel oppressed, dominated, as you say, smothered.' He took a short breather. Looked back with some pride at the distance he had covered, and forward with some trepidation at the next sentence stretching out before him. He was about to come to natural soundness. He knew something about the natural soundness of students' judgements but he wasn't going to say anything about what he knew to Cora Peck. Instead he crumpled his forehead and wrinkled his nose and sucked at his tongue and sampled her arguments as if he were about to take his first bite from the tree of knowledge. 'Whereas,' he continued, painstakingly, 'what I ought to be doing — let me see if I've got this absolutely straight — what I ought to be doing is leaving the student to the intrinsic health, one might even say to the natural soundness, of his own judgements.' Sefton wiped his brow. 'Am I right so far?'

After a long silence, very trying to the sweet, pupillary look on Sefton Goldberg's face, Cora said, 'I heard you were sarcastic.'

Sefton threw up his arms. Not only is she not knowing, he said to himself, she also spells things out. But he only said, 'Well, there are some things you have to find out for yourself.'

'You must think I'm very naive.'

Sefton couldn't tell whether Cora was about to cry or to hit him. He knew he didn't want her to cry. 'No, I don't think you're naive. Though it might be that you could do with a little more experience under your belt.'

To his surprise, to his alarm even, Cora appeared to assume that that very loose and general phrase had a very exact and particular application. If he was not mistaken her eyes actually travelled down her body and rested on an area of herself which, if she had worn a belt, no one would have disputed was under it. And indeed her fierce retort, 'I am a lot more experienced than you think,' was of a specificity so unmistakable that Sefton feared (and perhaps he even hoped) it could only be followed by the solecism, 'And a terrific lay.' In the event she managed to be more original without being less specific.

'I'm an expert,' she averred.

Sefton stared. Merriment, ribaldry, ridicule and that whole jolly gang flashed a message to Sefton's brain that they were on their way up, but for the moment stupefaction held sole sway over his features.

Cora saw only derision. 'I'm an expert,' she repeated, with all the frustration of a defeated schoolmistress falling back on her qualifications. If she had been standing up she might have stamped her foot.

Sefton experienced a warm sensation in both his sides. If his memory served him correctly what he was experiencing was pleasure. Already he was shaping an account of his evening for Peter Potter. He noticed that the lager in his glass was agitated. 'I thought your area was the modern experimental novel,' he said, putting his glass down carefully.

'That was the subject of my thesis,' said Cora. She spoke with a kind of swingeing laborious exactness. She had the air of someone who had already said too much but who was prepared, just once, to sacrifice reserve in the interests of clarity, and of course — Sefton had no doubt that he was being shown how much he had missed — revenge. 'I'm also,' she went on, 'an expert at masturbating men.'

The following day, when he was attempting to render this moment for Peter Potter, Sefton confessed that if he had to write about it he wouldn't know how to begin to evoke the impression of wan ineptitude conveyed by Cora's boast, or the simultaneous amazement, horror, delight, pity, self-consciousness, hilarity and shame experienced by himself. If he didn't laugh out loud, he said, it was because he couldn't bear to draw any more attention to Cora and him; he wasn't sure whether the awful word (he didn't mean expert) had been overheard but he didn't see how some whiff or echo of it could not have made its way by instinct into the primitive collective unconscious at the bar. But what he didn't even try to describe to Peter was the extent to which Cora's language emptied life of all its meaning for him, robbed romance of all its charm, left libidinousness itself without a dread or quiver. He had long ago decided that masturbation was so irredeemably ugly a word that it should never be used; but Cora was able to reveal levels of bleakness and desolation in it which even Sefton didn't know it possessed. On her lips it evoked all of humanity's most damp and inglorious physical ills: it evoked rheumatism and sciatica and rickets and artificial limbs and trusses and congested passages and the thousand unwelcome juices and fluids which made men cold and wet and full of dismal needs. He didn't attempt to describe this to Peter Potter because he felt sure that however much Peter would want to understand all that he meant as it related to Cora Peck, he would balk at the idea of dismal needs, as they related to Miranda.

There was another significant omission, too, in Sefton's narrative. He couldn't find any way of explaining to Peter that notwithstanding everything else he felt he also felt curious. It was not possible to sit at a small table in a public place with a young woman of recent acquaintance and have that woman claim to be an expert at bringing men to the point of ecstasy (and perhaps beyond) without one's being — well, curious. It was possible, either, for the object of those highly specialised skills, or at least the particular potential object which belonged to Sefton Goldberg (and which she was letting him know would never, alas, enjoy a standing that was anything *but* potential), not to be, as it were, on the table before them. Throughout the evening, during all the fluctuations of Sefton's desire for Cora, Sefton's member had, in its usual independent and indiscriminating way, retained a steady if not an intense interest; but upon Cora's declaration of her dexterousness it had taken cover. It was on the table as an idea all right, but Sefton could not have said where else it was or whether, in its corporeal form, it was even still alive. Which could only mean that his curiosity — the curiosity he could never have admitted to Peter Potter that he felt — existed solely in the mind. Cora had excited him mentally at last. Not that he would ever let her know that she had, or Peter Potter know that she had, or, if he could help it, himself know that she had. That was to be nobody's dirty little secret.

As he did say to Peter, he couldn't laugh out loud at Cora's boast for fear of attracting even more attention to their unconventional *tête-à-tête*. What he did was to look around the room in mock terror, put his finger to

94

his lips, and say, 'Hush! Not here. This is Wrottesley, not Oxford. These are very basic men.'

'Don't worry about them,' said Cora, sweeping the room with her expert's eye. 'They probably all read my articles anyway.'

'Your articles?'

'My articles.' Cora was giving nothing more away.

'On the modern experimental novel?'

'On masturbation.'

'I see,' said Sefton, looking straight in front of him. 'You write on the subject as well. That means you are an authority as well as an expert?'

'Yes.' Cora expelled the word as if it were pointed and poisonous, like a pigmy's dart.

'And where do these articles of yours appear? I might have come across them. *Notes and Queries*? *Essays in Criticism*?'

'I doubt whether you have come across them. And you only want to know so that you can use it against me.'

Sefton had never looked more innocuous. 'Use it against you? Why should I do that?'

'I've told you too much already,' Cora lamented, more to herself than to Sefton. 'I'm going to regret ever saying a word to you about it. I don't know why I did.' She brought her little white hands up from her lap and made a joint fist of them on the table.

In the circumstances Sefton felt that he owed it to them both to try very hard not to look at Cora's hands. 'Don't tell me you write for *Playboy* and *Penthouse* and things like that?' he said with boyish zest.

Cora nodded. 'Things like that.' She was white with strain. 'Look,' she added, 'are you going to talk about this?'

'Who would I talk about it to? Anyway, what difference does it make? If people read your articles they already know . . .'

'I don't write under my real name.'

'Good God, you aren't —?' And Sefton went on to

name some of those lady writers whose regular columns in the glossy men's magazines he made a point of reading all he decently could of while collecting his *Education Supplements*. She wasn't. She was somebody else entirely. And she wasn't going to say who. She'd keep that to herself, at least.

Sefton couldn't make up his mind whether he should be excited to meet his first lady pornographer or disappointed that the first lady pornographer he met should be Cora Peck. Speaking simply for himself Sefton was disappointed; but as it concerned his obligations outside of himself — his obligations to a good story and to Peter Potter, for example — he considered he'd had a good time.

Zipped up against the night and Sefton Goldberg, Cora had nothing to say as she was being driven home except, 'I know I'm going to regret this. I should never have told you.'

And Sefton had nothing to reply except, 'A lady's secrets are always safe with me.'

Sefton stopped his car at the corner of Cora's street. A complicated one-way system prevented his driving into it and dropping her at the house from which, a mere couple of hours before, he had picked her up with his heart full of hope. She lived four or five doors from the corner.

She showed no signs of moving from her seat. 'Will you drive me home, please,' she said.

Sefton pointed out her house through the passenger window.

'Will you drive me home, please,' she insisted.

'If you're determined that I drive half way round the town in order to get into your street from the other direction and drop you ten yards from where you are now, I will. But it seems a terrible waste of time. For you, I mean. If you were to walk home now you could be well into another article in the time it would take me to drive you there.'

Cora sat very still.

'Wouldn't you say?' Sefton persisted, coaxingly.

'I don't like being out on the streets at night,' was what Cora finally said.

Sefton made a quick calculation of the distance Cora would have to walk; ten yards might be a slight under-estimate, but from where he was sitting he was confident he could have hit Cora's window with a crumpled paper bag. Still, as he had said once tonight, this was Wrottesley and not Oxford and even he didn't like being out on the streets of Wrottesley. But still again, Cora had offered herself as being above those considerations and her eyes had swept over the Wrottesley men in the bar — her readers — with professional contempt. Sefton wasn't feeling punitive, but there really did have to be some facing up to consequences in these matters, didn't there? Women really were going to have to decide whether they were frightened of men or whether they weren't.

'Look,' Cora went on, as Sefton sat with his arms folded on the wheel, 'It wasn't too much trouble for you to drive to the door when you picked me up.'

Sefton thought this was conventional of her, but fair.

'I didn't know then,' he said, 'what I know now. Now I feel secure in the knowledge that if an attacker jumps you, all you have to do is tell him your name — I mean your pen-name — and he'll drop everything in return for your autograph.' Sefton thought this was conventional of him, and unfair.

'I knew I should never have told you anything. I just knew. Please drive me home.'

'I'll walk you.'

'Please drive me.'

Sefton put his car into gear. 'Well,' he said, 'I'd never have picked you for the frightened type. Peter Potter yes, you never.' And he drove her the long way home.

She slammed the car door like any girl without a degree and a foreign language and she walked along the little path to her flat. Sefton could see the movement of her breasts from behind. He leaned across the passenger seat and called out to her as she was putting her key in the lock. 'Is everything all right? I won't leave until you're inside. Perhaps you could flash your lights on and off when you get in so that I'll know for certain that you're safe.'

'Sefton Goldberg,' Cora shouted back (and Sefton did not at all like the way she filled her mouth with Goldberg), 'you're thirty-five years old and you're a nobody!' It sounded very much, from the clang in her voice, as if whatever it meant she meant it.

'I'm thirty-three,' Sefton returned, in an injured tone, but she was gone. She didn't even flash her lights to let him know she was safe.

Thereafter, their professional relationship went steadily downhill. Whenever Sefton ventured an opinion at a staff meeting Cora screamed it down, and whenever Cora offered a suggestion Sefton brushed it aside like a charging rhino. Ultimately Sefton settled into a view of her as just one more highly-strung and humourless female intellectual who couldn't cope with his easy-going convivial Jewish belligerence, and he thought he was a fool ever to have expected anything of her; but secretly he was still very curious: no one likes to squander a chance with an expert.

Now that he really was thirty-five and a nobody and Cora was about to have published everything she had written (Sefton had not had the presence of mind to ask Peter whether that included the articles she had alluded to a couple of years before), Sefton accepted that his position, viewed from some angles, might have a distinctly derisible look. He had fought his daily battles with people on the working assumption that if he didn't win at the time he would win handsomely in the future when his book or his act or his reputation or whatever it was he was going to be notable for, finally materialised. The secret subtitle of all his literary and creative endeavours was *Sefton's Revenge*. Vendettas and reprisals were not normally considered to be the

98

chief spurs to art but they lay close to the source of his inspiration and he suspected that they didn't lie all that far from the source of Cora's. In which case — if she did indeed share his insights into the relations between art and aggression and publication and revenge — then it was *she*, with her royalty cheque in her pocket, who had routed *him*. And he couldn't honestly expect her to be generous or discreet. It was even possible that she would show him the cheque, wave it under his nose while he drove her to Peter's. He didn't have to close his eyes to see the colour of it or to feel the little draught it would make, cold on his defenceless throat. His only hope was that the sum it promised to pay would be modest. It couldn't be anything else, could it? There was no money in experimental writing. It might be published but it wouldn't be read. He remembered how little he'd been paid, years before, for a story structured like a symphony which had appeared in an anthology. 'They're giving you how much?' his friends from Manchester, the ones who imported shirts from Hong Kong and made trousers for Marks and Spencer, had asked. '*How* much? Well, I suppose you do it because you like it.' They were not impressionable, Sefton's Jewish friends from Manchester. They would have taken one look at Cora Peck and offered her a job making the fires on Saturday. Sometimes Sefton wished he hadn't gone to Cambridge but had stayed instead in the hard bosom of his people. But for the moment, at least, out on the blank streets of Wrottesley, he had seen his way of giving Cora, if she gave him trouble, trouble back. '*How* much are they paying you? And they want you to suffer the inconvenience of exposure and publicity for *that*? Do you want me to have a word with them? I think they use my accountant.'

He became so fond of these sentences, after he had rehearsed them a half-a-dozen times, they seemed to guarantee him such imperviousness and indifference, that he didn't see why he had to wait until Friday to put them to the test. It was some twenty minutes since he had left the Polytechnic car park, and he was now not much further from Cora's flat than he was from his own. It was simply a matter of deciding whether he would turn left to Cora's or keep on in the direction he was going for home. There was nothing waiting for him at home and he had to arrange to give Cora her lift and he really ought to offer her his congratulations, so without thinking about it much he turned left.

He had only seen the inside of Cora's flat on the night he had picked her up to get to know her better a couple of years before. She had only just moved into it then and as she said she had hardly had the chance to stamp it with her personality, but Sefton had been struck by how much sitting on the floor on cushions she was clearly planning to do, and how many fringed lace shawls she was intending to drape and how many photographs of suicidal lady poets and novelists she had already placed on walls, and how very many more odds and ends of porcelain and stitchery and other bygone femininities she possessed, than you would have supposed so modern a girl had any use for. Since then he had been vouchsafed regular glimpses of Cora's flat through the intercession of rumour, hearsay, and gossip. She often invited students back, either singly or in carefully selected groups, and they all reported their experience to their friends with wide eyes and the air of not expecting to be believed, as if they had to explain that they had been whisked away by the fairies and had spent the evening under their hollow hill, listening to incantations. Which in a sense they had. Cora played them very wistful pop music on her record-player, most of it performed by literate groups she had known and cared for in Oxford. (Sefton was amazed at the freedom with which Cora talked of Oxford to the deprived and under-privileged students of Wrottesley Polytechnic; *he* went to the most extravagant lengths of circumlocution to avoid using even the word Cambridge and when perchance it slipped or was forced out of him, he felt as if he had dribbled sherry trifle in the sight of the starving.) And she read them her favourite poems and stories, often again by friends of her student days and some of them written expressly to her or for her or about her. She permitted them freely to read her own pieces which were placed about the floor for guests to try or leave alone, like bowls of nuts. She encouraged them to offer criticisms of her work and she would look them straight in the eyes with unflinching bravery when their remarks were harsh and she would nod her head and agree and be grateful to them. Sefton discovered that this sort of thing was going on not just in Cora's flat but also in her writing classes at the Polytechnic. Before Cora's arrival the only signs that students enjoyed any intimacy with one another were the brown and yellow bite marks on their necks; but now there was discernible on some of them that nervous exhausted look which comes from the excessive practice of candour. Sefton spoke out against it in staff meetings. He offered it as his belief that, strictly speaking, it was a matter for the police.

'It wouldn't be so bad if you didn't have to touch each other.'

'We don't touch each other,' Cora screamed. 'We are uninhibited in our reactions to one another's work.'

'It amounts to the same thing,' said Sefton.

He watched with dismay as Cora gathered around her a small circle of intuitive sympathisers; students and research assistants and young lecturers who did not merely sympathise with her ideas, but sympathised with *her*. They understood her loneliness and dedication; they could tell when they awoke whether the day was to be fair or foul for Cora; they could sense when they were in another room if she had a headache, and they breathed a little quieter for her; and they knew at once when she was, as a woman, indisposed, and they seemed to draw some creative inspiration from their knowledge. If they had all been women Sefton wouldn't have cared how inspiring they found her indispositions,

101

but he hated seeing men so attentive and attuned to the vicissitudes of Cora's hormones. He didn't consider himself to be at all talmudical in his attitudes to women; he had, when he took his Jewish bride, forgone with equanimity his rights to shave her head or send her off, at the appropriate times, for ritual purification. But as he trod the path to Cora's front door, as he thought of all those who had trodden it before him, bearing their oblations as to a menstrual shrine, he wondered if this really were a proper place for a Jewish boy to be.

5

'H — h — how much?'

Sefton actually heard himself make the noise which, whenever he saw it laid out in print, he didn't believe anyone made. He didn't believe either that smiles froze on faces, or that jaws instantly dropped, or that hearts fled into stomachs, but his did.

He had been compelled to try out his new indifference and imperviousness much sooner than he had expected, in fact while still standing at Cora's front door. She had greeted him with such unashamed ebullience on this her big day, and she had been so surprised but yet not all that surprised to see him after all that had happened or rather not happened between them, and she had been so busy on the phone with this one and with that one, and it was now becoming so clear to her what Henry James was on about in all those stories concerning writers whose talents were spoiled because they were lionised too soon which she would have to guard very carefully against, that Sefton began to fear for the strength of his resolve. Already the skin below his nose was tightening up. Soon it would be the skin inside his throat. From where he was standing he could see up a short flight of stairs into Cora's flat. The bottom half of a male form in a fine coat was just visible. Sefton concluded that it was Melvyn Bragg's. He couldn't chance leaving it a moment longer.

'Cora,' he said experimentally, 'I am really delighted for you. But are they looking after you properly? I know what some of these university publishing houses are like. They think they're doing you a favour. Don't take any shit from them. Insist on an advance right away.'

'I've got one,' said Cora.

Sefton laughed. 'Yes, I know the sort of thing. Have that to be going on with and if we sell any copies we'll send you a bit more. What have they given you, two, three hundred?'

Behind Cora's spectacles something twinkled. 'It's quite a shock actually,' she said. 'You see they've been auctioning them off to American publishers. *Slowly Dying* and *The Sick Rose* have already been bought, and the bidding is still going on for *Terminal Case* and *The Amputee*. So far it's looking like I'm guaranteed ninety per cent of −' and because she knew it wasn't ladylike to mention sums of money aloud she put her lips to Sefton Goldberg's ears and blew into them a couple of numbers quite modest in themselves but yoked to a sequence of zeros which she shaped like smoke rings, each one rounder and warmer than the one before.

The words, 'I suppose we do these things because we enjoy them not because we want to be rich,' died on his lips. The same lips on which, at the same time, the smile was freezing, and just below which the jaw was dropping. He would have liked to nip back quickly to Manchester to ask them what he was supposed to say now. But on his own he could only fumble like a *nebbish* with his aitches. 'H − h − how much?'

He hoped it wasn't because he looked faint, or strained, or bitter, or anything that was indifferent and impervious, that Cora asked him up for coffee. She explained that she had a surprise visitor.

Sefton couldn't face Melvyn Bragg. Not now. Not today. Another time, when *Penelope's Warp: In Praise of Incompletion* was completed. Then they could sit and talk about negative affirmation. But not now. So he declined coffee and congratulated Cora again and made his arrangement to pick her up and take her to Peter's party.

'I'm really looking forward to it,' Cora enthused girlishly. Spontaneous delight in simple things did not come any easier to her than to other intellectuals, but like them she worked on it. 'I could scarcely believe it when Peter invited me. I always thought he didn't like me.'

'That just shows you how wrong you can be,' said Sefton.

'I only hope it won't be spoiled by what Sidewinder's done.'

'Ah, you've heard about that? Lectures in the terraces. No, we'll all be over it by then. Anyway, it will be your job to cheer us up before you leave.'

Cora smiled confidently. She was dressed as the early Garbo, in a white beret. She had a naked optimism on her. Today she could cheer up the dead. 'Oh, by the way,' she said, as Sefton was about to go, 'you don't mind giving a lift to a friend of mine as well do you? I'll check that it's all right with Peter of course. I don't think either of you know him. He's a nice bloke actually.' Cora, like all well-brought up girls with degrees who wanted to use the word bloke, pronounced it blook. 'He teaches over in languages. He might be going to translate *The Growth* into French for me. He's called —'

'Walter Sickert Fledwhite.'

'Wally Fledwhite, yes. How did you know?'

'I guessed,' said Sefton.

'You know him then?'

'I've met him briefly.'

'So you don't mind giving him a lift?'

'No,' said Sefton. 'No, no. The more the merrier.'

As he walked down her path, drying his ear, he wondered how she had come to know about Side-winder's proposal if she hadn't been to the degree ceremony, and he knew she hadn't been to it because Peter had run into her outside his room while it was still

on. Sefton had only got to hear about what had been
proposed because he had been mooning about his room
late and had been caught by his head of department.
Something made him turn and look up at Cora's
window. Staring out and watching him go was a face
which could only have been Melvyn Bragg's if Melvyn
Bragg had been the double of Charles Wenlock.

6

Sefton had always been ashamed of something he was doing; being ashamed of everything was a difference only of degree. So apart from those feelings of unabatable depression and intense humiliation, which he carried with him in his luggage anyway, he was not unduly taxed when he first arrived at the town of Wrottesley in order to teach in its Polytechnic. He knew what to do. He knew to keep his coat on and his passport ready and to go about with an absent air as if trying, above the din of other people's settled lives, to hear if his train was being announced or his flight called. He knew not to find a local doctor, not to put himself on the electoral roll, not to join libraries or organizations, and not to open accounts with stores. His present existence had nothing to do with him; it had simply attached itself to him accidentally, like a talkative drunk. It was shaming but one looked the other way. Similarly, as he wasn't staying, there was no point in making himself physically comfortable; so he rented the first flat he could find and did without a telephone and a fridge and a continental quilt, and failed to memorise his post code. So temporary was to be his sojourn that he kept his suits in cases and his socks in laundry bags and his books in bundles of string and himself on the edge of his chair. Perched, on the top floor of a wet Victorian house, ready for flight. He had been perched for five years. Some of his books were now out of their string but there was still no quilt and no fridge and no telephone. To have bought or had installed any of those material equivalents to happiness would have been tantamount to acknowledging that he did indeed live in Wrottesley and that this was indeed his life he was living in it. Whereas he didn't and this wasn't. He kept his bed rumpled and uninviting so that he had rather to sleep on it than in it, and he did without cushions lest he should be tempted to sink back in his chair. If he had been comfortable he would have been even more miserable than he was.

'Vile, isn't it?' he had once challenged Charles Wenlock to deny, on the occasion of the latter's paying him a rare visit for the purpose of a little light lamentation.

'Yes. Why do you live like this?'

'Because I hate it here.'

'Then why don't you move out?'

'Because I might forget how much I hate it.'

Charles Wenlock could never understand why Sefton didn't move to the country. The opportunity to live out of Wrottesley seemed to him to be the best if not the only justification for having a job in it. Nor was he alone in his reasoning. Apart from Cora who was writing, and Sefton who wasn't staying, and those who were expiating some ancient social sin or acting out some contemporary social fantasy by dressing up as Chartists and living cheek by jowl with hands and operatives, the members of the Department of Twentieth-Century Studies drove home westward every evening to converted barns and cottages. Charles Wenlock was forever dropping estate agents' literature on Sefton's desk.

'Charles, I'm Jewish. What am I going to do in the country? I don't own a pair of wellingtons.'

'What do you do in the town?'

'I wait for something to happen.'

'And what happens?' Charles Wenlock could be as pitiless as Socrates.

'Very little, but that's not the point. There's always the chance that something might.'

There was always the chance, for instance, that Fiona McHenry, the diminutive Scottish nurse who lived on the next floor down from Sefton, would not bring her scrutable Chinese boy friend back and fill the house and the night air around it with the most comprehensively explicit miscellany of moans and whimpers and sighs and grunts that Sefton was rather humiliated to admit he had ever heard; in which case there was also the chance that Ron Penn, who lived next door to her and directly below Sefton, would not attempt to drown her out by banging all his doors and playing his Tom Jones records at maximum amplification. There was always the chance, but it was slim. Fiona McHenry, who seemed to Sefton to be too small and frail to be any use as a nurse — surely she was too weak to squeeze a syringe let alone carry a bed-pan — had settled into a ritualistic pattern of behaviour. First came the liver and onion fry-up, then came the teach-yourself-Chinese cassette, then there was faint laughter followed immediately by the sound of curtains being ripped, and then the racket began. Sefton sat on the edge of his chair in his laced up shoes and wondered if the first radio had struck its listeners as being as miraculous, for the irrelation of its size to its capacity to make noise, as Fiona McHenry struck him. This in turn made him wonder whether people had always needed to be so vociferous or whether the need had arrived with the death of God, the First World War and D.H. Lawrence.

'Do you think she's frigid?' he would yell at Ron Penn if he met him on the stairs, cupping his hands around his mouth to make a megaphone.

'I don't know about frigid,' Ron would yell back. He often began his sentences with the promise of balance and wit but he always collapsed at the caesura and tried to look the joke he couldn't find. Alternatively he would slide into oblique complaint. 'I don't know about frigid: I've got to get up in the morning.'

In point of fact he didn't have to get up in the morning at all, because he had nowhere to go and nothing to do. He had been unemployed for the five years Sefton had shared a bathroom with him and there was no reason to doubt he had been unemployed for five years before that. 'Things are bad,' he would say to Sefton with his defeated Wrottesley nasal rattle. It was a persecuted, subjugated sound; a cry of complaint from something smaller than the man — something bad-natured but in trouble at the back of Ron Penn's nose. 'Things are real bad.' He blamed the current political situation but it was difficult to imagine what there would have been for him to do if things had been good. He claimed he was a painter, self-taught, but he couldn't get going again until he had finished the easel he was making out of bits of furniture he had picked up or been given. Sefton couldn't remember a time when the easel wasn't being made.

'It'll cost me nothing when it's finished.'

'Why don't you make some to sell?' Sefton asked him.

'I would,' he replied, 'but it's the time, you see. Time's money, isn't it?'

They met and talked on the stairs as infrequently as Sefton could arrange it. Sometimes, when Ron was desperately lonely, he would come up and tap on Sefton's door. Sefton would immediately whip the cover off his typewriter, bang a few keys, call out, 'I won't be a minute,' and stagger to the door in the attitude of a distracted author. Ron was always sorry to be a nuisance; Sefton always rubbed his eyes and found him a few spare moments.

'It must be funny being a writer.'

Sefton thought. 'It is,' he said.

'I suppose it's a bit like my painting.'

'Must be very similar.'

'Do you have to be in the mood?'

'Absolutely.'

'I find that with my painting.'

When he wasn't finishing his easel so that he could get going again with his painting he did exercises to the music of Tom Jones. He did press-ups and lifted weights and squeezed metal springs in his fist with more or less ferocity according to the excitement of the rhythm. He was roused by Tom Jones and had his hair permed to look like him. Once Fiona McHenry started screaming Ron Penn turned up his music and stepped up the tempo of his exercises. Well into the early hours of the next day Sefton wold hear him, maddened by isolation and drumbeats, thumping his chin on his floor while Fiona McHenry split the ear of the morning with her gasps and her shrieks and a slut called Delilah drove men to violence and despair.

Thither, long after others had sped out of Wrottesley to the wholesome hush of the elfin-named villages beyond, did he nightly repair. He had a little habit, a kind of fetishistic tic, which he never failed to honour, of following up the collection of his mail by feeling first under the mat and then behind the curtains of the unlit hall just in case any really important letter had somehow fallen, slipped and slid, or somersaulted, ricochetted and lodged. No one currently studying The Long Novel with Sefton could have been in any doubt as to his low opinion of the works of Thomas Hardy in which, he explained, peasant morality triumphed over peasant ambition through the agency of peasant superstition and an unreliable postal service. 'We expect a little more from Tragedy,' he used to say, 'than the non-arrival of a parcel or the accidental misdirection of a postcard.' But in fact there was no tragedy which Sefton feared more at present than the accidental non-arrival of the letter which was to take him out of Wrottesley; and there had never been a peasant living on the face of the earth, let alone in the pages of Hardy, who believed as unshakably as Sefton in the mysterious will in such a letter to go astray. The postal system was so vast and casual and arbitrary that it was a kind of madness to entrust a get-well card to it, let alone an invitation to an interview or an outright offer of a job.

He had missed out on he knew not how many offers and appointments because of the vagaries of the post, the malevolence of the postman, the incompetence of some sorter, the sprightly independence of the letter itself. He was always amazed at the fatalistic readiness of people to take the non-arrival of an expected or a hoped-for letter as a rejection, when the little pink envelope containing 'I do, I do' was probably all the while sitting at the bottom of a forgotten bag on Crewe station.

Tonight, with his head full of football and Fledwhite and failure, it seemed more than usually important to him not to mislay a letter. He fell on his knees and felt below the mat; then he felt below it again in case he had pushed something aside with his first feel. He was in the frame of mind where he could spend half the night on his knees checking himself checking, verifying his verifications. There was a strong smell of cats in the hall, which awoke him to another of the thousand natural threats to his mail and his future. Did cats eat paper? In the main he was proud to be Jewish and know nothing about animals, but sometimes he became bored and irritated by his own ignorance. His parents should have prepared him better. He didn't want to know all the different breeds of cats that there were and he didn't want to learn to distinguish their markings; but it would have put his mind at rest to have known, for certain, that the insinuating blotchy-looking thing which purred around Ron Penn could not have been climbing trees and digging holes in people's gardens with an offer of a Vice-Chancellorship for Sefton Goldberg in its stomach.

As he climbed the stairs the smell of cat merged into the smell of frying liver and onions. From Ron Penn's little room came the sound of amplified drum-beats, monotonous, insistent, rousing. His door was half open which either meant that he was angry and wanted to let more noise out, or that he was lonely and hoped to catch Sefton as he crept past. He caught him. He was a short man in tight unfaded jeans and a skimpy tee-shirt. His

112

biceps were pumped up high and hard. His permed hair was fluffed out. He looked shiny and excited, as if the tom-toms had got to him.

'There's a friend of yours here,' he informed Sefton, smirking and sagacious.

Sefton looked up and down the stairs. 'Where is he?'

'It's a she.' Ron Penn grinned with a kind of nostalgic wickedness, like Tom Jones reminiscing about his adolescence in Pontypridd. 'I've got her in here.' He announced that as if he were boasting that he suffered from some obscure but itchy ailment: 'I've got trinear.'

He was beckoning to Sefton to enter his room and see the surprise but by this time she had come to the door, a big friendly girl with strong white teeth. Sefton was very pleased to see her.

'Jacqueline! Well! How nice! You haven't been waiting for long, I hope.'

'No. I was just passing and I thought I'd pop up to see you. Ron heard me ringing and he very kindly let me in and played me some music.'

Ron shone. Knowing and intrusive. He had his thumbs in his belt, like Tom Jones. On his record player was some savage sentimental song about home.

'That was indeed very kind of him,' said Sefton, shepherding her out and up.

'Yes, thanks Ron,' she called over her shoulder.

'That's all right Jackie,' he said, through his nose. He called up the stairs after her, 'Any time.'

Jacqueline was an infrequent visitor to Sefton Goldberg; her time was limited because she had a regular boy friend and Sefton's time was limited because he was writing a book. But her visits, when she did make them, followed a set pattern. She always popped up for a coffee as she happened to be passing and she always stayed the night. She never intended to stay but she always had with her the woman's little necessaries for staying. She never intended to stay because she had a sense of duty to her parents, a sense of loyalty to her boy friend, and because she had been brought up to believe that a man liked a small show of reluctance from a lady; but she just allowed Sefton to see that she saw that he saw she was going to stay for all that, as a concession to the other point of view, that men also liked a lady to show willing.

She was a librarian in the town and before that she had been one of Sefton's students. They had declared their regard for one another at a party just before she left the Polytechnic, when it was safe for him to admit that he had delivered his lectures only to her, and when it was safe for her to admit that now he came to mention it she had noticed. She was taller than him which he liked, and she had lots of fair hair and lots of feature and lots of teeth. She spoke nicely, her father was an architect, and she came from Knutsford. That last was most important. Cheshire, where the Q.C.s and the surgeons lived, was an enchanted place for people growing up in Manchester, and Sefton's parents would often drive him out on Sundays just to stare at lovely Homes; but Knutsford had a special magic for him. Mrs Gaskell had written a novel about Knutsford and therefore she had thrown about the spot, for the bookish Sefton Goldberg, the idealized Protestant charm of English Literature. Girls from Knutsford would have silk ribbons in their hair and sweet natures and a working knowledge of the English Poets. They would talk of duty. They would be discontented with their rural lot but they would conceal their discontent.

Jacqueline's discontent was disturbingly well-concealed. In the year or more that she had been occasionally visiting him he had discovered nothing, beyond a few little things he did or didn't do, that caused her any lasting displeasure. She loved the people she knew, she loved her boy friend, she had loved the Polytechnic and she loved Wrottesley. She even preferred it to Knutsford although she loved that too. She would enthuse over her job at the local reference library and she would tell Sefton how much she liked working with people.

114

'People!' Sefton used to exclaim. 'How can you like working with people?'

'They're nice.'

'Nice? In a reference library? They're all crazed with disappointment and grievance in reference libraries.'

'They are not. They're just ordinary.'

Jacqueline did not merely like ordinariness, she had an ineradicable ideological commitment to it. She read books about rabbits that talked, she went regularly to Stratford to watch the Royal Shakespeare Company, she wept the night John Lennon died, she wrote messages on Snoopy notepaper, and she believed that if it wasn't for politicians people would live in peace and harmony with one another.

Sefton never knew where her niceness was next going to strike. During lovemaking (he made it and she was appreciative) he had to be on constant guard against her slipping into baby-talk. Excessive endearment lay between them like a sleeping third person; and the moment Sefton felt it stir he would bury Jacqueline's mouth in his hair or he would glue his ear to her shoulder, or he would find some completely new and unexpected positions for their bodies from which all verbal communication was impossible. Vigilance made him versatile. It would have been easier by far if he had called her Jackie as she wanted, but he couldn't bring himself to say it. It belonged to other vile diminutives he would never allow to cross his lips, like Debbie, mummy, willy, panties, potty, or bra. He had noticed that Ron Penn had called her Jackie without a qualm — but then bra would have come easily to the likes of Ron Penn (whom Jacqueline, incidentally, thought very nice).

Sefton wasn't proud of his niggardliness, particularly as Jacqueline (who called herself a giving person) bore him no grudge. She would rise from the bed on one elbow and she would shake her hair over him as though she were the goddess of the morning and she would produce the words he wouldn't with the most marvellous clarity from the pursed-up O of her mouth, as if they were newly strung pearls, useless but priceless gifts for a man who had everything. Tonight she sat with her chin resting on her knees and stared into Sefton's face, willing his eyes open.

'I think his songs are lovely, though,' she said.

They had been talking about Leonard Cohen, or rather Jacqueline had been talking about Leonard Cohen and Sefton had been grunting.

'Don't you?' she persisted.

'No.'

'Why not?'

'Because I'm not impressed by the people who like them.'

Jacqueline wrapped some more sheet around herself and moved closer to her critic-lover. She looked excited and engrossed, as if this was what she had really come for — talk.

'That's not a proper reason,' she said. 'And anyway *I* like them, and you're impressed by me.'

'But I didn't know you when I decided not to like them.'

'Well then now you can change your mind.'

'You mean I should stop being impressed by you?'

This was the signal for Jacqueline to become playful. She would never know, and Sefton was never going to tell her, that a mountainous blonde with muscles and sharp teeth was every Jewish boy's dream of perfect bliss. It would not have occurred to her that she was capable of giving Sefton the thrashing of his life, and still less would it have occurred to her that Sefton was capable of enjoying it. She was as unknowing as anyone else in Wrottesley. But at least she was clumsy and Sefton could rely on her to roll over him a few times, compressing his windpipe, fracturing a rib or two, raising bruises on his soft and unused skin. It wasn't precisely what he wanted, but it was close.

What Jacqueline wanted was to return to the discussion. This was disappointing to Sefton and he knew

116

how Arthur Miller must have felt when it got to bed time and he found himself giving tutorials. 'Seriously,' Jacqueline continued, as Sefton fought for his breath beneath her, 'do you really judge things according to what you think of the people who like them?'

'Mmmmnnnghaaaaimes,' said Sefton. He was in bad shape. 'Sometimes,' he repeated.

'Then when don't you?'

'When I take the trouble to read or listen to them myself.'

'Does that mean you haven't listened to any of Leonard Cohen's songs?'

'Not a single one. Life's too short to listen to Leonard Cohen's songs.'

Jacqueline was scandalised. 'How do you know if you haven't heard them?'

'Life's too short to find out,' Sefton explained.

Life's too short was a phrase Sefton had picked up as a student at Cambridge. He had spotted at once both its immediate and its future usefulness. At the time it served to fill in, in one application like plastic cement, all the gaps in his knowledge; so that it should appear that what he didn't know he didn't know by choice. And for the future it seemed to promise all the satisfactions of austere discrimination while allowing him to stay an extra hour in bed. But the phrase had only sentimental value now — in fact there was time for anything. There was even time to tease nice girls. And have them put one right on art.

'If life's too short to enjoy things then it's also too short to criticize them. You're too critical. You enjoy not liking things too much. We all used to say that about your lectures. Half the time you didn't like the books you were teaching and even when you did it was pretty evident you didn't like us. You were always on about how boring teaching was and how much you hated the Polytechnic. That didn't make us feel too confident. And none of us agreed with you. I used to say that you were just saying things you didn't really

117

believe in order to provoke us; but the others thought you were just cynical. We'd sit around over coffee after one of your lectures arguing about whether anyone could actually *be* as cynical as you were. Sally Roberts thought there was a secret tragedy in your life, but Roger Church was convinced you just hated students because you were old.'

Sefton watched in amazement as she moved her mouth and made real words and sentences. She seemed too young to know how. And she gave the impression of inhabiting such a bright, fresh world that Sefton felt as if he were listening to the rabbits talk. He leaned back on his pillow and closed his eyes. 'Jackie, Jackie, Jackie,' he sighed, 'what on earth is going to happen to such a nice girl as you?'

'Darling!' she cried, smothering him in kisses. 'You said it! Three times!'

Because she had to be up and about in her bright, fresh world before he had to be down and out in his old, stale one, she would wake first and bring him tea in bed. 'You've slept well,' she would tell him as if it were an achievement, as if he had beaten everyone else at sleeping. And then she would begin to dress herself, telling him now to turn away, and now to cover his face, and now to put his fingers in his ears, in obedience to her mother's advice that men like a lady to retain a little mystery; but permitting him some fleeting intimate glimpses too, in obedience to the other teaching that men like a lady to be a trifle free.

She sat before the mirror combing out her hair like a mermaid and singing songs to herself, probably by Leonard Cohen. Sefton flicked through the pages of a woman's magazine she had brought up with her. She had been doing a quiz to see if she was a properly adjusted modern woman: not too compliant but not too aggressive either. She seemed to have scored quite well. He continued to flick through the photographs of anorexic girls striking poses in Delhi and Dubai until

118

there fell out of the pages a letter addressed to him. It was postmarked Cambridge, it was thumb-stained as if it had been handled by a delinquent, and it had his name spelt Gouldebergg.

'This for me?' he asked, holding it up to Jacqueline. She had finished her hair and was pulling on her boots.

'Oh Sefton, I'm awfully sorry. I found it on the mat downstairs last night. I forgot all about it when Ron invited me in. I hope it's not important.'

Sefton looked at the back of the envelope. It carried a crest and the embossed words

THE MASTER'S LODGE
HOLY CHRIST HALL

Sefton tossed it aside. 'I shouldn't think so,' he said.

Jacqueline was ready to leave. As always Sefton experienced profound relief while at the same time thinking he'd never liked the look of her more. He admired the way her hair fell lightly on her broad shoulders, the way her lipstick glistened, the way her leather shoulder bag sat perfectly on her hip. She wasn't really out of *Cranford* but she was close. Sefton wondered whether, if he had not been introduced to Gudrun and Hermione so fatally early in life, he would have been quite so relieved whenever Jacqueline said goodbye.

As soon as she was gone he reached for his letter. Inside the envelope was a scrap of paper, similarly embossed, on which was scratched, with an old fountain pen, the following:

Dear Ghoulburgh,

   The Governing Body has read with interest your application for the Disraeli Fellowship. Perhaps you would be so kind as to dine with us some time soon, say next week, say Wednesday.

   If there are likely to be any dietary complications attached to your dining with us perhaps you would

be so kind as to make your stipulations to the Chief Butler; and if you feel that you would like expenses the Bursar is the man to see.

Please let us know if this date happens to fall on some Festival or Holy Day or if you are unable to dine with us for any other reason.

Thank you for the interest you have shown in our Disraeli Fellowship. I myself would have preferred the nomenclature Lord Beaconsfield, and so, I am sure, would he, but there you are.

And it was signed Professor the Right Reverend Sir Evelyn Woolfardisworthy — which was to be pronounced, as Sefton later learned, Woolsery, like the village in Devon.

The old terror gripped Sefton Goldberg (spelt, as he was later to explain, Goldberg, and pronounced similarly). Jacqueline's friend Sally Roberts had been right about him: he *did* have a ghastly tragic secret in his life. It was called Cambridge. He thought he had put it behind him like fear of the dark, but here it was again with all its ancient eccentric assurance and all its exclusive poisonous dottiness, having stolen into his room in a crumpled crested envelope under the cover of Jacqueline's *Cosmopolitan*. The deceptively insignificant crest and the majestic informality of the handwriting added a familiar insult to an old injury; it had affected him similarly when the Vice-Chancellor swayed past him on a bicycle, or when Dr Geoffrey Tolcarne had swum under him in the nude. They were never discountenanced and he was never anything else. They would forget his name and he would appear the foolish one; they would bang into him in the street and he would feel he was clumsy; they would sneeze in his face and he would apologize. Already, as he merely looked at the letter, that metamorphosis of himself from freeman to menial was beginning. Already his shoulders were rounding and his palms were running with sweat. In a moment dandruff would leap from his hair and dirt would fly into his fingernails and the breakfast he hadn't eaten would appear in wet stains down his front. Then would he be ready to dine with the Master of Holy Christ Hall, straining to hear what was said to him over the rush of his own perspiration. And these were no more than the anxieties he would bring with him; what would he do when he came to the resident terrors of High Table — the rituals of precedence, and prayer, and port?

Prayer!! What were they going to get him to say? Who were they going to get him to thank? Would there be anything involving candles or hymnals or biscuits? Could it be that he himself was to be dunked?

Well, he was in no position to do anything but submit to whatever they wanted to do to him, and they would have to take him as he was; that was where, after much further deliberation and a cold bath, he came out. There was no point in worrying. And in the meantime he was going to have to refresh his memory of his application. He would have to find the copy. He had no idea what he said he was working on, where he said his special interests lay, what he said he'd done, who he said he was. He could not remember having heard of the Disraeli Fellowship let alone applying for it. But he felt that this was the very position he'd been chasing all his life, and if it wasn't that he believed he was bound not to get whatever he acknowledged he wanted, he would have acknowledged he wanted it.

7

It was Open Day at the Polytechnic, Wrottesley.

Strictly speaking it was never anything else, for like the Windmill Theatre during the war and the Salvation Army at any time, the Polytechnic held it as sacred that it should never close its doors to the curious or deny its facilities to the needy. In its brochures and its prospectuses, in its advertisements on the buses and its sixty-second commercial on local radio, it described itself as 'standing square in the centre of the vigorous town of Wrottesley — a position it is perhaps not fanciful to see as symbolic of its involvement in the working life of the community'; and indeed so reciprocal was this involvement that there was nothing — from an exhibition of sculptural forms in the Faculty of Purposeful Art and Design to a lunchtime lecture on the Micro-processor and You — which the working people of Wrottesley were not invited and even urged to attend. They were to understand that it was *their* Polytechnic. But today it was open not merely in the functional and hospitable sense; today it was casting aside its reserves and laying bare its secrets and showing everything it had. Recruitment was the official word for what was going on, but the pressing concupiscence of the Polytechnic Directorate, done-up and glistening, with its name on its lapel, suggested an older and more immodest form of invitation; while the expressions of cruel indifference on the faces of those with whom the Polytechnic wanted its way — the coach-loads of sixth-formers who were still athirst for knowledge but who had not as yet been snapped up by any of the first twenty institutions of their choice — appeared to support Jacqueline's mother's contention that a little mystery is no bad thing. Whether the Polytechnic would have wooed more successfully if it had wooed more subtly, or whether it would have recruited more if it had not wooed at all, who can say? These were difficult times and beggars couldn't be choosers. No one knew this better than the sixth-formers themselves. They had come along for the ride, to get a day off school, to humour a teacher, to please a parent, to accompany a friend; what they had not come for was to cringe or wheedle or beg or bow or scrape or in any way do the sorts of things which Sefton Goldberg remembered as being mandatory in the days when he sought admission. Sought admission. That dated him. It was a long time since the Polytechnic had put anything like admission between itself and rapidly dwindling student numbers. Admission had gone the way of selection and rejection. And if the sixth-formers didn't all know when they boarded their buses they certainly all knew when they got off them that it was they who were interviewing the Polytechnic, and not vice versa. Why else was it that the only ones who were cringing and wheedling and dressed up uncomfortably in their best suits were the lecturers? Those same sixth-formers might not have known that Dr Gerald Sidewinder, the Polytechnic Accountant, had all that week been explaining to his staff the very latest method of dividing the number of teachers into the number of taught and coming up with the answer redundancy; but they could have guessed as much from all the fizzy drinks and the ham sandwiches that were being given away.

By the time Sefton turned up for work, senior officials were flitting in and out of one another's rooms, the strain of occasion showing on their faces despite (or was it because of?) their attempts to give the twin polytechnical impressions of old-style unhurried academic privilege and up-to-the-minute technologically oriented inter-modular relevant relatedness. In their pressed suits they most resembled delegates of an obscure trade union, down from some remote corner of the country, popular in the bar but without much muscle. Outside his room the Director himself was in urgent conference with Sidewinder. Sefton noticed that the Director's trousers were hitched higher than ever above his spit and polished pit-boots and that he was wearing a new cloth cap. And even Sidewinder looked dusty in a fresh way, as if he had arranged for clean grit to be deposited in the creases of his cheeks.

The younger, more junior staff were escorting groups of unbelieving school-children around the building, explaining the organization of courses, discriminating between modules, pointing out the generous provision of staircases and toilets, slighting the universities, hinting at pleasures not in the prospectuses. Entice-ments such as, 'If you lean to your left and stand on tip-toes you can just see Wales' and, 'Yes, field trips are a compulsory component of unit GEO II and they are subject to a . . . well, a form of assessment; but mainly we all go to the Lake District and get pissed', floated across to Sefton Goldberg as he made his way to his room. Lounging against radiators, boys in leopardskin school uniforms and chains and coloured hair eyed off secretaries who for the rest of the year went about their business unnoticed. In a corner of the corridor which led to the annexe which led to the fire-escape which led to his room a Hogarthian group of schoolgirls, sluttish beyond dream or fantasy, waited for someone to talk to them about micro-film resources. They seemed to be exchanging experiences of physical disease and corrup-tion. They hooted and snorted as Sefton passed. Thank God I'll be out of here soon, he said to himself, thinking of Holy Christ Hall before he had time to remember that he shouldn't.

On Sefton's door was the usual message from Nick Lee explaining that he wasn't going to be able to get in today. But somehow he had been able to spirit on to his desk a mass of notes for students, marked essays, reading lists, apologies, testimonials, duplicated articles, suggested sources of reference, and detailed instructions for reaching him, should there be anything he was urgently required to talk over, via letter, telegram, telephone, telex and long wave radio.

On his own desk there was less to wonder at, but there was a surprise. Someone had left him, where he couldn't fail to notice it quickly, one of those exceedingly conscientious radical journals on the covers of which there was always a fuzzy photograph of a freedom fighter or a mother and her baby being tortured. It was printed on that sort of morally desirable cheap or even re-cycled paper and in that sort of clandestine type-face reserved only for the telling of the real truth — an indictment, in its very appearance, of the meretricious glossy lies of capitalism. Sefton flicked through its pages and came to an article on Israeli atrocities. 'Fledwhite,' he said to himself, and threw the truth into his wastepaper basket.

Otherwise his desk was as usual. His application forms were piled as high as ever, and he was just able to postpone telling himself that he might soon be able to throw them away too. Waiting for him also was an exhausted memo from Charles Wenlock wondering if there was any chance whatsoever of a meeting getting itself called for later in the day in order for there to be discussed by whoever might care to discuss them 'certain crucially disquieting developments regarding accommodation for the staff of the Department of English Lit. — oops, crossed out, sorry — Twentieth-Century Studies.' And a note from the Dean of Applied Arts requesting a few moments of Sefton's time, whenever convenient. Sefton supposed this had something to do with his refusal to escort sixth-formers around the building and show them Wales.

'I'll happily interview any number of them to see if there's a single one worth having,' he told Pat Ellis, the person responsible for Staff Resource Deployment on Open Days, 'but I'm fucked if I'm going to be involved in an exercise designed to help them to see if a single one of us is!' Sefton knew that he was packing into his resistance all the prejudice he couldn't help harbouring against men called Pat.

'So you won't mind when you end up with no students and no job?' Pat Ellis asked him, while crossing him off his list.

'Mind?'

Sefton knew that there was a word going around to describe his unhelpfulness in this matter. It was a word which often went around to describe the unhelpfulness of most of Charles Wenlock's department in most matters. Sefton took it for granted, therefore, that he was to be carpeted and that what he was to be carpeted for was élitism. The Polytechnic was pretty decisively down on élitism. The Dean had had occasion already to let Sefton Goldberg know that. On the other hand he had wanted Sefton to understand that he (the Dean) was not as fiercely opposed to it as Sidewinder and that he was even prepared to turn a blind eye to it provided that it was practised in moderation and without too many people being involved. So Sefton didn't expect to be dressed down too severely. Nonetheless he wanted the interview out of the way as soon as possible. He had a highly developed respect for authority and even the slightest telling off made him feel queasy. He didn't at all like this submissive quality in himself and he tried to disguise it by barking at menials whenever he could and by bullying and frightening students, but in the still reaches of the night, when there was only him and his humiliations, he was prepared to admit that had he run into him in the street, in uniform, he would have said *Sir* and maybe even *Heil!* to Hitler.

In order to get to the Dean's office in order to get the telling-off over, he had again to pass the group of schoolgirls. They appeared to have progressed from putrefaction to a discussion of sado-masochistic cannibalism. Whatever they found funny about him from behind they found even funnier from the front. They splurted and choked. Thank God they'll be going to Sussex and Lancaster, Sefton thought, remembering this time not to tempt providence by thinking of, and thanking God for, where *he* was going.

Humming a tuneless tune and feeling about five years old, Sefton arrived at a door marked Ray Grassby, Dean of Applied Arts, whereupon he knocked, waited, cleared his throat, knocked again, rattled the knob, called out 'Ray' and did, in short, what everybody did when calling on the Dean — gave him fair warning and plenty of time. Not that it ever made any difference. All the warning and all the time in the world would not have saved Ray Grassby from being caught, by whoever called on him, in some inexplicable act of furtiveness and stealth. When Sefton finally entered he found Ray Grassby marooned in the middle of his long bare room apparently just on the point of burgling it. There was not a single item worth taking, but nothing short of his being thwarted in an attempt to palm a sideboard or swallow some rare manuscript without the aid of water could account for the extraordinary contortions of his body and the look of unspeakable guilt, disappointment, and discomfort on his face as he registered Sefton Goldberg. Other visitors had found him sniffing his walls or putting light bulbs in his ears or trying to stuff the carpet into his socks. But it seemed that providence had seen to it that he would always be interrupted in time: nothing was ever reported missing.

He was a large dark man on whom, once, people might have depended. He struck Sefton as having been one of those indispensable presences in all those emergencies which sort men from boys and which Sefton himself had spent his whole life avoiding for fear of where the sorting process would leave him. Ray Grassby, he was sure, would have known how to tie a tourniquet and where to find the sand-bags and when to open the sluice-gates; he would have been strong enough to hold up the roof for that extra hour and go without water for that extra day. If some old person had collapsed in the street or the supermarket he would certainly not have looked the other way, as Sefton always did. But Ray Grassby was himself not young any more and he had upon him that deathly yellowish waxen look of intense self-absorption which comes from a wrecked digestive system or a shattered confidence or hopeless and eccentric wife. In Ray Grassby's case it came from all three. He had arrived at the Polytechnic years before it was a polytechnic, when it was just a friendly little tech with something of the working men's institute atmosphere about it. He was then the solitary arts man in the place, a figure in amateur dramatics, a raconteur and a monologuist of some repute. He would enthral local audiences with readings from Macaulay and Ruskin, and once, in a pair of silk pyjamas and with a towel round his head, he had given a recitation from memory of Fitzgerald's *Omar Khayyám* to the Wrottesley Literary and Scientific Society of which, for a while, he was President. At about the same time that his wife (who had herself been something on the local stage) received the first of her 'messages', the tech became the Polytechnic; professionals with degree courses and discriminations and prescriptions began to arrive; and Ray Grassby turned his face to the wall and gave up his days to administration and ulcers.

He had been born and had grown up in Porlock, and he claimed that it was his great-great-grandfather who had disturbed Coleridge while *Kubla Khan* was coming to him. He told and re-told this story, with embellishments, to the members of Charles Wenlock's department, as a means of maintaining some literary connection with them; but to Charles Wenlock he told it as an act of aggression. For in Charles Wenlock he had found the only person living or dead, and not excluding Coleridge himself, who could take exception to it.

Sefton was continually amazed by the failure of his head of department either to be indifferent to, or to arm himself against, Ray Grassby's anecdote. At the first mention of Nether Stowey or the Quantocks or Ray's family, Charles Wenlock's chest would heave and his cheeks would blaze and his lips would set white like a dead man's, as if it were *his* fleeting fragile inspiration that had been broken in upon and Ray Grassby himself, never mind his great-great-grandfather, who had been the gross intruder.

If Ray Grassby's story of his great-great-grandfather's unintended act of vandalism was the means whereby he retained some form of contact with the world of arts and letters, the means whereby he retained some form of contact with the world of men and women — or people, as Jacqueline called them — was beer. Not so much the drinking of it as the descriptions of the drinking of it. If you visited the Dean you expected first to catch him red-handed in the middle of his room and then you expected to hear, in some detail, what he had asked the price of, asked the weight of, bought, smelt, sipped, held to the light, tasted, and finally drunk the night before in a new pub he had discovered through the pages of a new Real Ale guide which had been recommended to him in the pub he had been advised to go to the night before that. Today, on the occasion of Sefton's turning up to be carpeted, he took only as long as was absolutely necessary to finish palming his sideboard before embarking on a winding acclivitous journey, through the beers of his uncritical youth in Porlock, over the frothy illusions he had foolishly followed as a soldier in Germany, into the marshes of excess and disappointment, up the slopes of false optimism and vain anticipation, to the best Wem bitter, at last, that he had ever held to the light. Sefton went as far with Ray Grassby as he could. 'Really!' he would exclaim, at sudden and surprising turns in the road, but it wasn't easy for him, being Jewish, to feign much interest for long. Being Jewish he was as uninformed about beer as he was about flowers and birds. Even in the days when there had been nothing to know about beer he had known less than anybody else; but now that a pint was about gravity and purity and politics, was judged by the laws of mathematics and morality, he felt especially disadvantaged. When he was thirsty he drank any one of those lagers in which Ray Grassby for a while had lost his way, and when he wanted to taste something he drank whisky. He had been brought up to spot a gentile as someone who ordered pints in pubs, and although he had come to find flaws in that method of identification he still recognized in himself a lack of passion for the subject of beer that was so fundamental it could only have been tribal. It was a lack of passion in every way comparable (if lacks could be compared) to his lack of passion for flamingo's milk or monkey's brains. And he always tried to let this be known about himself early on in his relations with other men — with other men who were not Jewish, that is — so that they shouldn't come to feel he had passed himself off as one of them when he wasn't. Too many cold hurt glances had come his way when he had interrupted a call for 'Ten pints of XJ11 please' with 'Could you make that nine, and one half of Heineken?' It was best all round if he put his cards on the table early; and if he had been really courageous while he was at it he would have included, as further possible bars to friendship, his lack of passion for hearing people fart, for being heard to fart, for making qualitative distinctions between farts; his lack of passion for discussion of piss, whether just popping out for a or couldn't half do with a or nothing like being on the; his lack of passion for the idea of inebriation (as opposed to the thing itself for which he did not lack a passion), for nostalgic evocations of past inebriation, for running bulletins on the progress of present inebriation; his lack of passion, in short, for all the little frills and folderols of what, if he had mastered the idiom, the gentiles called being on the ale. But he wasn't really courageous.

He certainly couldn't have brought himself, for example, to tell Ray Grassby that he thought his enthusiasm for beer was in fact no greater than Sefton's own, that it was written all over his sad, uncomfortable yellow face that he only talked beer because he was damned if he knew what else to talk to another living soul about, and that for all Sefton or anybody else had actually seen to the contrary Ray Grassby might have been a teetotaller all his life. It was altogether easier simply to let him finish.

'But,' the Dean said at last, pushing his fingers through his hair, 'I haven't asked you here on such a busy day merely to talk about Wem bitter. A couple of things. The first one I don't attach much significance to, but I have to bring it up with you briefly.' Ray Grassby rocked his right hand as if he were shaking a cocktail in slow motion. It was a gesture designed to suggest a man bigger than his office but mindful of his obligations to it, too.

Elitism, thought Sefton Goldberg.

'I had an official complaint made against you this morning —'

Fledwhite, thought Sefton Goldberg.

'— by a young woman, well not such a young woman —'

Cora? Lynne Shorthall??

'— called Peel, I think.' Ray Grassby consulted a small black diary. 'Yes, Val Peel.'

'Val Peel?' Sefton's ability to remember the names of his students had never been great and it had always been declining, but recently there had been a drop into something like hysterical amnesia. He needed information more particular than a name. They all had names. Was she tall? short? fat? thin? ugly? pretty?

'Second year student,' the Dean helped out. 'She mentioned that she had done a year with the Open University. About forty. Got two or three children.'

A dim outline formed itself at the back of Sefton's

mind — shortish, fattish, uglyish — and slowly filled out into the person of Val Peel, mature student, mother of three, part product of the Open University. Sefton tried to think of what, in especial, he had done to Val Peel of late. He was pretty sure he hadn't made fun of her in lectures. And it didn't seem likely that he would have invited her on to his floor. If his memory served him correctly, she had cried recently, in a tutorial — but then all mature students cried. It was in the nature of the terrible sacrifice they were making, of their time, their marriages, their children, their shopping, that they should be on edge. No matter how competent they were they lived in constant fear that one day they would come face to face with the one book they couldn't understand or the one essay question they couldn't answer and then it would all have been for nothing. Sefton taught a whole class of them. They would all arrive together, in their smocks and pinnies, ten minutes late, having done the week's washing and prepared their husbands' breakfasts and dropped the children off at school. And within seconds the pill popping would begin, the little plastic container of valium being passed from shaking hand to shaking hand under Sefton's very nose. And Val Peel *was* a little jumpier than the rest.

'I've given up a lot to come here,' she would tell Sefton Goldberg, her eyes wet behind her spectacles, the holdall which she clutched and jiggled on her lap spilling too many books and folders and pencils and nappy liners and tins of mashed peach with strained rhubarb.

'I know that,' Sefton would reply, trying to think of Val Peel's cold hearth and neglected starving children, but being capable only of wondering whether it was for this he had been so excited when he had won a place at Cambridge so many years ago. 'I know that, but I am only proposing that you move a comma.'

'If you think I'm not honours degree material I'd prefer it that you tell me now.'

'On the contrary. I expect you to do very well. All I'm suggesting . . .'

'Because it isn't worth it. It isn't worth my going on if you think I'm stupid.'

It was during those moments when Sefton was able to restrain himself from bawling, 'Just move the fucking comma!' that he felt that he might have been cut out to be a teacher after all. Only the other day he had been so remarkably restrained as to say not a word to Val Peel but only to lean over and cross out with his red pen the offending mark and re-insert it where it should have been, with his black.

'What I liked about the Open University,' Val Peel had surprisingly burst out, rising and brushing wet tissues from her pinny into her holdall, 'was its respect for students' scripts. Not once, during the whole time I was with them, did they do what you've just done. Their criticism was positive, not destructive.' And stuffing her essay into her nappy liners she had stormed from Sefton's room.

'Val Peel? Yes, I think I've placed her. What was her complaint — that I fiddled with her punctuation?'

Ray Grassby had the look of a man who was not going to take sides. 'She said you scribbled over her essay.'

'I didn't. What else did she say?'

'I explained to her, of course, that sometimes there isn't room in the margins or at the bottom of the page for a marker to write everything he wants to.'

'Ray, I didn't scribble on her essay — though even if I had . . .'

'Yes, yes. That's what I thought.' Both the Dean's hands were now shaking cocktails. He was very anxious for there to be no trouble. 'I said this to her. I've marked essays myself and I know that it's easy to get carried away.'

Sefton found himself feeling quite upset. 'Ray I *didn't* scribble on her essay. I moved a comma.'

'Well, I calmed her down anyway. But, you know, be

a bit careful. Particularly with the older ones.' He was placatory, indulgent, avuncular, conspiratorial even — perhaps he and Sefton might have a night out some time soon and scribble on a couple of older ones' essays together; but not for one moment or for one syllable did he believe Sefton Goldberg. It wasn't personal, as Sefton himself could see. It wasn't even workaday cynical. It was simply that he had complete faith in the truth of an accusation because the energy that was required to make one impressed him. A rebuttal was reasonable and understandable, but it was no more than a response; it came second. Whereas an accusation was initiatory: it started something. And to someone who had become as morally indolent as the Dean had become since turning his face to the wall, the energy to start something was awesome; therefore he confused it with rectitude.

Sefton knew that nothing he could say would ever shake Ray Grassby's belief that he (Sefton) had fallen on Val Peel's essay, with a red ballpoint pen in each hand and another between his teeth, and had not released it until every blank space had been filled and every original word obliterated; but he also knew that it was a part of Ray Grassby's same moral indolence not to have an attitude to that brutal and gratuitous act. He was not in the slightest degree censorious of what he unshakably believed Sefton had done; his only concern was that it shouldn't lead to anything in the way of student bother. He lived in daily dread of student revolt, and when he wasn't summarily doubling complainants' marks or handing them out degrees on the quiet, he was practising concealment from them on a massive scale. If he had possessed the moral energy to formulate a motto it would have been: Give them Everything and Tell them Nothing. With the latter part of that undeclared policy Sefton had no difficulty agreeing; he too believed in keeping as many secrets as possible from students, although he felt that he had reached this position by a different route from

134

Ray Grassby's — the Dean had come the lazy way, desiring only peace and quiet; Sefton took the more strenuous path of wishing to be punitive. In the matter of students' record cards, for example, it would have been much simpler for Sefton to have accepted Cora Peck's proposal that they should be made available to the students themselves as it was their futures which were likely to be affected by them; but Sefton had argued, above Cora's screams, that the sorts of things that he derived pleasure from writing on students' record cards, and indeed the sorts of things he derived pleasure from reading off them, were intended to be confidential and would lose their distinctive pithiness and verity the moment they were intended to be anything else. This had resulted in an arduous ideological struggle of the kind for which Sefton had a seemingly tireless enthusiasm and which was resolved, finally, in the compromise of everyone's record cards being made public, except Sefton's.

Sefton took very seriously the responsibility thus enjoined upon him of being the only person left in the Polytechnic to keep alive the art of termly (or rather, now, semestral) disassemblage of students' characters and personalities; and there were times when he put in more hours on his record cards than on his book on failure. It even occurred to him to keep copies of these cards as other people desirous of celebrity kept copies of their letters, so that when his hour arrived, they might be collected and published. He could not therefore, take too much exception to Ray Grassby's conniving assurances that he had cheated the students of a grievance and covered up a crime, even if the crime that was being covered up had never been committed. Sefton felt like one of those petty felons he had seen on investigative television programmes who claimed (in silhouette or with their backs to the cameras) that they were in the habit of confessing to what they hadn't done just to keep their relations with the police on a sound footing and as a kind of guarantee of good faith against the time when they would have to deny doing what they actually had done. If Sefton didn't too strongly protest his innocence of the charge of ruining the lives of Val Peel's hungry children, things might go easier with him when it came to élitism.

It seemed, though, that the Dean was in no hurry to come to it. 'But anyway,' he said, with both his hands in front of him and cupped downwards, as if he were lightly keeping a couple of lids on things, 'that's not what I want to talk to you about. I asked you here to find out your opinion of Kevin Dainty.'

'Kevin Dainty?' The thought occurred to Sefton Goldberg that the Dean was planning to go through the names of every student at the Polytechnic in order to see if Sefton recognized a single one of them. 'I'm sorry Ray, I can't place him. What have I done to him?'

Ray Grassby assumed that Sefton was joking. He didn't know why Sefton joked as often as he did but he supposed it had something to do with his being Jewish. Living in Porlock, then in Germany after the war, then in Wrottesley, he hadn't met many Jews. He smiled briefly to show he hadn't missed the joke. 'When I say I want your opinion of him I mean I want your opinion of his writing.'

Sefton was desperate to be helpful. 'Look Ray, off-hand I can't tell you. But if you like I'll nip over to my office and check my records. What year did you say he was in?'

'What year? Kevin Dainty? The footballer? You don't know Kevin Dainty, the captain of Wrottesley Ramblers?'

Sefton shrugged, ashamed. In the reflection of Ray Grassby's eyes he could see what Ray saw — a twisted yellow thing, a musty indoor creature that shunned the light and was inimical to all things wholesome. 'I certainly didn't know I was teaching the captain of Wrottesley Ramblers,' said the creature, in a gravel voice.

'You aren't!' Ray Grassby suddenly saw that the

point of Sefton's jokes was that they weren't funny. 'He isn't a student. Who said he was a student?'

'You asked my opinion of his work?'

'His writing,' the Dean corrected. 'As well as being a footballer he also happens to be a novelist.' Whereupon he reached into the drawer of his desk, pulled out a thick book in a shiny slip-cover, and pushed it across to Sefton. 'There!'

Kevin Dainty's novel was square and bulky and heavy in the way that Sefton remembered adventure books for boys being in the days when he read and enjoyed them; but although the cover showed a muscular and heroic looking footballer heading a ball past the desperately outstretched fingers of an equally muscular but rather less heroic looking goalkeeper (they were identical as far as looking incorruptibly gentile was concerned), there was something about the glint of sexual invitation which the first footballer somehow contrived to flash from his eyes even as he was soaring above the bemused opposition and thumping his head against that lump of leather, that told Sefton that this was not the sort of adventure book for boys he used to read and enjoy. It was called *Scoring* and as Sefton flicked the pages he was quickly able to understand the ingenious quibble of that title.

'Well?' asked Sefton, returning the book to the desk.

'Well?' echoed the Dean.

'You want to know what I think?'

'You're the long novel man. Gerald Sidewinder thought you were the natural one to ask.'

'Gerald Sidewinder?' Damn! Sefton told himself that he must try to stop repeating, and with such surprise, every name that Ray Grassby mentioned. But he *was* surprised that Sidewinder had thought of asking *him* anything. He also wondered whether this had anything to do with the proposed move to the football ground, with Charles Wenlock's suicidal resistance to it, and with Gerald Sidewinder's having once been given a trial by the team of which Kevin Dainty was now, when he

137

wasn't writing, captain. Was *Scoring* being passed around to prove to Charles Wenlock and his staff that they didn't have a monopoly of literacy? Was Sidewinder to be offered a belated contract in return for Sefton's good opinion of the novel? In which case, was Sefton to give it and get rid of him, or withhold it and thwart him? For a split second Sefton tasted the sweets of power. But he didn't really have any option. 'Why does Gerald Sidewinder want to know what I think?'

'He believes it would help if there were some expert enthusiasm for Kevin Dainty's writing within the faculty. The novel has been very well received, of course, but if we could say that *we* liked it — well, Sidewinder feels it would help.'

'Help what?'

Ray Grassby impatiently flicked his wrists as if he were momentarily letting the lids off something. 'His nomination to the Board of Governors.'

Backward and short-sighted as well as Jewish and a failure, Sefton Goldberg peered into the gloom. 'How does my opinion of Kevin Dainty's novel help Gerald Sidewinder's nomination to the Board of Governors?'

'Not Sidewinder's! Sidewinder is already on the Board. Kevin Dainty's.'

Damn! thought Sefton, as he heard himself repeating, 'Kevin Dainty's?' He wanted to be clear, however. 'Kevin Dainty has been nominated as a Governor?'

'Yes.'

'Of the Polytechnic?'

'Yes.'

'But he's a —' Sefton searched for the one word which would pack in all his abhorrence but he could not do better than the word which was to hand '— sportsman!'

Ray Grassby's dark eyebrows formed themselves into disapproving question marks, but he only said 'And a novelist.'

Sefton reached for *Scoring* and held it aloft. 'Ray, this isn't a novel.'

Ray Grassby shook his head. Here they still were

138

then, the discriminations and the prescriptions which had sent him into administration. He had made the right decision; he hadn't turned his face to the wall a moment too soon. 'What do you mean it isn't a novel?' he demanded. 'What else is it?'

'Ray, it's unbelievable crap.'

'How can you say that when you haven't read it?'

Sefton felt that he was picking up where he had left off with Jacqueline. Fair-mindedness — you never knew where you were going to find it. Oh well, Sefton thought, in for a penny. 'I don't have to read it,' he said, leaving out, 'Life's too short.'

'You can tell by just looking?'

'I can tell by just looking.'

Whatever it was that was black and that came up from Ray Grassby's stomach and took over his face the minute Charles Wenlock started reciting poetry at him, was visibly on the move now. 'I think it would be best,' he said gravely, 'if you took it away and read it. Gerry Sidewinder is of the opinion that someone in the faculty should be in a position to talk knowledgeably about Kevin Dainty's writing in the event of any questions being asked about it. He would prefer it, of course, if that person were to be enthusiastic, but,' and here the Dean turned from Sefton Goldberg and addressed the rest of his remarks to the wall, 'it is fairly certain that the nomination will go through regardless. Kevin Dainty is an accomplished athlete and a highly regarded member of the local community. He's also a successful business man and a philanthropist. There isn't likely to be any opposition to him that counts.'

Sefton had always wondered what he would do if he found himself enmeshed in a tangle of blackmail and corruption, and he was interested to discover that he probably wouldn't do anything. Perhaps it would have been different if he didn't have Holy Christ Hall at the back of his mind — but he didn't (did he?) and therefore it wouldn't (would it?). The idea of inviting a footballer to enter an educational institution (even *this* educational institution) let alone to govern it, struck Sefton as an indecorum verging on criminality and madness, but once the idea was granted the politics of its implementation didn't bother him. Perhaps because he was Jewish he wasn't at all upset by machination. He was the only person he knew whose attitudes were at all reasonable who had not been up in arms about Nixon and Watergate — he had always assumed that that was how things were arranged, more or less, in high places. Harold Wilson's accent and latterly Margaret Thatcher's cadences occasioned him, personally, far more pain, and seemed to him a greater cause for national alarm. So it was mainly out of loyalty to Charles Wenlock, and his own youth, and all the principles he had briefly cherished at Cambridge, and also because he didn't want Ray Grassby to feel that he had turned black for nothing, that he did what he could to sound like someone nosing out foul play. 'There is some connection, I take it, between Kevin Dainty's nomination and our going over to the football ground?' was the best he could manage.

But it was enough. The last traces of yellow vanished from the Dean's features; even his lips turned black. 'Ask Gerald Sidewinder,' he snapped.

Hello! or funny! Sefton might have thought, if he had belonged to a different literary tradition. But he taught long nineteenth-century novels, skipping only the natural descriptions, and he cared about hurting or not hurting people's feelings rather than catching or not catching them out. Long after other boys his age had finished uncovering all Britain's dirtiest atomic secrets and had moved on to the activities of the CIA in New Zealand, Sefton was still feeling for Miss Bates. How could he not, therefore, feel for Ray Grassby as he paced with big clumsy steps the length of his room and parried the most innocuous questions with 'Ask Sidewinder?' Besides, this might be his last conversation with the Dean; he didn't want it to end on a sour note.

'I only meant that there seems to be so much coming and going between us and the football club that anyone would think we're being ... I don't know, twinned or something.' Sefton produced the ridiculous word comically, to show he was free of the usual cantankerousness associated with Charles Wenlock's department.

Ray Grassby started. 'What do you know about that?'

'You've just been telling me —'

'What do you know about the twinning?'

'The twinning?' The Twinning? The phrase suddenly had status; had a formal, even ceremonial ring, like the Coronation or the Last Supper. Hello! Funny!

The Dean was not waiting for Sefton to understand the question. From a drawer in his desk, the same drawer which had held Kevin Dainty's *Scoring*, he drew out a bundle of white cards held together by an elastic band. He tugged one from the top of the bundle and flashed it smartly at Sefton Goldberg. He looked as comfortable as an Asian producing his documents at Heathrow. 'Do you know anything about this?' he demanded.

In the thousandth of a second he was granted to look at it Sefton was able to make out from the frill around its edge and the embossed gold of its characters that is was an invitation, not all that unlike what his parents had sent out to friends and to family on the joyous occasion of their first son Sefton Lawrence's barmitzvah; but what it was an invitation to he couldn't discern. He shook his head.

Ray Grassby stood lost in thought, holding the bundle of invitations behind his back. 'You're sure?' he asked at last.

'I'm pretty sure. I'd be surer if I knew what it was.'

'Well, I suppose you might as well see it now,' he said, sadness contending with his anger. He flicked the card on the desk for Sefton to read. 'You'd have to see it sooner or later anyway. You're invited. Everyone's invited. Except Charles Wenlock.'

Sefton read. What everyone except Charles Wenlock was invited to was the Official Twinning of Wrottesley Polytechnic with Wrottesley Ramblers Football Club, to be held in the presence of his worshipful the Mayor, on a date which Sefton calculated to be only a little over a fortnight from today, in a place which, if his eyes didn't deceive him, could only have been the football ground itself, at a time which wasn't difficult to compute as half-an-hour before kick-off.

Sefton read the invitation a couple more times before replacing it on the desk. Then, in response to a gesture of the Dean's reminding him that the invitation was now his, he tucked it in the inside pocket of his jacket. A great calm had descended. In the middle of his room Ray Grassby stood on one foot, rhythmically plucking at the elastic band which kept all the other invitations close to one another. Sefton was very quiet, working hard at remembering how little he was upset by machination. 'This is actually to take place in the stadium?' he checked, unexceptionably curious.

'Before the fans, yes. It should be a capacity crowd.'

'I thought attendances were quite low over there at the moment.'

'They'll be playing Manchester United on that day.'

'I see,' said Sefton. Outside Ray Grassby's door an urban geographer could be heard inviting some of the visiting sixth-formers to the pub and being refused. 'So it should be good for recruitment?'

'Exactly. That's Sidewinder's plan. Take the Polytechnic to the people. Meet them where they live.' Ray Grassby shrugged his shoulders. Sefton knew for certain that in the time it took him to make that movement the Dean had weighed the advisability of adding, 'Get down to nitty-gritty.' The man could not be all bad who decided against saying that. 'It's the only way we'll keep our jobs,' was what he said instead.

'And what's in it for the football club?' Sefton asked, showing that all his qualms had been satisfied as to

142

what was in it for the Polytechnic.

'Revenue. We rent their empty spaces. And they'll have full access to our duplicating facilities.'

It seemed a good deal all round.

'But why us?' Sefton asked, still very quiet, after a pause.

'Why you?'

'Why is it our department that has to go over?' He did everything he could not to make that sound like a complaint. He might have been asking why the sun didn't shine at night.

'Space. You're the only one that will fit. All the others need equipment and laboratories. There isn't the room. You don't need anything.'

The modesty of Sefton's department's needs had always been a sore point with Administration. There wasn't any money for anything if the department had wanted it but Administration liked at least to have something to refuse. There was something a bit uncanny about teachers who didn't requisition things.

'Just a few books?'

'Just a few books, yes.' Ray Grassby tried to remember from his own teaching days what it was one taught with. 'And a bit of chalk.' For a moment his face took on a melancholy expression as if he were thinking of those other teaching aids of his, the towel and the silk pyjamas.

'And Charles isn't to be invited even though it is his department which is blazing the trail?' Sefton knew how much exquisite pain Charles Wenlock would derive from his exclusion, and he resolved, good friend that he was, to inform him of it at once so that he shouldn't lose a moment's moaning time.

Ray Grassby wasn't prepared to discuss Charles Wenlock. He turned his back on Sefton, made an impatient clicking noise with his teeth, and began to look covetously at his curtains. 'That's the Director's and Sidewinder's ruling. They won't have him interfering with the ceremony. He's lucky that that's all

143

that is going to happen to him.' He took in some air. 'I consider that Gerry Sidewinder has been very good about all this. He's tried to explain his position. He hasn't had to do that. Asking you to read Kevin Dainty is an attempt to create some mutual understanding. He didn't have to do that.'

Breathing deeply, the Dean propelled himself to the furthest corner of his room. Sefton supposed that he was ready to begin burgling it again, so he tucked Kevin Dainty's novel under his arm and made for the door. He had one more question. 'Ray, now that we're to be twinned do we have any guarantee that this,' he patted the protruding half of *Scoring*, 'won't suddenly appear on the syllabus?'

The Dean seemed to be measuring up the corner of his room in order to work out the best method of slipping away with it later. 'Just read it,' he said, into the cream institutional paint.

And as Sefton closed the door after him he thought he heard the Dean add, 'And try to like it.'

8

Sefton read Kevin Dainty's novel a couple more times on the way back to his room. It struck him as being rather light on construction, not so much wrought as slicked and smarmed together with some kind of moral pomade or brilliantine. Even the fouling and the fucking were oleaginous. And Sefton soon realised why. Kevin Dainty was a Londoner. He might have been playing his football in Wrottesley but he had been born within the requisite distance of all the bells and clocks and towers, all the streets and pubs and markets, all the docks and marshes and cemeteries, all the sights and sounds and fishy smells, about which it is the mark of the true Londoner to be tedious. And he wasn't just born close — he was born in the living centre of the throbbing heart. And therefore he was as bright as morning on Hackney Downs, as breezy as a coach trip down to Brighton, and as full of blubber as a plate of jellied eels. Why was it that no one dripped like a Londoner? Sefton wasn't certain but in his heart he thought it was probably all the fault of Dickens. Ever since he had invented them, Londoners had been unable to see themselves as anything but sentimental warmints, coves and dodgers, as energetic as a tugboat and as home loving as Toodle, fly and artful, but not nat'rally wicious. So once Sefton ascertained where Kevin Dainty came from it wasn't really necessary for him to flick a fourth time: there was only one novel a Londoner could write.

In the event there were a couple of small surprises.

Instead of being the expected aphoristic Jewish market-stall holder (life is one big gaff) from Shoreditch, the hero's best and oldest friend — who was devoted to the hero ever since they'd come up the hard way together but who wasn't going to stand idly by and see what fame was doing to the hero's life and what the hero's tireless womanizing (what's wrong with the one you've got, you *shmuck*?) was doing to the one he'd got, the *shmuck* (a real little lady with a warm heart and a nice bum and more love in her little finger than he had power in his right boot, the *shmuck*) — was in fact an aphoristic West Indian cab-driver (you see the world in your cab, mon) from Leyton. And, perhaps as a consequence of this first departure from convention, the hero's wife Elaine — the one with the warm fingers and the nice heart and all the love in her bum, whom the hero had sobbingly to confess (even while he was slipping it to the bunny from Bromley) that he loved and didn't deserve even more than he loved and didn't deserve his old mum who had had nothing all her life and the baby Trevor for whom he wanted something better and the as yet unborn (but you could hear her kicking, like her dad) Mitzi who was going to be a real little lady like her mum but with a good husband and not some *shmuck* of a world famous footballer who wasn't good enough for any of them — perhaps as a consequence of her husband's best and oldest friend being the West Indian rather than the Jew, Elaine was not able to confess during the final reconciliation, when everyone was promising to stand by everyone else although it wasn't going to be easy, that she had spent an evening and a night, during her deep distress when she had nobody else who understood to turn to, with her husband's best and oldest friend. Sefton thought it was shrewd of Kevin Dainty to have calculated what his hero could and couldn't cope with, and shrewd of Elaine to have calculated likewise. The Jewish stall-holder, a temporary consolation rather than a rival, would not have been too impossibly difficult for the most jealous of husbands to manage mentally, now that Jews were making themselves sexually harmless and going in for having heard of Christ, compassion, and interpersonal human relationships. The idea of your wife whiling away an evening (you're with the bunny from Bromley yourself) in the company of someone as benign and philosophical as David Kossof, or even lasting the whole night in the arms of a boy-genius like Bernard Levin, submerged beneath his megalo-saurian wit, submitting her grammar to his correction, is not insupportable. An ordinarily possessive husband might feel no differently if his wife's consolation were to take the shape of Sir Keith Joseph or David Jacobs or Mr Silkin. But a West Indian cab-driver putting out the light is an altogether darker proposition. A husband might shudder and draw the line at that.

Sefton sighed a little wistfully as he slid Kevin Dainty onto his bookshelves, just before Dante. There had been a time when his race, too, had occasioned phallic terror in the minds of English gentiles. It would be nice to bring a bit of that back. He, for one, had been far too accommodating. Hiding and stooping and apologising and being grateful. It was time to reassert himself. He thought he might begin by not making himself so manageable for Peter Potter this lunchtime, as a preliminary to not making himself so manageable for the Master of Holy Christ Hall. He experienced a little rush of patriotic, Judaic fervour, not unlike what he had experienced when he saw a film of the Six Day War, before he realised that those fierce dark men with the moustaches and the berets who made his heart leap were in fact the Syrians.

But by the time Peter Potter came to collect him for lunch (lunch had been getting earlier and earlier over the years and now began at about quarter to eleven) his spirits had dropped. Popping his head around the door, Peter found his friend slumped against his filing-cabinet with a sheet of paper hanging limply from his hand like a suicide-note or a rejection slip from a painstaking publisher. Peter Potter couldn't believe his luck; he had hoped to find Sefton still smarting from Cora Peck's success but he hadn't counted on catching him in the full flush of an even fresher disappointment.

'Bad news?' he asked, his eyes shining with expectation.

Sefton started. Then he pretended not to know what Peter was referring to. 'Oh, this,' he said at last, waking up to it. 'No, this is nothing. Where do you want to go, The Marquis of Queensberry or The Slough of Despond?'

Sefton was telling the truth. What had caused his spirits to droop was not a rejection or a refusal but a copy, in his own hand, of his application for the Disraeli Fellowship. He had fished it out of his filing cabinet where he was acustomed to stuff whatever he didn't expect to have to look at again: minutes of meetings, messages from Charles Wenlock, used copies of *The Times Higher Education Supplement*, those student essays about whose precise degree of freedom from plagiarism he couldn't make up his mind, and all the details concerning all the jobs he ever applied for. He couldn't remember when he had last had to look for anything in his cabinet; normally he only opened a drawer to shove something in it, and he could do that while he screwed up his eyes and looked the other way as if he were handling a tray of thoroughly excavated kitty-litter. But now that Holy Christ Hall wanted him badly enough to be prepared to watch him eat, he had to lower himself into that graveyard of hope and ambition in order to find what he'd written, remind himself of the means by which, this time, he had contrived to make a virtue out of a lifetime's non-achievement. It was no fun in there, but it was even less fun when he found what he was after. Unfortunately for him his gift for speed-reading always deserted him when it came to his own writing; his own page wouldn't flick and his own words clung to him like frightened children. Towards anything he had written himself he was in that state of consanguineous antagonism — loathing it because it was his — which most parents experience when they first behold their offspring, before they decide, like Kevin Dainty's hero, to call it love. And whatever it was he actually wrote to the Governing Body of Holy Christ Hall, this is what he read:

> ... from which it will be apparent that I have in no way sought to conceal from you the unconventional, academically unencumbered nature of my career to date. I rejoice to concur with the non-specialist reader and lover of literature; and indeed I take some pride in my unlettered condition; in the possession of but one, solitary, unremarkable degree, and, with the exception of a short study of the reticent heroine from Fanny Price to Amy Dorrit which appeared in the women's pages of the *Sydney Morning Herald*, no scholarly publications.
>
> Let others revel in the trappings of office and the ticker-tape of qualification. I stand before you like Lear on the heath — bareheaded!
>
> Ours is not, I maintain, a discipline which is best served by the forms and the rigours of scientific research; and therefore I have not undertaken any. Teaching itself has ever been my first enthusiasm, and when what one teaches had been as broad and as common as what I believe what I have taught has been, then one is never, as it were, not, in the fullest sense, researching. By the same token, if I have lectured have I not (in that fullest sense) published? if I have enlightened a few have I not contributed to the knowledge (knowledge *felt* rather than merely acquired) of the many? and if I have at all times distinguished and discriminated have I not *lived* those articles which I have only by the most literal interpretation of the word writing not written?

Sefton's first thought, once he had reached the bottom of the page, was that not another living soul should ever read this. His second thought was that the Fellowships Committee of Holy Christ Hall already had. What on earth were they doing then, asking him over to eat with them? Either they were sadistic, in which case he would be well advised to stay right where he was, or they were genuinely interested in hearing him develop further his ideas on felt research, in which case they were more in need of frantic diversion than he was. Had Peter Potter not popped his head around the door at that precise moment Sefton might have invented some dietary complication as an excuse for not going to Holy Christ Hall, but the look of profound self-satisfaction Peter still wore brought Sefton to his senses and reminded him that it wasn't just for himself that he was applying for jobs — there was also the misery he could cause Peter to consider. Ten minutes later he had taken the first frame in the lounge of The Crown of Thorns, and had come down from 301 in only five darts.

'Nothing's the matter, then?' Peter had resumed.

'No, absolutely nothing. In fact,' Sefton paused to collect five pounds from the fruit machine, 'I think I can even say that I've had some good news.'

'Oh?'

'I'm not, as you know, sanguine by nature, but it does look as though I've got a fighting chance of getting out of here.'

Peter Potter bit a chunk out of his glass and spat beer on to the cribbage board. 'What, out of here?' he asked, making a comic gesture with one of his hands which embraced the lounge of The Crown of Thorns, its slashed seats and the bits of crisps and peanuts which had been ground into the old carpet like mosaic.

Sefton laughed in a lordly fashion. 'Here too, I hope. But I meant the Poly.'

'Tell me more,' said Peter, bravely.

'Well, it's not one hundred per cent certain, but it looks as though I've got an offer of a job at Cambridge.'

Peter swallowed with difficulty. 'What, at the tech?' he managed to ask, but he seemed to use up all that was left of the fluids in his throat in order to ask it.

Sefton Goldberg threw one hundred and eighty-one in three darts and sank all his seven balls plus the black from the break. Every one of his dominoes was a double and as he leaned accidentally against the fruit-machine it disgorged a treble-jackpot into his back pockets. 'No,' he eventually replied. Full of the joys of vengeance as his heart was, he still felt that this was one of the cruellest things he had ever had to say. 'No, Peter. Not the tech.'

'The *twinning*?' The Department of Twentieth-Century Studies, or at least that proportion of it which had bothered to read Charles Wenlock's note and to turn up to the meeting which Charles had not quite had the energy to call and was not quite having the energy to chair, was unanimous in its amazement.

'My reaction exactly, at first,' continued Sefton Goldberg. He was enjoying being the bearer of hitherto undivulged intelligence. It was an unaccustomed role. Being the first to know gave him some unexpected insight into the workings of power. If he had been on the opposite side of the table listening to someone else unfolding the terrible tale of what Sidewinder intended, he would have been groaning and thumping his forehead and burying his face in his hands and threatening defiance and planning to do absolutely nothing about it exactly like the rest of his department; but because the details were already familiar to him he had become more or less attached to them. Hearing them under attack, he even felt obliged to defend them. Thus must men privy to a nation's secrets learn to cherish schemes that would appal them if they came upon them in the common way. The twinning of the Polytechnic to the Football Club was looking better to Sefton Goldberg with every protest; and it was not without some perverse pleasure that, with his colleagues exhibiting around him every stage of educated disapprobation from gesticulation to collapse, he took the serene and easy-going point of view. 'My reaction exactly. At first. But why don't we give it a go? I know we are under a traditional obligation to oppose any scheme of Side-winder's, but if we can just forget where the idea comes from we might be able to see some merit in it, we might even discover some good reasons of our own for going along with it.'

'Which are?' These faltering words from the wreck-age of Peter Potter. He knew something about Sefton's reasons, such as that they should all go over to the foot-ball ground because he was going somewhere else. But it was not going to be possible for him to find his voice for long enough to lay that charge. He was only upright because he had laced his wrists and ankles through the slats of his chair. Too much noise, too much vibration, and he would topple. Sefton knew that his secret was safe with Peter for a while.

'Which are? Which are what I thought we were meeting here to decide. But if you want to know what I think, I think it won't do us any harm to be a little more robust about what and how and where we teach.'

'You!' Charles Wenlock pointed an accusing finger at Sefton. His face was scarlet with the consciousness of insult, slight, treachery, and betrayal. 'You . . . You!' was all he was able to exclaim. But everybody knew what he meant.

Arthur Twinbarrow laid the palms of his hands upon the table with some resolution. Even the hairs on his knuckles were white with the worry of his calling. 'What I still don't see,' he said, 'is what possible connection there can be between a football club and a university.'

'Arthur, we aren't university.'

Arthur took this badly. 'You know what I mean.'

'All right. The connection I see is that we are all show-men together. Furthermore we are all playing to empty houses.'

Charles Wenlock winced. '*You* might be a showman,'

he said. He was always very defensive when it came to styles of teaching and lecturing. He knew that there was a certain oratorical demonstrativeness abroad these days, a mixing of eloquence and familiarity, but his preference was for something more meditative and his own delivery was marked by a kind of ruminative absenteeism.

Arthur Twinbarrow wasn't having it either. He gave one of those death-rattle laughs that only diffident men can manage. 'I agree with Charles,' he said. 'We're not all showmen.'

His lectures were also quiet affairs, but unlike Charles Wenlock's they were well attended. After an hour of Arthur students would be astonished by how many notes they had taken and what a complete comprehension of the symbolic structure of the work in question they now possessed. Arthur Twinbarrow could find a symbol anywhere; not a flower grew but it was symbolic of regeneration, not a leaf fell but it was symbolic of spiritual desolation, not a ball bounced but it was symbolic of the irrepressibility of the human spirit. Nothing was ever the thing it was and everything was always something else. Symbols drove Sefton to distraction. To him they were like fleas in the double bed of literature. He was aware that they might be in there somewhere but he could never find them himself. And even when he was determined to pass an undisturbed night he was pestered by the scratchings of somebody else. He waged a bitter war against Arthur's influence, telling his students that they had better not go on a symbol hunt when he was around, but he knew that they went charging after them the minute his back was turned. It irked him that although he was constantly demonstrating the wildness and folly of Arthur's ingenuity the students still agreed with Arthur. He didn't like to hear himself, either, raising his voice to some quiet but obdurate pupil who wouldn't see that he was right; it seemed to him that there was something a trifle defeated about having to bang the desk and bawl, 'Why can't it just be a fucking albatross, you berk?'

So he wasn't going to have Arthur Twinbarrow making a virtue out of his lack of showmanship, in a calm voice.

'More's the pity, Arthur,' he said. 'We might all have been less vulnerable to Sidewinder's threats if we'd put on a better show. I'd have thought we had an obligation to be entertaining. But instead of that we mumble and whisper and wince and start. I know that we wouldn't be teachers of books if we weren't by nature sickly; but that doesn't mean that we have to show it all the time. Those footballers across the road might be just what we need to help us to be,' here Sefton hesitated slightly and took a deep breath, 'healthy and well adjusted in body as in mind. I think we should go over there and pick up a few tips about ... well ... you know ... ordinary ... er ... life.'

'You!' Charles Wenlock generated so much heat so quickly that he had shot like a rocket out the other end of rage. The spectacle of Sefton Goldberg, who had never been known to say a word in favour of life, let alone ordinary life, trying to make a fish with his soft Jewish fingers and advocating friendship with footballers, struck him as so amusing that he became humiliated by the extent of his own mirth. He seemed to be on the road back to rage when another voice interposed. It was Cora Peck's. She had arrived late for the meeting (probably kept by Melvyn Bragg), but just in time to hear Sefton on the superiority of the sporting life to the literary.

'That's not only a popular misconception,' she said — and she seemed to have begun the sentence even before she had opened the door — 'it's a dangerous one. I see nothing peculiar about lying in bed reading books. I still do it. Kicking balls about seems to me far more neurotic. There's more ordinary life, as you call it — though I happen not to believe that life is the province of the critic — but there is more of it in one line of

154

Nabokov or B.S.Johnson than there is in thirty blooks chasing after one another on a muddy field. Sport's the real sickness.'

Cora had not included her own name in the list which began with Nabokov and ended with B.S.Johnson, but that was only because she didn't need to. As she appeared before them in an old black silk dress which might have been Katherine's and long net gloves which might have been Edith's and a string of pearls which might have been Virginia's and a black woollen cloak which was almost certainly Sylvia's, she exuded from her person all that ordinary life which was not the province of the critic but about which there had been so many popular and dangerous misconceptions.

Like everybody else, Sefton tried to keep a smile on his face the whole time that Cora was speaking, so as to demonstrate that her success (news of which had been circulating the department all day) was not painful to him. All around the table beams and grins were going off like photographers' flash-bulbs. But her little harangue had put him on the spot. He couldn't retreat now and abandon footballers after all that he had been claiming for them simply because he didn't want to appear antagonistic to Cora; but nor could he explain to her that he hadn't really meant anything he'd been saying and that it was unbelievably literal-minded of her to take him up on it, because such an explanation would have been unbelievably literal-minded of *him*. He worked out on the spot what it was that infuriated him about Cora (apart, that is, from the little matter of her having all her books published): she had no instinct for the irresponsible playfulness of conversation; she had no imagination of any kind of discourse other than that wherein convictions and principles were exchanged and scrutinized. She had all the weaknesses of the political mind: she supposed that God had given her language so that she should have something to express her opinions in. Even Charles Wenlock, who had been redder than the sun for the last half-hour and cooling nothing like so

155

rapidly, had never supposed that he had been in some battle over dogma. He knew perfectly well that it was people that irritated and enraged and betrayed and humiliated him, not ideas. Like Sefton himself, Sefton felt, he had too much respect for ideas to get personally caught up in them.

And it was Charles himself, significantly, who quickly intervened in the battle between Cora and Sefton just as Sefton was poised (reluctantly, let it be said, but what else was he to do?) to send in the whole of his armed forces and any others he could muster for a blitzkrieg on art, artists, the life of the mind, Nabokov, women novelists, women, women who got published, women who wore cloaks, women who had no feeling for the irresponsible playfulness of conversation, and anything else that was close to the target. Charles Wenlock's intervention was significant, Sefton believed, because it was not unconnected with Cora Peck's window and with Charles Wenlock's having been at it. Sefton would have been prepared to swear that when Cora Peck entered the room there was superimposed upon Charles Wenlock's already burning brightness the roseate hue of a lover's blush, and that when she had finished speaking there was discernible in his already confused and embarrassed expression the additional discomposure of a lover's shame. All Charles Wenlock did was to spread out his arms like a pacific parent, and all he said was, 'Now come on you two,' but he wouldn't have done it or said it in the days before he took to appearing at Cora's window. And what is more, in those days it wouldn't have worked.

Sefton was curious, grateful, and disapproving. 'Is she worth it? Thanks for getting me off that one. What about your wife?' would have been his way of expressing what he felt. But on balance he was now prepared to let Charles have what he'd been saving up for him. It only needed his head of department to reassert his authority over the meeting and ask it to consider what attitude it would like him to take and in what manner it

156

would like him to comport himself, on its behalf, on the day of the official twinning ceremony, for Sefton to find his opportunity.

'Er, Charles,' he said. 'There's something else that Ray Grassby mentioned to me. You're not invited.'

Because Charles Wenlock believed he was still a young and slim person he wore shirts which were inclined to be rather more on the fitted side than the loose. As Charles pushed out his chest, as if to receive the full force of this information where it would do most damage, his shirt burst open at his navel. Sefton noticed that this was fringed with the same distinguished grey hairs which formed little tufts high up on each of his cheeks, and that it was likewise a smoking pool of perspiration. He was not able to discover whether the sight of this was stirring or familiar or both to Cora Peck but he was aware that at the other end of the table Peter Potter was showing all the signs of returning to ironic life. There was nothing like an exhibition of the unmanageableness of other people's flesh to get the humour lines working on Peter's face.

'It's the most deplorable victimization,' Charles said at last.

'It is,' Sefton Goldberg agreed.

'Can they do this?'

'They seem to think they can.'

'Did Ray give you any reasons?'

'They can't chance letting you be there, Charles. It's because of what you did to Sidewinder the other day. They're frightened you might do it again.'

A smile of infinite sorrow indistinguishable from a smile of infinite satisfaction passed across Charles Wenlock's burning face. 'They're paying me back.'

'Yes.'

'You said they might.'

'Yes.'

'It's Sidewinder, isn't it?'

'I suppose it must be.'

'And this won't be the end of it either.'

157

Silence from Sefton. He was still something of a puritan. He believed that people had to earn their pleasure.

'Will it?' Charles added.

That was better. 'I doubt if it will,' said Sefton.

Charles gave out a sigh which seemed to come from an enormous depth, as if there were more of him under the floorboards.

'The b******!' he said. And then, because it felt good, he said it again. 'The b******!'

Just before the meeting came to an end a secretary arrived with a cable from Nick Lee. He was sorry he couldn't make the meeting, he'd been unavoidably detained. He would agree with the wishes of his colleagues and would cast his vote with theirs. Nick Lee claimed he had been detained in Gornal, but the secetary said she thought the cable had been sent from Montevideo.

The wishes of his colleagues were finally quite clear. They were that Charles Wenlock should seek to be invited to the twinning ceremony or seek to know the reason why he wasn't, and that if his application should be unsuccessful (as they were all convinced it would be) then Sefton Goldberg, as the person with the strongest and most positive views on the subject, should represent them on the big day. He was the one with the understanding of footballers.

It was Peter Potter who had been the most persuasive in urging Sefton's suitability for this office. His self-confidence had come flooding back to him in that almost inexplicable way that self-confidence does, and with it the conviction that things might well work out the way he wanted them to for the simple reason that he wanted them to.

'I didn't bring up the matter of your job at Cambridge,' he said to Sefton as they left the meeting together, 'because I think you said that it wasn't quite finalised. I take it I did right?'

'You did.' The tide of Sefton's confidence had gone out just as rapidly as Peter's had come in.

'It seems sensible not to mention these things until one's absolutely certain that they've gone through. Just in case ...' Peter brought his own sentence to a halt with the most exquisite tact. A little furrow appeared across his brow; a sympathetic gesture in advance, lest the very worst he couldn't bring himself to imagine happening, happened.

'Just in case they haven't,' said Sefton.

'Let's not talk about that,' said Peter. 'Do you know when you'll know?'

'Middle of next week.'

'Well look, why don't I postpone my party so that it can be a double celebration? For Cora and you?'

Sefton hesitated. He wasn't sure where this was taking him. 'That's assuming, of course, that I get the —'

'It's *insisting* that you get the job.' Peter Potter twinkled with vivacity. He was urbane and arch and merry and magnanimous. 'I'll start to make another cake tonight.'

Sefton didn't like it. Peter seemed determined that his party was going to be a roaring success. Sefton could guess at whose expense.

9

It is pretty well established now that the Gestapo was never fully operational in Manchester in the 1950's. But that did not prevent Sefton Goldberg's early years from seeming every bit as fraught as Anne Frank's. The faintest rustle in the porch used to be enough to throw the Goldberg household into scenes of such unforgettably terrifying confusion that even now, whenever his doorbell rang, Sefton Goldberg wanted to throw himself under a table and wait with thumping heart, just as he did then, for his mother to peer through infinitesimally parted curtains at the retreating back of the milkman or someone collecting for the NSPCC and assure him that the coast was clear. What she feared was not the secret police but something far worse — prying neighbours; and Sefton believed he must have been fourteen years old before he saw the front door opened to anyone but his father. His own front door was seldom tested these days, but although it was his contention that he was nothing like his mother and really welcomed visitors, it only took the old-fashioned bell to twitch and rattle on his wall for him to be on his hands and knees looking for somewhere to hide.

A call after midnight might have been expected to cause him more than usual alarm therefore, except that a call after midnight prompted other associations. He'd been living on his own for long enough now for the news to have reached all those Australian girls whose love for him had foundered on the rocks of his marriage; it

was only a matter of time, surely, before he found someone with jet-lag and a tan pulling away at his bell in the
dead of night. He wasn't exactly waiting up for her but
he wasn't going to waste any time letting her in. However, what he found when he opened his door was not
Kerry or Rozo or Judy or Janine but Charles — Charles
Wenlock, wrapped up against the ravages of the cli-
mate in a fine woollen scarf, but distinctly bare to the
ravages of just about everything else.

Whatever the time or the place or the circumstances,
Sefton was always disappointed when a visit or a note
or a message turned out to be from a man and not from a
woman. This was one of the ways he knew he wasn't a
homosexual.

But he wasn't a churl either. 'Charles!' he said.

Charles Wenlock greeted Sefton with a red face and a
succession of moans and an indulgent laugh against
himself, as if he were not at all ashamed of whatever
misdemeanour or misadventure lay behind his visit,
but considered himself, on the contrary, to be the more
engagingly human for it. Sefton recognised this air of
defiantly glistening culpability and knew it to be what
husbands wore when they were thinking of leaving
their wives for passion. It was also round about the
time that they were thinking of leaving them, Sefton
recollected, that they took to calling on their friends at
midnight. And staying until dawn.

'Any chance of coffee?' Charles Wenlock asked, and
he looked so excitably awake that Sefton (who only ever
bought small jars of Nescafé because he wasn't staying) wondered if he was going to have enough.

As they passed little Fiona McHenry's room sounds
which could only have come from brontosauri wrestling
caused the two men to pause and exchange glances.

'Is that the one you were telling me about?' asked
Charles. 'The one with the liver and onions?'

'Yes,' said Sefton, just as a submission was followed
by a couple of falls, 'but I think something must have
been slipped into the onions tonight. Only oysters stuffed

with ground rhino horn and marinaded in minotaur's milk could be responsible for that.'

Charles Wenlock, following Sefton up the stairs, reddened audibly. 'That sort of thing works does it?' he asked, just by the by as it were.

Sefton knew that he was definitely not going to have enough coffee.

'I see,' said Sefton, after about half an hour.

And then again, at approximately ten minute intervals, he said, 'I see.'

In fact he didn't always see because although Charles was voluble tonight and had about him a suggestion of recklessness, he was also oblique. Sefton was pleased with him for not being gross in the way that many gentile men were when it came to justifying their defections ('Do you know, she wouldn't even — '), but Charles Wenlock's discretion made comprehension difficult at times. His decision not to call parties by their names, for example, seemed to Sefton quite exquisite, but it wasn't always easy, as a consequence, to know who Charles meant by 'we'. Was he alluding to something that had been awful with Joyce Wenlock or something that was now breathtaking with Cora Peck? It seemed important to Sefton to get this right. On more than one occasion he had looked down sympathetically and said, 'I see, I see,' when the proper response would have been to open his eyes wide and say, 'Really?' And whenever Charles rounded off a particularly involved stretch of narrative with the decision 'we' had taken to try (or not to try) a little longer, or the understanding of one another's needs that 'we' had (or had not) come to, Sefton found himself with nothing at all to help him in his struggle to ascertain whether that meant that Charles Wenlock was happy or was miserable to leave or to stay with either Cora or Joyce.

Nor was Sefton's task made any lighter by Charles Wenlock's propensity to pronounce the language of joy

162

and the language of misery identically. If one were simply listening to sounds or watching the play of his features as he made them, then one could have found little to choose between the 'sterility' of his relations with his wife and the 'geniality' of his relations with his mistress — unless one had decided that on balance 'sterility' was the more enticing for sounding the less pinched and defeated. Charles didn't, of course, employ the words wife or mistress, but made do with 'she' for both; so it was some time before Sefton could make out which of them Charles found 'vital and buoyant' and some time more before he realised that Charles did not mean to imply by that that she was as inert as a drowned rat.

But he got there in the end. By dint of hard listening and some careful ambiguity of sympathy. Charles was going to leave his wife because his marriage was sterile, because she didn't read or quote from books, because she fell asleep in company, and because she wasn't excited any more by his perceptions and discriminations. He hadn't realised it until he had met the other one but he'd been lonely for some time now.

Once he felt that it was both safe and appropriate for him to do so, Sefton put up some not too offensively principled protest at this rough treatment of Joyce Wenlock. On the few occasions he had met her, all of them at dinner parties over which she had presided, he had been taken by her affability, her large, sleek good health, her freedom from any of her husband's irritabilities, and her cooking. She cooked simply, in order to cut down conversation about ingredients, and served up innumerable courses in immeasurable quantities in order to cut down conversation about everything else. Maddened by the preoccupation of his guests with food when he had some story about Sidewinder or some judgement upon Keats to deliver, Charles Wenlock would rise from his table and walk round and round his garden, whereupon his wife was able to regale the party with as many anecdotes as there were courses about life

163

with her husband. She was genuinely a country woman, unlike Charles who was rural only because he wasn't quite urban; but she had none of the English country woman's complacency, none of her country wisdom or country officiousness or country penuriousness. She was as bored and as contented as it was proper she should be living out of town, and she gave off what was to Sefton a very soothing air of stocked larders and soft beds and unapologetic self-indulgence. Even though he didn't own a pair of wellingtons, Sefton looked forward to being invited to the Wenlocks at the bottom of whose garden the very cows didn't really look like things that belonged to the country but seemed instead to have been let out of Joyce's kitchen for the time being, until she should get round to doing something simple but tasty with them. Sitting at her table, Sefton had not been aware that her limited interest in books diminished in any way the pleasure of the occasion; and comfortable in one of her armchairs afterwards, when Charles had come in from the garden, he found nothing personal in the way she would intermittently drop off, and detected nothing pointed or intrusive in her snoring. In short she was a model wife for someone who was old enough (as Charles was old enough) not to want romance, appreciation, gratitude and art-prattle.

Not that he could imagine Cora Peck offering much in the way of any but the last of those. Why should she, poised as she was for celebrity, be grateful to Charles Wenlock who was twice her age, who couldn't remember the name of the department he ran, and who hadn't published anything? Since seeing Charles at Cora's window, Sefton had tried not to ask himself any of those questions which related to what Cora might have wanted from, or even seen in, or planned to do to, Charles Wenlock. He didn't trust himself with those sorts of questions. They weren't, strictly speaking, decent, and he had never really understood, anyway, what women saw in any man. (This was another of the ways he knew he wasn't a homosexual.) The one question Sefton couldn't help posing to himself wasn't all that decent either, and he didn't think at all highly of himself for posing it, but he *was* curious still about Cora's expertise and he was concerned lest Charles should at any moment tactlessly allude to it. Should even crow.

He was sure, however, that no undeclared interest of his own in any way influenced his determination to fly the flag for Mrs Wenlock.

'Charles, you've got everything you want at "Alfoxden",' he said, attempting to emulate the slow and solemn tremble with which Charles himself pieced together the separate syllables of the name of his house.

Charles smiled a smile of irresistible wanness. 'I haven't been happy for some time.'

'Happy? Who said anything about happiness? What's wrong with just having everything you want?'

'I haven't got everything I want.'

Sefton put up the fingers of both hands and began to count off everything that Charles had. 'You've got Joyce, you've got the house, you've got seniority, you've got Joyce, you've got a big fight with Sidewinder, you've got a colour television, you've got a letter of thanks from E.M. Forster, you've got tenure, you've got Joyce . . .'

Tapping his chest, as if he were his own physician and had bad news for himself, Charles Wenlock interrupted. ' "The passion and the life" — that's what I haven't got.'

Sefton stared — Charles should have been grateful that he didn't have 'the passion', so likely to cause physical enervation and nervous irritability and a general tightening of everything that ought to have been loose, did he make it sound. But it didn't mean, just because he couldn't say it, that he didn't want it. He wanted it all right. Sefton could tell that from Charles Wenlock's air of fervid vulnerability, his pursed lips, his too pugnacious eyes, the glistening grey hairs which were even now springing out from wherever they could find an exit in his cream silk shirt. Sefton decided that it didn't make a pretty picture, to be wanting something that badly when you were over fifty. God grant me that I don't look so urgent or so tremulous when I reach that age, he said; God grant me that I don't become amazed by some girl's youth and spontaneity or interested in her insights; God spare me from sexual fucking wonderment.

He said this, of course, to himself. What he said to Charles was, 'So you want bliss?'

Charles winced. It mattered which words you used. 'I don't want to be with Joyce.'

'Like I say, you want bliss.'

A spiteful look crossed Charles Wenlock's face. This usually meant that he was preparing to quote poetry. He stared hard and in an uncomfortably personal way at Sefton, and then he delivered what he had to deliver with thin bardic fastidiousness, rapture and umbrage so close as to be interchangeable.

She gave me eyes, she gave me ears,
And humble cares, and delicate fears;
A heart, — the fountain of sweet tears —
    And love, and thought, and joy.

It didn't sound much like Cora, and for a fraction of a second Sefton wondered if he'd got the wrong she again and if this was a description of what Joyce had given him and why he therefore couldn't stay a minute longer — but Charles' expression was so naked and splenetic that he could only have been describing what he wanted. It was Cora who could give him eyes and ears. Poor Charles! He wanted bliss. He wanted to be the first Adam, in a Shropshire garden. And poor Joyce, who gave him a comfortable house and huge piping hot dinners — it was a bit hard on her that Charles had suddenly decided that he wanted to be made to see the world freshly, instead. No, Sefton definitely didn't like it. He didn't like it in this particular instance and he didn't like the trend. Even the middle-aged Jewish heroes of middle-aged Jewish novelists were eschewing sedentary cynicism and unfolding themselves sensitively to teenage girls and nature, offering their cocks to near babies as if they were prize flowers picked in a *goyische* garden. They used to be inventive. Now they were tremulous. Behind all this Sefton believed he could detect the hand of D.H. Lawrence. Sefton wasn't a devout Jew. He drove his car on Saturdays and ate bacon sandwiches whenever he could, even on festivals. But his race had its sexual pride to protect, and he drew the line at D.H. Lawrence.

He was beginning to feel that he ought to draw the line at Charles Wenlock also. He looked ominously fresh. And packed with quotations. Sefton felt that he had done what he could for Joyce Wenlock for the time being. The quickest way to end the evening (even Fiona McHenry had fallen quiet now, and Ron Penn and Tom Jones had called it quits) was to bless the new union, hope it would all work out for the best, promise a bit of support, offer a few examples of similar associations which had prospered — that sort of thing. He could leave it to them to discover what a lousy time they were having.

'So when do you think you'll make your move?' he asked, beginning to wind things up.

'In the next day or two. It won't be easy.'

'Of course not. And what will you do, move into her place? Or will you find something else together?' Sefton thought it prudent not to be too curious about what would happen at the end of the year when Cora would surely be off on her fellowship.

'Well that's a tricky one. There are difficulties with her place. We're thinking of a caravan.'

A caravan! It had been hard enough trying to envisage Charles Wenlock in a flat. But Charles Wenlock in a caravan! Where would his shirts go? What about the spaces and the privacies which must have been even more necessary for a man of fifty than for a man of thirty-five, and especially so, surely, for one who was as instinctively un- communal as Charles? Or was the very absence of these a pre-condition for the re-education of his sight and of his hearing? In that case it wouldn't be long before he would be wishing that he was blind and deaf again. A caravan looked the quickest way of getting him back to his wife. So Sefton was not going to try to talk him out of one. On the other hand he owed it to Charles to demur a little.

'A caravan? Is that necessary?'

Charles narrowed his eyes to suggest intensity. 'It's expeditious.'

'I see.' Sefton looked away. There were some urgencies one had no right to have an opinion about. And there were strong forces at work here. But Cora's flat would be quick, too. And if Charles moved in she would presumably take down the pictures of suicidal poetesses for a while, and perhaps bring the cushions up off the floor. Sefton suddenly felt very sorry for Charles. This was probably the last splash he was going to make. Sefton didn't see why he shouldn't be comfortable while he was making it.

'Is the flat really impossible?'

Charles looked puzzled. 'What flat?'

'Cora's flat. Won't that do until you find something better?'

Sefton started at his own trepidation. He had mentioned the other woman's name, brought the other half of the new 'we' into the room as she had not been in it before.

But he didn't start as suddenly as Charles Wenlock.

'You know that I've been seeing Cora?'

What was this? Was Charles going to add coyness to obliquity?

'All I know is what you've told me, and that you were there the other night.'

'She hasn't said anything to you?'

'Not a word.'

168

'Then how do you know that she has offered me her flat?'

Offered? 'Haven't we just been . . .?'

'She said she wouldn't mention it to anyone.'

They were fighting already.

And already Sefton was mediating. 'She hasn't said a word to me, Charles.'

With an air of rueful magnanimity Charles Wenlock decided not to pursue it. 'It was a genial offer,' he said, instead. 'She's been surprisingly helpful.'

Charles was renowned for the eccentricity of his vocabulary, but even allowing for that, just about none of those words made any sense to Sefton.

'She's a friend, of course,' Charles added.

As in, she's a friend as well as a mistress? Leading to, I respect her as well as desire her? Could Charles stoop that low?

'They've been friends for a while. They've got a lot in common.'

They? Cora and Joyce? Cora a friend of Joyce? Could Charles stoop *that* low?

'They're both, you know, a bit militant.' Charles coloured and laughed, man to man.

Joyce Wenlock militant? Not by any stretch of the imagination. She might soon be, of course, once she discovered the thanks she got for offering a choice of sweets every night. But she wasn't yet. And even Charles, who was understandably not seeing things clearly at the present, couldn't suppose that she was. Somewhere along the line, Sefton decided, one of them, Sefton or Charles, had confused the other.

'So,' he said, taking the conversation back, 'you feel it would be tactless, all considered, to move into the flat?'

'Not tactless, impossible. There isn't room for the children.'

Children? Evidently, Sefton had not taken the conversation back far enough. Charles couldn't possibly be referring to his own children who were grown up and teaching and moving in and out of flats of their own.

And Cora couldn't possibly — could she? — have been keeping a little family secret. If she had had children Sefton didn't believe she could have forgone strapping them to her back when she came to work and suckling them in seminars. Even without them she never left one entirely free of the impression that she might at any time pull out at least one breast, on a matter of principle, as it were. Sefton Goldberg, flinching and unnatural, lived in permanent dread of having to witness spontaneous motherhood in a confined space and he had schooled himself to recognise the preliminary signs so that he could slip out before anything else did. Cora Peck moved in her seat and darted her eyes around a room ominously; there was no doubt in Sefton's mind that only the absence of something hungry and hers stood between Cora and a feed. So he could only stare at Charles as he had been doing for the last ten minutes and ask, without wanting to sound too stupid, 'Which children are they, Charles?'

'Matthew, Emma, and I can't remember the name of the other one.'

Charles was impatient. It seemed a pretty silly question.

Sefton was astounded. 'I had absolutely no idea that Cora had children. Have they been living elsewhere or something?'

'I don't know anything about whether Cora's got children. What's Cora got to do with it?'

Sefton took a deep breath. 'Charles,' he said, as if one or other of them were retarded and ought at last to come clean about it, 'are you or are you not about to leave your wife for Cora Peck?'

If umbrage was the word for what Charles normally took then there was no word in the language for what he was taking now. 'Cora Peck?' He was mortally offended. The blood rushed to his face. His lips seemed to vanish altogether in distaste and reprehension. 'I most certainly am not!'

The idea was so preposterous to him that Sefton felt

170

ashamed not just of his mistake but of his ever having been interested in Cora Peck himself. He was highly susceptible to the opinions of other men when it came to women; he didn't want to want what wasn't already wanted. And indeed, Cora was so obviously not what Charles wanted, was so far from being what he would have wanted even if he hadn't wanted someone else, that Sefton fell to wondering what kind of tremendous beauty she must be then, and with what distinctions and exemptions and qualifications, who had torn Charles from his wife and his home and taught him such high standards. On the sudden he felt quite queasy. He had no desire to see Charles miserable and uncomfortable, but that didn't mean he wished him to go too far in the opposite direction.

Sefton was only human; there were limits to how much happiness he wanted for his friends.

'In that case,' he said, meeting heat with heat, 'we've been at cross-purposes for some time. I assumed you were referring to Cora Peck. I must admit I thought it was strange. Accept my apologies for the mistake. But are you going to tell me who "she" is then? Do I know her?'

Charles was still deeply insulted. 'Cora Peck!' was all he said. Sefton could imagine him still repeating the name, whenever they met, twenty years from now. The calumny had been that hurtful. 'Cora Peck!'

But at least, while he was being kept in suspense, Sefton had the opportunity to retrace his steps through the maze of Charles Wenlock's narrative. Whoever she was she wasn't Joyce's friend but Cora's. It was she and Cora who were the militants. Joyce had nothing to do with it. To all intents and purposes she was still dozing quietly in her kitchen at 'Alfoxden'. And because she ('she', not Joyce) was Cora's friend Cora had been doing the decent, militant, sisterly thing: promoting passion, offering support and sympathy and a place for the lovers to meet. That was the explanation for Charles's unlikely appearance at her window —

he was hovering around the nest, perhaps waiting for Cora to go out, perhaps giving her money to go to the pictures, perhaps seeking expert advice. Sefton took some comfort from her being Cora's friend. One somehow knew that if she were Cora's friend she would not be all that beautiful or accomplished. It was becoming oddly important to Sefton that she shouldn't turn out to be all that beautiful or all that accomplished.

'You aren't going to tell me, then?' he ventured at last, after Charles Wenlock had said 'Cora Peck!' a few dozen more times.

'Whether you know her?'

'Yes.'

'You know her.'

'Well?'

'Well what?'

'Do I know her *well*?'

Charles considered this question with a kind of inscrutable weightiness. He looked as if he might have much to say about the impossibility of anyone's ever knowing another person *well*; but he said, instead, 'You aren't nice to her, if that's what you mean.'

Sefton tried to think of who he wasn't nice to.

'You've been particularly not nice to her lately,' Charles went on.

Sefton loved all guessing games but he was especially partial to those which entailed guessing something about himself; so he put to one corner of his mind, for future deliberation, the now obvious truth that whatever else Charles had called for he had called (and might even have been sent) to get Sefton to be nice to whoever-she-was. Illicit lovers could always be counted upon to make a nuisance of themselves in this way when they went suddenly public; Sefton couldn't remember how many times he had been expected, without a moment's warning, to shower welcomes upon the mistress, usually just as he had finally come round to reconciling himself to the wife. But in this case the mistress wasn't going to be all surprise to him. It seemed they shared a little history. He didn't have to arrive at being nice from being ignorant; he had to arrive at being nice from being not nice — an altogether longer and more inconvenient journey.

And it was clear from Charles's rather pink and peevish expression that he was going to sit and watch him make it.

But who had he been not nice to — *particularly* not nice to — of late? Jacqueline's visit had gone off reasonably well, and it couldn't possibly be her. There had been no women in Fledwhite's party in the car-park, or at least none that he had noticed in the gloom and the excitement. There was, of course, Fledwhite himself. He was both a friend of Cora's and a militant. But the idea was too fantastic. Sefton sneaked a quick look at Charles Wenlock. Well — perhaps it wasn't, after all, quite *so* fantastic. There wasn't an English gentile living whom it was really impossible to imagine in the part. In fact, if one considered for a moment, it was more difficult to imagine them in any other. Take Peter Potter. Who did he think he was fooling? But no, not Wenlock and Fledwhite. Not Charles and Wally in a caravan. So who did that leave? Sefton racked his brains. It could be argued that he had not been very nice to Val Peel, recently, though strictly speaking it was she who had been not nice to him. Besides she was a student, a dumpy jumpy mature student, who wore pinnies and shed shredded paper hankies as she stormed out of lectures and tutorials in tears and dudgeon. And she had children. Three, if he wasn't mistaken.

Three children! Something cold, like certainty, passed over Sefton's body. Val Peel! The idea was horribly plausible. It would be just like Charles to make his first, last, only dash for freedom in a caravan with a frumpish, lactic, ex-Open University student who was as touchy and as irritable as he was and who had three

173

children. It would be just like Charles to make a mess of being irresponsible.

Sefton hoped that he had got it all wrong again and that Val Peel would fare no better as a guess than Cora Peck had done. Indeed, he was beginning to wish that it had been Cora Peck after all. Or someone mindlessly young. Some slip of a thing who was as knocked out by Charles' perceptions and discriminations as he was besotted with the firmness of her flesh. He could forgive that now. He believed he could even entertain the idea of Fledwhite. Anything was preferable to the image he was forming of Charles Wenlock trying to keep himself clean in a caravan while his concubine sniffled over the marks she had got for her essays and his concubine's three children, Emma and Matthew and whatever the other one was called, fought over the Lego and the Farley's Rusks. If Charles were to tell him that he had in fact fallen for a fifteen-year-old with orange hair, Sefton believed he would promise his undying loyalty and support.

So there was nothing Sefton could do to keep both trepidation and dolefulness out of his voice once he had found the courage to put the dreadful question, 'It isn't Val Peel, is it?'

But Charles was as deaf to nuance, as contented by mere familiar signal, as a fed computer. He had a peculiar smile on his face. Vilely proud, like a parent, Sefton thought. 'What took you so long?' he asked.

10

He was glad when Charles finally got around to leaving. It was just about morning. Already a pale Saturday light was stealing into Sefton's temporary encampment, casting an uninquisitive grey eye over the tied-up bundles of books and the half-packed suitcases and the laundry bags spilling socks. Charles turned up the collar of his coat and arranged his scarf about his throat. He didn't make it clear whether he was going to drive the thirty-five miles back to 'Alfoxden' or put up at Cora's place or pace the streets; but he struck Sefton as having the air of a man who was about to look at caravans. Sefton escorted him down the stairs, with the intention of taking a morning stroll himself. But there was nothing outside which he could persuade himself was essentially preferable to what was in. Even at that hour Wrottesley remained stubbornly resistant to any impression of mystery or expectation or surprise. There was nothing and nobody out there. The place was unvisited, as ever. Sefton opened his mouth, stained brown with instant coffee, and inhaled a little of something he wasn't much convinced was good for him. Then he returned upstairs, past Ron Penn's cell and Fiona McHenry's chamber of debauch, both silent, and went to sleep in his suit on the edge of his chair.

Within minutes he was on the edge of the penalty area, in mud, and the crowd was on its feet; a beautifully threaded pass from Kevin Dainty put him through, found him in space, exposed the opposition's naivety, caught its defence square and napping, and left Sefton Goldberg with only the goalkeeper to beat. Or so it seemed. So it was bound to seem to the steep banked terraces of rude Wrottesley mechanicals and storm-troopers who chanted like Methodists and swayed in unison like chorus-girls. What did *they* know of all the other things there were in the world to beat besides goalkeepers? They had white, hairless bodies which were impervious to pain, they had buttons for noses, extra bones where Sefton had migraines, and foreskins (*foreskins!* — Sefton had never been able to bring himself to look, but he had been told). Put a ball in front of any one of them and he would drive it at thunderous speed between any two objects which could be imagined to be goalposts. And ask questions later. No wonder their mouths dropped open when Sefton laid his foot on the ball which had been delivered to him with such sweet accuracy and fell to pondering all the things in his history and his nature which were preventing him from kicking it. How could they know, for example, that Sefton had never in his life, not even in his dreams, been physically comfortable; had never been certain, from one moment to the next, that any particular part of his body was going to function? And for this reason had never once — not even *once* — turned a somersault! (Even when he was with girls he liked to keep his head the highest part of himself.) And how could they possibly comprehend, dressed as they were, with tattoos on their fingers, and emblems of war and death rivetted in steel studs to their backs, that Sefton wanted no trouble either from the advancing goalkeeper or from the advancing goalkeeper's friends and family? If he needed the ball that badly (if *they*, his relatives and *machatonim*, needed the ball, that badly for him) — here! Have! And then there was the question of Sefton Goldberg's own needs and desires. Another word for goal was objectives. Sefton was only thirty-five; wasn't that a bit young to be certain what it was you wanted? Twenty thousand *goyim* might have wanted him to score; he — Sefton — needed a bit more time to think about that, thank you. Centuries of bitterness and persecution determined every move he made; so where was the hurry? Besides, he'd been here before — this wasn't the first dream he'd had. He knew perfectly well that if he were to start pounding the ball in the direction of the goal, the goalkeeper would start leaping and stretching and pounding it back again. Sefton didn't have the remotest hope of beating him. That wasn't faint heart speaking; it was experience. This was Sefton's dream — he worked the goalkeeper, too.

But then, if it was his dream, how was he to account for the odd turn it subsequently took? If it was his dream, what did it signify that on his return to the changing rooms, after he had left the other players on the field exchanging shirts and for all he knew addresses, he found Val Peel waiting for him and already running a shower? Smelling of milk and ink and rusks and carrying a box of tissues (or were they liners?) under her arm. If this was *his* dream, why was Val Peel helping him off with his shorts?

And why was he not objecting, but actually . . .?

As a rule Sefton wasn't appalled by his own subconscious. He had known and accepted for a long time that his dreams were as unselective, as easy for absolutely anyone to get into, as the Polytechnic. And what happened in his head when he wasn't using it didn't seem to have very much to do with him. In this regard, as master of his little ship, so to speak, he was democratic, easy-going, and indulgent in his relations with the crew. He went his way, his subconscious went its. Or so he had thought until this morning. But it was looking unlikely now, after the completely unexpected appearance of Val Peel where she should distinctly not have been, that he could go on denying responsibility for what went on below deck. Val Peel had not materialised from nowhere. His subconscious had not found her lying latent in the structure of thought or language; it had not dredged her out of any ancient reservoir of race memory; it had not even discovered her in myth or ritual or legend — it had got Val Peel from him! It looked to him for its raw materials and Val Peel was the best he could provide. Sefton was ashamed. He owed the other half of his divided self something a little better to work with.

He wondered where it had all gone wrong. Would his dreams have been any more exotic if he had gone to the London School of Economics instead of Cambridge? Would his inner life have been the richer — would his fantasies have been the wilder — if he had mixed with sociologists and monetarists and executives from Lever Brothers instead of those provincial spinsters who were the chief characters of every English novel ever written? Still in his suit and still on the edge of his chair, Sefton unashamedly apportioned blame. He was harder on those two *shiksas*, Fanny Price and Little Dorrit, than even their respective families had been. But he badly needed a bigger adversary, like God or the Midianites or Hitler.

The first Tom Jones record of the weekend, requested and played by a Mr Ron Penn of Flat 2, Paradise Villas, Wrottesley, got the day rolling by touching off something primitive in Fiona McHenry's Chinese boyfriend, at present residing at Flat 1 of the same address. Sefton Goldberg, religiously refusing to tempt providence by thinking of Holy Christ Hall, rose from his chair and cleaned himself up in a perfunctory sort of way — like a man who was not anticipating anything primitive stirring in him today. Then, by some devious twist of logic, out of some need that was not entirely or even partially obvious to himself, he descended the stairs (listening neither to the left nor to the right of him), started his Avenger, and drove to Manchester to see his parents.

'Hello, dad.'
'Hello, stranger.' Sam Goldberg, strong and menacingly jovial, extended a giant hand. Watching his

own hand disappear inside his father's, Sefton was reminded of how this form of greeting had always made him feel as if he were his father's stooge, invited nightly from the audience ('You've never seen me before, have you sonny? Just turn this way a bit') in order to be dispossessed of his watch and braces. Funny he should still feel that. Or rather, alarming. He was thirty-five; wasn't it about time the son was more robust than the father? Most of his Jewish friends had little yellow men who had to be kept quiet and in one place for fathers; and most of his gentile friends had chalk-white shufflers, obscurely aggrieved, coughing up pit-dust. ('Wi' all yo' fancy ways, tha's bin nobbut a disappointment ter me and yo' mother.') Sefton wasn't excessively or unreasonably Oedipal — he didn't want his father entirely out of the way; but it wouldn't do any harm if he just moved to one side a bit. Or occasionally took to his bed. ('Don't upset yourself, dad. Lean forward and let me fluff up your pillows.')

He eventually released Sefton from his grip and slapped him around the shoulders and the stomach in a paternal sort of way. 'You've put on weight,' he said. Then he nodded in the direction of the stairs, 'Your mother's in the bathroom.'

Sefton wasn't surprised to hear that. It was only lunchtime; his mother spent the whole of every morning and most of the afternoon locked away, circumventing the world's determination to stare at her with prying eyes by turning herself into someone else. He could hear the sound of taps and dryers. If he listened really carefully he could hear the squeezing of tubes and tweezers. He was pleased to have some time alone with his father. He wanted to impress him with his manliness. He was never entirely free of the impression that his father believed his mother was still writing him excuse notes. So he chatted away in what he hoped was a confident and independent manner about his car and the weather and the job he was about to be interviewed for in Cambridge. 'I think I've got a

179

pretty good chance of getting it,' he concluded, in a deepish voice.

Sam Goldberg looked puzzled and preoccupied. It was unmistakable, from the distant expression in his eyes and from the way he was fumbling in his pockets, that he was preparing one of his tricks (or effects, as he had lately taken to calling them) to show his son. 'How do you mean you're going for an interview for a job at Cambridge?' he asked.

'What do you mean how do I mean I'm going for an interview for a job at Cambridge?' Sefton was shouting as loud as if he'd never left home and lived with gentiles. 'Which bit do you want explaining?'

'I thought you'd already got a job at Cambridge.'

'No, dad, I haven't already got a job at Cambridge. I never have had a job at Cambridge.'

'Oh.' He wasn't going to fight about it. He had that air of far-away concentration which comes with trying to repair or manipulate objects which you cannot actually see or easily get at.

'Where are you now, then?' he asked, as if he ought.

'I'm at Wrottesley Polytechnic, dad.'

'Wrottesley Polytechnic?' He wasn't prepared to say that this was entirely new to him. But it was puzzling. 'I could have sworn we came to see you at Cambridge.'

'You did, dad. Thirteen years ago. When I was a student. You came to see me get my degree.'

'And don't they give you a job for that?'

In the time it took him to reply, Sefton Goldberg imagined the sort of life he might have had had he been lucky. In such a life, as well as being golden haired and tall and turning somersaults, he had a father he called father who smoked a pipe and talked philosophy to his children in his quiet, book-lined study, and taught them the names of plants and flowers, and played them mediaeval music on his recorder, and remembered who they were and where they worked, and wasn't such a cretin as to suppose that degrees and jobs were the same things — except that if he'd had such a father they would have been. 'No, they don't give you a job for that.'

'I see,' said Sam. He was looking bored as well as busy, as if he too might have been imagining another life in which he had a son who wasn't prolix. 'So that was your degree we came to see you get?'

'It was.'

'I see.' His lips were pursed with other-worldly concentration. There was intense activity in and around his breast-pocket. But he had remembered something which struck him as germane. 'Didn't we hire a car especially?'

Didn't we hire a car? It was a bit like Paris, son of Priam, asking if he hadn't once borrowed someone or other's wife. *Didn't we hire a car?* Didn't a chap called Duncan once stay the night with us, in the guest room? Sorry to be a bore but did somebody say, 'Where three roads meet?' They had hired a car all right. Or rather, Sam had. Sefton could see it now, gliding through the gates of his college, vast and sleek and silent, like a hearse for very senior royalty, only silver — the most expensive car in the world, on hire for as long as was necessary, so that Sefton Goldberg shouldn't feel let down by his parents.

'Well, what do you think of the jalopy?' Sam asked his son, in the hearing of three college porters. He had on his check Archie Rice suit and the black bowler he wore for *simchas*.

In the back seat, behind the tinted glass, Sefton's mother sat with that air of cataleptic nonchalance she assumed whenever she was out of the house, pretending that nothing untoward was happening. But she was clearly in an advanced state of shock. Extravagantly and wildly dressed, she resembled from a distance the Maori or Samoan delegation come for the coronation.

After putting his wife to bed in The University Arms, Sam Goldberg spent what was left of the afternoon chauffeuring his son in style through the narrow streets of Cambridge, knocking some of the finest minds in Europe off their bicycles. Thereafter, once he had been persuaded to park the car (and found five adjoining empty parking spaces to park it in), he communicated with Sefton almost entirely through the medium of the camera lens. If Sefton pointed out some interesting building or landmark, Sam photographed him pointing at it; if Sefton ran into friends or tutors and introduced them to his father, Sam extended one hand and filmed the introduction with the other.

'This is the famous library built by Christopher Wren,' Sefton said at last. 'Why don't *I* take a photograph of *you* standing outside it?'

Sam Goldberg tossed him one of his cameras, but when Sefton put it to his eye he saw that his father was filming him filming.

The graduation parade itself was an irresistible challenge to Sam. Not for as long as he lived would Sefton ever forget the sight of his father bounding along in his bowler in front of the procession on King's Parade, tearing from one side of the road to the other, disappearing down alleys and materializing again in shop doorways, shouldering aside Proctors and Praelectors, in order to get the best possible snaps of that purple-faced ingrate, Sefton, in his gown and hood. Nor was he ever likely to erase from his memory the sound of strictly forbidden flash-bulb in the Senate House, the sharp blue light and the POP, just as he knelt to grasp the finger of the Vice-Chancellor, held out to him with waning elasticity like a well-milked teat. There was another boy holding another finger at the same time, but the Vice-Chancellor did not need to ask for whom the bulb flashed — it flashed for Goldberg, not for Goy.

Yet how could any of these mere incidental indignities hope to vie with the shame that enveloped Sefton as he caught sight of his father setting up his little collapsible table on the college lawns, where families and fellows had gathered for a celebratory sherry, and removing from his pockets the dice and the silk handkerchiefs and the lengths of string which Sefton had relied upon his mother to persuade his father to leave behind? She was nowhere to be seen — gone into hiding. And Sefton would have hidden likewise had he been able to make any part of himself move. But the mesmeric power of filial humiliation held him quite still. Only when he saw his father beckon to a small bald figure with an apocalyptic profile, did he move even his lips. 'Not him!' he pleaded. 'Oh no, not *him*!' But that was all he did, and still he watched as his father fluttered his hands in the air like a pantomime wizard, muttered the magic words, 'Abracadabra, hocus pocus, bim shallabim', and produced an egg — a large, white, new-laid egg — from F.R. Leavis's ear.

'Yes, dad, now you come to mention it, I seem to remember something about a hired car myself.'

'So do I,' said Sam, but that appeared to be all he did remember. Besides, he had no reason to go on idly reminiscing; his trick was ready. 'I think you'll like this one,' he said to Sefton, as he drew from the inside of his pocket a wand, a wallet, a pack of playing cards, a cigarette lighter, and a five pound note.

'Oh, you're not going to show him *that*!'

Both men started. In the doorway stood one whom Sefton could only suppose to be his mother concealed in clouds of voluminous materials, hidden behind powder and paint and a pair of diamante studded spectacles which seemed to have dropped upon her face like some exotic lost bird; his mother — out of the bathroom and invisible at last under earrings and bangles and chokers and wigs. It was his mother all right, he could tell that from the way his father was beginning to age.

'What aren't I going to show him?'

'That silly trick.'

'He's interested.'

'He's not interested in *that*. How are you darling? You've lost weight.'

'All right,' said Sam, as he tried to blow out the fiver he had just set alight. 'All right. You'll get no argument

183

from me. He's your son. You know what interests him and what doesn't. You're the one that writes the notes.'

'Notes? What notes?'

'*He* knows what notes.'

When Aubrey Kershaw and Sefton Goldberg first discovered that both their mothers suffered from agoraphobia they thought it might be a good idea to try to get them to be friends.

'My mother has not talked to anyone but me and my father for ten years,' said Aubrey, as the two boys sat polishing trophies on the school platform.

'Same here,' said Sefton, 'only with mine I think it might be longer.'

'Well I can't go out, so she'll have to visit me,' said Mrs Kershaw.

'I'm not going anywhere,' said Mrs Goldberg, and as she suffered from claustrophobia as well, she added, 'and I don't want her coming here.'

So Aubrey and Sefton discovered that it wasn't easy, bringing agoraphobics together.

As it turned out it was Mrs Kershaw who was by far the severer case. Only last year, on a previous visit, Sefton had walked past Aubrey's house and seen him, bald now and short sighted, trying to push his blindfolded mother into the back of a Thames Trader. 'Aubrey, where are you taking me? I feel dizzy. The ground is opening out in front of me, Aubrey. Aubrey, why are you pushing me over a cliff?' 'Mother, I'm just trying to help you upstairs.' 'So what's that engine I can hear?' 'That's the television, mother. There's a motoring programme on the television.'

Whereas Mrs Goldberg, now that she had hit upon the ruse of wigs and caftans, was prepared to go almost anywhere provided she didn't have to cross the channel or take an aeroplane.

It was only to be expected, of course, that she should preserve some of her old attitudes and habits. As witness, for example, her insistence that the house

184

should never be quiet. Even today, as Sefton had discussed his future with his father, he had been compelled to do battle not just with the washing-machine and the stale air extractor and the pressure cooker, he had had to make himself clear over the television and the radio also, both of them on in the middle of the day not to provide entertainment but to prevent whoever was downstairs hearing whoever was up. For Sylvia Goldberg had never limited her domestic precautions only to the dangers of being seen. The hell of being human was not alleviated, for her, simply by becoming invisible — there was also the problem of being *heard*. One needed to be inaudible, too. And the only way of drowning out noise was more noise. Sefton was well advanced into manhood before he discovered that not all children had a mother who led them in community singing the moment any one of them made a move in the direction of the toilet. 'Where are you going? How long are you going to be? O.K., on the count of three . . . *O Susannah, don't you cry for me* . . .' And that not every family staggered its bed-times, slept behind tightly close doors with its fingers in its ears, and rose and used the toilet on a rigidly structured rota system, so that under no possible circumstances and by no tragically unforseen mischance should any one of them get wind of any other. Sefton's mother knew of no greater or more urgent service to perform than to save her family from all the horrors of the body: to disguise her own and to silence theirs. One tiny sneaking misdirected inadvertent little fart — and all would have been up with the Goldbergs!

The years had not relaxed any of the rules governing personal privacy in the Goldberg household, and Sefton would have been disappointed if they had. He had come to enjoy the hot little conspiracy, the unwhispered assumption that he and his parents had something important to hide from one another. It was like visiting again the first formative minutes of his psychology. Not surprisingly, therefore, it was change rather than continuity that was likely to upset him; and there was one very particular change in his mother, this weekend, which caused him consternation. She had found herself friends! Worse, she actually invited them to the house!

Sefton scrutinized his own reactions to this new state of affairs most conscientiously. And no, he did not feel that he had been cruelly ripped from the breast; he experienced neither hunger nor cold nor unaccountable desolation. Nor did he feel nostalgia for the good old days when the faintest scratch at the front door sent his mother and him scrambling into a wardrobe or under a bed. He looked that one over a couple of times, in order to be scrupulous, but no, he wasn't nostalgic. He wasn't, in fact, he was certain, anything but what a considerate son should be; he wanted her to have friends — hadn't he tried to secure her the friendship of Mrs Kershaw all those years before? — and therefore it could only have been that he didn't want her to have *these* friends. He watched them come and go and tried to work out why it was that he didn't care for them. By the end of the weekend he had arrived at a formulation which he believed was fair in every detail and left absolutely nothing out: they were the most hopeless collection of human beings he had ever met!

He wouldn't have minded if his mother had admitted that she was running some kind of hospice for the physically underprivileged and the emotionally needy. He might even have enjoyed being the son of a Mother Theresa of North Manchester. But far from even merely intimating that she knew her visitors weren't perfect, she insisted as she introduced them each in turn to Sefton, that they were paragons and prodigies.

'Sefton I want you to meet Bernie. Bernie makes the most beautiful envelopes, don't you Bernie? Bernie, show Sefton one of your envelopes.'

Bernie had one shoulder higher than the other and seemed to be missing an ear. He carried a manilla folder pressed tightly to his side. From this he produced and offered for Sefton's inspection 'my latest'. Sefton guessed that it had been cut with great precision from a sheet of stiff wrapping paper. A galleon struggled under a lowering sky, but lo!, when you lifted the flap, the storm clouds had passed.

'Well?' pressed Mrs Goldberg.

'Well I think it's the best envelope I've ever seen,' said Sefton.

'It's marvellous, isn't it? And the work! — the work that's gone into it!'

Danny had also put some work in. He knew the routes and the departure times of every bus in Manchester and Salford. Sefton was made to test him with a number.

'Reddish, Denton, Audenshaw and Droylsden. Every twenty minutes until seven, then every hour till midnight.'

'Isn't that fantastic?' asked Sefton's mother.

Danny weighed over twenty stone and was scarcely able to walk without asistance. When she supposed he wasn't listening Mrs Goldberg nodded in his direction and whispered in Sefton's ear, 'He's going into hospital next week to have his mouth wired up.'

'Is he?' Sefton replied.

'He's a lovely person,' Mrs Goldberg said, with just a touch of firmness, as if she'd detected criticism.

But the loveliest person of all was Jean from Eccles. 'My oldest friend,' Mrs Goldberg called her. She was a wasted middle-aged woman with very little hair and charcoal-coloured circles round her eyes. Sefton gathered that she had just had something removed. He also gathered that she'd had a terrible life with men. She always trusted the wrong ones. 'If 'e 'its me again it'll be the last time,' she told Sefton.

Mrs Goldberg took Sefton to one side. 'Well what do you think of her?' she asked. 'Don't you find her charming? I think she bubbles like champagne.'

On Sunday morning Sefton took a stroll down the

187

street to buy *bagels* from Reubens the delicatessen. Fay Reubens, the daughter, whom Sefton had known and had laughed at when she said she wanted to be a famous jazz singer, was now a famous jazz singer, torchy and raunchy, and there were blown-up coloured photographs of her biting her microphone as if it were a pretzel on the walls of the shop. Sefton was admiring her wild eyes and bare olive shoulders and thinking that she still didn't have what it took to make it into his mother's circle, (say a hump or a hare-lip) when he was accosted by an old friend he hadn't seen since his schooldays. It was Barry 'Basher' Casofsky who had been the slowest boy, or at least the slowest Jewish boy, in his class. He wore a blue blazer with gold buttons and he was brown from a lifetime of lying in the sun. In contrast to the colour of his skin the whites of his eyes had the texture of milk. He wore a diamond ring on his little finger.

'So how are you?' Barry Casofsky asked. He spoke with a Manchester Jewish drawl which gave an urgency and even a suggestion of desperation and panic to every question. He *really* wanted to know how Sefton was. He'd heard that he was a professor now.

'Something like that,' said Sefton Goldberg. 'But how are you? You're looking prosperous.'

Basher Casofsky shrugged his shoulders. He surveyed the whole length of the street with his soft suspicious brown eyes. 'I mustn't grumble,' he said. And then, when he was certain that there was nobody in earshot who might come and take it all away from him, he added, 'Thank God I'm doing all right.'

He sounded for the moment like an old man; as superstitious as the peasant his grandfather had undoubtedly been. If there had been something holy to kiss, some tassel or scroll, he would have dropped to his knees and embraced it. In gratitude and fear. Because, thank God, he *was* doing all right. That was clear from the way his shirt cuffs protruded stiff and white from the sleeves of his blazer. Most of the world had reverted to buttons, but Basher Casofsky's cuffs were fastened by gold links on which the initials BC were engraved in an elaborate script. And this was only a Sunday morning. Sefton wondered what kept his shirt cuffs together in the week when he was doing business and needed to look his best. And not just for business, either. Basher Casofsky was married and had three children on whom he doted and through whom he was to be made eternal; but there could be no doubting that he also treated himself occasionally to girls from Rochdale and Bury. He sparkled and shone like someone who was getting more of everything than he could possibly need. Superabundance gleamed from him like the diamond on his little finger and the gold studs at his wrist. Poor deprived Sefton Goldberg wanly surveyed his old friend. The pure whiteness of those cuffs defeated him entirely. He had never been able to get his shirts to do that. There was no point now in his even trying. It was too late. You had to stay with what you'd chosen.

At Cambridge, people who were impressive were referred to as minds. They didn't just *have* minds, they *were* minds. Sefton had chosen to be a mind.

He walked back with the *bagels* and chopped herring and found his father sitting up at the breakfast bar in the kitchen, practising tearing telephone directories. His mother (alias, this morning, Dolly Parton, Montsarrat Caballé, and the Supremes) was listening simultaneously to the radio, the television, and the dishwasher. The Goldbergs had a lounge and a dining room, just like the gentiles, but they spent all their time in the kitchen. The rest of the house, though only a very modest example of contemporary provincial Jewish rococo, had not been designed for the comfortable accommodation of human beings. Over the years Mrs Goldberg had contrived to fill every conceivable space — for Jews, like Nature, cannot abide a vacuum — with those sorts of flashing sparkling gewgaws a taste for which the Jews share, though they'd be horrified to

189

have it pointed out to them, with the *schvartzes*. For less than half of the loot in Mrs Goldberg's front room native chieftains had once bartered continents.

'It's not brute strength, you know,' Sefton's father explained. 'A child could do it, actually. You've just got to know how to fold the pages.'

'Shush!' demanded Mrs Goldberg. 'I want to hear this.'

On the television Brian Walden was forecasting that nine-tenths of the world's working population would be unemployed by the end of the decade, which was five years after the date he had given in his programme the week before for the total destruction of mankind by nuclear war, pollution and starvation. On the radio David Jacobs was playing all Sylvia Goldberg's favourite popular classics. In the dishwasher the glasses and cutlery were getting their final clear rinse.

'Have you tried it out in front of an audience yet?' Sefton asked his father.

'Not yet. The trouble is that Manchester's got two directories now.'

'Well you don't have to tear both, do you?'

Sam Goldberg had no patience for half measures. 'It'd be more effective.'

'So what will you do? A to M first, then N to Z?'

'No, I'd like to do them both together.'

'Shush!' said Sylvia Goldberg.

On the television a union man and someone from management, brought together by Brian Walden, were making it impossible for one to envisage any future for Britain short of civil war and anarchy. On the radio Herbert von Karajan was whipping the Berlin Philharmonic through the best bits of Tchaikovsky's overture to *Romeo and Juliet*.

'You'll rupture yourself,' Sefton warned his father.

'I've told you, strength has got nothing to do with it. It's the way you hold it.'

'Oh, I love this,' said Mrs Goldberg.

Von Karajan was throwing caution to the wind. So

was the union man. They were both going the whole way.

'It's so beautiful. I don't know why you don't like it, Sefton. *Our love, dee dee dah dah dah dum, dee dah daaah dum . . .*'

Sefton felt his mother defying him to disapprove of her. She was doing with Tchaikovsky what she had been doing with Bernie and Jean. She had been diffident long enough. She was sick of feeling cowed and bullied. She would take on now only what she was confident she could handle. The impulse might not have been all that different from what took Sefton to Fanny Price and thence to Wrottesley, and kept him there.

Sefton handed his father a plate of buttered *bagels*. Hunched over the breakfast bar, he was still trying to prove that ripping a telephone directory in half was a matter only of deft touch. He seemed to be enjoying in advance the little stir he would make when he had perfected the effect, the applause and laughter and appreciation of Jean from Eccles and Danny with the wired-up mouth.

Was it only an hour ago, Sefton marvelled, that he had put the proposition to himself, while he chatted to Basher Casofsky, that he was now stuck forever with the choices he had made? Choices? He had flattered himself. Who did he think he was? An orphan?

11

Back at the Polytechnic and with only forty-eight hours to go before he was expected at Holy Christ Hall, Sefton found himself involved in an unpleasant and untimely incident. Gerald Sidewinder, passing him in the corridor, smiled at him!

Thereafter, wherever Sefton went in the building, he was aware of an atmosphere of almost carnival frolic. This was not what one expected in a polytechnic on a Monday morning but Sefton made strenuous efforts to think about it rationally. All this unnatural animation and merriment did not *have* to be at his expense. Sidewinder's behaviour, for example, could be put down to his excitement at the imminent twinning with the Football Club. The look of twinkling regional astuteness on the faces of the Director and his various Supervisors and Foremen could be attributed to the same source. As for Cora Peck, there was no mystery about the two glowing circles of confidence on her cheeks; a whole weekend had elapsed since Sefton had last seen her: time enough for her to have persuaded Melvyn Bragg to devote a complete series of programmes, or maybe even the rest of his life, to her extraordinary talents. (Cora Bragg — it had a ring!) And Charles Wenlock, patently, had more occasion for excitement than anyone. Sefton could hear him sighing and moaning all over the Polytechnic, wandering from room to room, letting every member of his department into his secrets, elated with guilt and indecision. On top of his domestic difficulties (Joyce had found out and was suicidal) there was the outrage of his exclusion from the coming ceremony at the football ground, which seemed to work like an aphrodisiac on him. The wild ecstasy of his sense of injury must have taken Val Peel's breath away, and Sefton could easily imagine her making the terrible mistake of reckoning what an even better lover Charles would be when he was happy. All this was explicable to Sefton without any reference to himself, but what had Bob Floss to smirk about, why was Walter Sickert Fledwhite suddenly ubiquitous and merry, and more significantly, why was Peter Potter moving in and out of lectures without his feet so much as grazing the ground? What did *he* have to be so delighted about?

His hair was cut for the new week like a school-boy's and he was dressed in the olive green suit which his wife had made for him out of material she wove and dyed herself. Peter claimed that every bit of it, apart from the buttons, came from their garden. And indeed he looked as if he had come from the garden himself. A little green imp. Impish, oh he was impish all right! And that, as far as Sefton was concerned, could mean only one thing — he was not afraid of what was going to happen to Sefton in Cambridge. Because he knew that *nothing* was. And how did he know it? Not by ringing up Holy Christ Hall and checking on Sefton's chances, nor by posting a twenty-five pound postal order (to fix you-know-what) to Sir Evelyn Woolfardisworthy, care of The Master's Lodge. He knew it because he was in tune with nature and the fates and the fairies and the way things were. He knew it in the same way that one of those little garden birds he resembled knew when it was safe to come hopping out onto the lawn. That's what Peter was doing in his vegetable suit — he was showing off his instincts and chirruping on the grass, friendly and fearless, because he knew in those amazing little organs of percipience of his that there was nothing out there that could harm him, not for miles.

Peter was too busy to talk for long. He was lecturing

all morning on one of those preposterous characters in Lawrence who don't like being touched, who aren't going to have the first desperate woman that comes along reaching for *their* little winkies, thank you very much. Peter was aware of meeting some resistance from his students. 'They don't have much feeling for male chasteness,' he complained, brightly.

Sefton thought about it. 'I suppose they don't,' he said.

'They're not the only ones, either,' Peter went on.

For a moment or two Sefton wondered whether this referred to some obscure act of unchasteness on his part, but Peter's eyes were rolling like a conspirator's and he realised in time that he was thinking about Charles. Peter couldn't, of course, approve of what Charles had done.

'Needs must,' said Sefton, tolerantly.

Peter Potter was somehow able to draw the skin tight across his face. He looked old and bitter. 'Needs!' he said contemptuously. 'Needs!' But he was quickly bright again, remembering that he had reason. 'When do you go?' he asked.

'Go?' For the moment Sefton was quite baffled. Was he going anywhere? Then it came back to him. 'Oh, go to Cambridge?' It really was the last thing on his mind, Peter had to understand. 'Wednesday morning.'

'So you'll be back for Friday night?'

'I'll probably be back Wednesday afternoon.'

'Come now,' said Peter, with urbanity. He wasn't having any false modesty. He knew a winner when he saw one.

'Yes, I'll be back for Friday night,' said Sefton.

'Good. We'll expect you about eight. Miranda's making the carrot champagne right now.'

It's a good job I am not superstitious, Sefton said to himself, or liable to fantastical misgivings; because the signs aren't good. The signs weren't good, even leaving aside Gerald Sidewinder and Peter Potter. The drycleaners had utterly failed to remove some mystery stains from the trousers of Sefton's interview suit, and they had somehow succeeded in laying it as a moral charge against Sefton that the stains were there in the first place. He had fared no better with the black shoes that went with the suit. The man behind the instant heel bar had turned them over with distaste. He was tattooed from head to foot and was clearly a man who had seen many things in life. But he had never seen anything like the undersides of Sefton's shoes.

'I'd throw 'em away and keep the laces if they was mine,' was his advice. Sefton tossed them into the first litter bin he came to.

It took him a day and a half to persuade anyone in the railway information office to answer the phone. Strictly speaking there were no trains to Cambridge, but if one was determined to be difficult one could catch the eight fifty-seven, changing at Birmingham, Leicester, Melton Mowbray, Lincoln, Peterborough, Spalding, March, Ely, and March again, arriving at Cambridge at four twenty-three.

'Would that be four twenty-three on the same day?' Sefton asked.

He had decided against driving. He would only brood at the wheel of his car. At least on a train there was the chance of an adventure to take his mind off things. He wasn't planning to prepare himself specially for what was ahead of him; he didn't want to work out answers to possible questions in advance. If they asked him how he thought he could contribute to the Christian life of the college he would have to rely on spontaneous wit and invention to carry him through.

So he took the train, prowling up and down the corridors in search of girls reading *The Rainbow*, and not finding any.

Cambridge. Scene in Sefton's time of the most staggering daily embarrassment. Not just in the mediaeval monastic cells of men like Dr Geoffrey Tolcarne, and not just on the river where at any bend the naked body of your tutor might come floating by you on its back, just the pink tips of nose and penis visible, like a couple of little bobbing corks, warning you to watch where you drove your punt pole — not just here, for these were places where you went expecting trouble, but out there anywhere, on the streets, in the shops, around the Market Place, along the Backs. The amount of turning aside and looking the other way and pretending not to notice that had gone on in those streets! The numbers of great and famous men who taught Sefton or signed forms for him or had rooms in the same college stair-case, to whom, when they sailed past him in their gowns or on their bicycles, he was afraid to say hello, because it was so abundantly clear, from the way their eyes darted about in their sockets like gnats on a summer river, that they were afraid to say hello to him!

Sefton soon realised that it wasn't personal. It wasn't so much *him* that they couldn't say hello to, it was *hello* that they couldn't say. They couldn't make the necessary noises the first time around and they couldn't sustain the strain of eye-contact long enough to try them a second. It was altogether easier to ride into a lamp-post or talk to the pavement.

The problem for Derek Muten was even more severe. He could not manage hello in his own house! Sefton had to go round to the Mutens once a week for a tutorial. If he was lucky Anita Muten would open the door. She couldn't say hello either, but it was clear to Sefton, who liked a trier, that she at least made an effort; her lips did discernibly part and from behind them came a faint rasping sound, somewhere between a gasp and a gulp. In the circumstances Sefton accepted this gratefully as both a greeting and a welcome. Derek Muten himself was rendered completely inaudible by the social difficulties which swarmed and multiplied between the threshold and the lintel of his house. Finding Sefton on the mat, waiting for his tutorial, Derek Muten would drop his head on his chest and run his hands through his hair. He never knew whether to lead the way to his study or allow Sefton to go first; consequently there was much confusion in the narrow hall, much hesitation and sudden propulsion, much jostling and collision, all of it mismanaged in deathly silence. If there was already a student in the study, Derek Muten would not know how to explain that his hour was up or be capable of asking Sefton to wait a short while; instead he would go to his window and stare out over Cambridge and absently pummel his face. Sefton had heard rumours that Derek Muten was once a pretty useful amateur middle-weight, and there could be no denying that he had the build of a boxer and a broken nose. Sefton therefore assumed that his habit of delivering left jabs to himself was an after-effect of the sport. Whatever the explanation, it didn't make things any easier for his pupils, most of whom, being boys from small provincial grammar schools and therefore highly susceptible to the idea that to be confident was to be crude, quickly adopted his mannerisms. Sefton could no longer remember how many times he and some fellow undergraduate had stood together unintroduced in the middle of Derek Muten's study, both of them with their heads on their chests and their hands in their hair, while Derek Muten stared out of his window and attempted to slug himself, with a combination of straight lefts and short rights, into a better or at least a less difficult world.

The tutorial itself was distinguished from all that had preceded it only by a marked increase in the level of communicated reticence and pain. It was a hard and hurtful business, thinking about literature; one was beset, if one was sensitive — if one could *read* — by so much anxiety, one was at the mercy of so many qualms and qualifications. It was a kind of crassness, therefore, to have anything to say. To be a critic, according to Derek Muten's example, was first and foremost to fret, and then occasionally to faint. Derek Muten was widely reported to have fainted the first time he saw

197

Macbeth and every time he read the Lucy poems. And there were stretches of some ten or fifteen minutes in any tutorial during which he allowed his head to drop between his knees, and his soul, in so far as one could detect the difference, to leave his body. With Derek Muten's example before him every week Sefton became ashamed of his own inability to pass out even briefly while he was reading. God knows, he tried. In all the proper places. The birth of Levin's child, the wounding of Prince André, the deaths of Hector and Lucy, the belated happiness of Anne Elliot. But it was no good. He couldn't keel over. It was only when he went to see a production of something or other at Stratford and found his eyelids drooping and his head dropping between his knees that he was able to believe in himself as a literary critic again.

However, even if Derek Muten's fits of responsive fainting didn't catch on, his inaudibility enjoyed quite a vogue during the time Sefton was at Cambridge, and many young men of his acquaintance soon became impossible to hear. Not uninfluential young men either. The President of the Cambridge Literary Society, for example, was always a Muten man, as indeed were most of the members — the offices of the Society passing from Mutenite to Mutenite at annual general meetings which were not so much secret as silent. Visiting speakers were astonished to find themselves introduced by a chairman whose lips moved but from whom no sound issued; and they could not fail to notice, conversely, that in proportion as *they* could be heard were *they* unpopular. It was no pleasant experience to find yourself alone in the midst of an angry and murmuring Mutenite crowd. Sefton had seen a few of the maulings which could follow a blatantly audible paper and they reminded him most of the sorts of beatings handed out in nightmares by unappeasable mobs of the handicapped and the maimed. A relentless assailant with dark glasses and a white stick had always been an image of the greatest horror to Sefton

Goldberg, but it was now replaced by something far more terrible — a Mutenite critic lowering his head as you spoke, silently disapproving, wordlessly disparaging, soundlessly appalled. Sefton Goldberg had been born with a big mouth; but by the end of his first term at Cambridge he had become noiseless.

Cambridge was different now. Now the place was full of sociologists and Italian girls from language schools. No awkward silences in the streets now, no riding your bicycle into the river rather than greet a colleague. Today it was all excitement and celebration — ejaculations of Neapolitan exuberance, protestations of unselfconscious Barnsley warmth. Sefton could feel the difference in the air the moment he got off the train. He wasn't sure that he liked it. He made a mental note of the new pizza parlours and waffle bars, and he supposed that once he was back living here he would visit them; but he felt a pang of nostalgia — it had been good, the old austerity and awkwardness and out-of-dateness. In the old days he had actually taught girls who had their hair pulled back like Charlotte Brontë how to twist; from a quick look about him he couldn't see anybody who needed that sort of tuition from him now. But he knew that it might all look different again once he put his nose inside Holy Christ Hall. It came as a little shock to him to remember what he'd come for. He consulted his watch and discovered it was already nearly five o'clock. He hadn't bothered to check what time he was expected for dinner, but if he remembered rightly they ate pretty early in college. Wasn't he always ravenous again by eight-thirty when he was a student? He quickened his pace and turned up his collar, like a hero on the last page of a novel, and before too long he was standing in the porter's lodge at Holy Christ Hall and wondering if he would be collecting his mail from here presently, as Disraeli Fellow.

'Good afternoon. I'm Sefton Goldberg,' he announced. It never came easy to him, saying his name, and he felt that it sounded more than usually ugly here, even in the porter's lodge where men went by the names of Victor and Norman. 'I am dining with the Master tonight and I believe a room has been kept for me.'

'Goldberg, you say?' The porter was the familiar Cambridge mixture of deference and effrontery. They were always locals — fen people. Aboriginals made into the slave class. Sefton was prepared to admit they had a grouse. But it wasn't the fault of the Jews. So why was it necessary to pronounce Goldberg quite like that?

'Goldberg, yes.'

The porter was running his eyes down the page of an exercise book. 'S. Goldberg did you say?'

How many fucking Goldbergs had he got written down there, Sefton wondered. 'S, yes.'

'Well all I've got here is a Goldblatt. S. Goldblatt.'

'That might just be it,' said Sefton.

'The address I've got here is Paradise Villas, Wrottesley.'

'That's it. That's me.'

The porter made a mark in the exercise book then he brought his face very close to Sefton's. He seemed to want to confide a secret. 'I lived in Wrottesley once. Couldn't stand it. I'm not surprised you want to come here.'

'It's an unlovely place,' Sefton agreed.

'It's a shit heap, if you'll pardon my French. I stuck it three years until I was the last white man in there. Then I left.'

'I know how you must have felt,' said Sefton. He wondered why there had been so few violent crimes against college porters over the years.

A pacifist himself, he simply asked for his key and enquired after the time of dinner.

'Dinner six-thirty sir, but the Master invites you to meet the other candidates over sherry at six, in the Master's Lodge.'

Other candidates! This was a sickening blow to Sefton Goldberg. It had never occurred to him that he was going to find himself in immediate competition for the Disraeli Fellowship. He knew that they might have had the odd other person in mind, but he hadn't expected that there was to be something as odious as a comparison afoot. Not here. Not in Cambridge. You went for jobs in Sheffield or Durham if you wanted any of that.

'Are there many other candidates?' he asked.

'Six of you altogether, sir, including yourself. Three tonight, three tomorrow.'

Shifts *noch*. They were coming in in fucking shifts! No wonder that prescient little prick Peter Potter had been in such high spirits. Maybe he'd be coming down himself in the next truckload, along with Ron Penn and Kevin Dainty. Sefton had all along been working on the assumption that for some reason best known to themselves — perhaps because they had found a happy congruence in the names Goldberg and Disraeli — the Fellows of Holy Christ Hall were inclined in his favour, and that provided he didn't spill too much food over himself or say anything detrimental to Jesus, the job would be his. He had even been quietly taking it for granted that the Fellowship was open only to Jews (thanks, perhaps, to some guilty bequest of Lord Beaconsfield himself); and if that was the case then where was the opposition — where were the *other candidates* — going to come from? This was England, not America. Here literature and criticism were still *goyische* pursuits, tied up with solemn attitudes to marriage and standards. Just about the only Jew teaching marriage and standards that Sefton Goldberg had heard of was Sefton Goldberg. But now it seemed there were six candidates. They couldn't *all* be Jews. Therefore his reasoning had been fallacious. It was open slather. The Fellowship might go to an Anabaptist or an Episcopalian or an Ultramontanist. In which case it was even possible that Sefton had been invited along just for the look of the thing — a token Jew, performing the same function as the obligatory

201

black policeman in American movies. Not that it mattered much now why he'd been invited. He was in no shape to face competition. He hadn't re-read any of the books he was supposed to be interested in, he hadn't even dipped into the one he was supposed to be writing just to remind himself what it was about. 'And are you working on anything original yourself at the moment, Mr Goldberg?' 'Yes, your holiness, I am, but I can't remember off-hand what it is.' Whereas, of course, the Episcopalian would be able to talk for hours about the contents of his card index system. And wouldn't the Anabaptist and the Ultramontanist have some interesting things to say about what they'd been reading on their train journey up? And they would have observed the countryside, would they not? Oh yes, they would not have let *that* whizz by the train windows without remark, not on this occasion they wouldn't, not given where they were going, not when they could safely bet a pound to a penny that there wasn't going to be an enquiry or a statement or a judgement made at High Table tonight that wasn't at bottom pastoral. Tragical-comical-pastoral for Sefton Goldberg. No use looking to him for suggestions as to where the geese were flying. He hadn't *seen* any geese.

By the time he had dressed for sherry Sefton was not exactly confident but he was calm. He discovered that he was enjoying being back in Cambridge again; in particular he was enjoying being back in a Cambridge college at this time of evening, with darkness coming down and the air filled with the sound of chapel bells — a wonderfully melancholy, alienating sound, if you were a Jew, calling you nowhere. Gowned undergraduates appeared and disappeared, flitting about the quadrangle like bats at dusk; and Sefton began to have trouble remembering what it was he hadn't liked when he was an undergraduate himself. He enjoyed negotiating an old narrow staircase again and letting himself in and out of the guest room through heavy double doors. The murmur of other people's interesting lives was just discernible, and it brought back the old sentimental hankering for a place in a community of scholars, for the very idea of collegiality itself. Why had he not liked it when he had had it? He must have been too young. He knew nothing of polytechnics then and he hadn't lived above Ron Penn. It would be very different now.

In this softened state he strode over to the Master's Lodge. Woolfardisworthy — it could be no one else — greeted him on the steps. 'So you must be Goldmann.'

Sefton was just able not to agree. 'Berg,' he said.

'Ah, Bergmann, I'm so sorry.'

This is the price of being pedantic, Sefton thought. But he couldn't retreat now. 'No, Goldberg.' He was conscious of being a dreadful nuisance.

Woolfardisworthy threw back his head and laughed. 'Welcome anyway,' he said, putting his arm through Sefton's. It was all rather theatrical, not unlike meeting Sir Laurence Olivier, Sefton guessed. With this exception: compared to Sir Evelyn Woolfardisworthy, Sir Laurence Olivier had the elocution of a publican and the refinement of a drayman and the bearing of an ostler.

And his looks would not have shown up too brilliantly either. Sefton did not normally notice these things but he was astounded by the youth and the beauty of the Master of Holy Christ Hall. He had been banking on a small gnarled cleric, but here was a man on the right side of fifty, erect like a guardsman, without a line on his face and without a crease in his clothes; blue-eyed, manicured, and smelling simultaneously of freshness — extreme immaculateness of flesh — and antiquity, not of person, but as it were of genealogy, of line. His individual fragrance was subtle and light, but he was heavy, too, with the odour of all that had gone before him and was his. Like a pine forest, his was a mixed pungency of new growth and old roots. Already routed on every front, with Sir Evelyn's hand holding him lightly as if he were a none too dangerous felon or a

203

soiled dishcloth, Sefton considered it unnecessarily bludgeoning of his host to have the advantage over him of both youth and age. Either one would have been ample. He overdid it in the matter of size, also; being at once much taller than Sefton, but somehow appearing to take up less space. He was more formal and more casual as well; and more cheerful and more grave.

The light trickle of perspiration down Sefton Goldberg's back had now swollen into a river. Already he couldn't distinguish his shirt from his skin. In another five minutes the cheque book in his breast pocket and the little wad of paper money in his trousers would be sodden. He hoped that he wasn't going to be expected to pay for anything before he had the chance to dry out. Sherry and dinner, presumably, were free; and a game of brag or poker didn't look imminent. But what if a collection plate were to be passed round at some point in the evening? Didn't Christians always have some nave or chancel (whatever they were) in need of repair? What then would be the effect on Woolfardisworthy (who had in all likelihood been kept away from Jews by a strict family and solicitous friends) of seeing Sefton Goldberg produce a couple of steaming oners from somewhere in the region of his groin? That would confirm an ancient Christian rumour or two, would it not?

In another moment, human time — that's to say after half a century, measured on the Goldberg scale — Sefton found himself ushered into a drawing room that was markedly less cluttered than his mother's and having to offer one of the hottest and wettest parts of his person for Lady Woolfardisworthy to shake.

He was in no condition to form any distinct impression of Sir Evelyn's wife. But he had the sense of a woman who had left the business of being tall and beautiful and successful to her husband. Her part of the marital bargain seemed to consist in her wrapping herself in layers of Scottish wool and rattling out her words with that staccato excitability expected of wives walled up in Oxford or Cambridge colleges. It was impossible to tell whether she was exceedingly confident and rude or exceedingly diffident and apologetic. One could be certain only that she was brusque, and that she might at any moment break off in the middle of a sentence in order to go and water the plants or make an entry in her diary. But while that fancy wasn't taking her she peppered Sefton and the air around him with little pellets of interrogation.

'Dr Goldberg, how do you do? What time did you get here? Have you come far? How dreadful. Has anybody shown you around the college yet? You must look at the azaleas. Did you stand all the way? Awful things trains. Why didn't you come by car? Indispensable. Especially if you've got children. Do you have children, Dr Goldberg?'

'Actually,' said Sefton, in an accent which he realised as he heard it owed much to early Gracie Fields, 'it's Mister Goldberg, not Doctor.'

'Oh, Mister!' Lady Woolfardisworthy peered the short distance down her own myopic tunnel and seemed to find something she very vaguely recognised. 'Oh, Mister!' she said again, and then she gave Sefton a wide conniving stare as if she had just caught him boasting but wasn't going to tell.

Sefton wondered whether this was or this wasn't an example of good breeding. But he never got around to making up his mind. Matters of far greater moment had taken over. Until now he had only been ashamed, humiliated and mortified. But here suddenly was alarm and premonition, *tremor cordis* . . .

Here, advancing upon him, with their arms sportingly outstretched, were the *other candidates*. Sefton had registered their presence in the room as Woolfardisworthy had escorted him in, but they had waited at a discreet distance while Sefton entertained the Professor's wife with his imitations of English as it is still sometimes spoken in the furthest western foothills of the Pennines. Only now, as they advanced, was he able to take them in and discover that he knew them. Yes, yes, he knew them! And what was more, or rather, what was worse, he didn't just know them — Ernest Weekley who had lived on Mykonos and who had just recently published a short novel about life in the confectionery trade, called *The Sweet Shop* (or perhaps it was *The Sweat Shop* — Sefton couldn't remember), and Gunnar McMurphy who had run off to start a new life with the wives of more senior academics than Professor Sir Evelyn Woolfardisworthy had had hot dinners at High Table — Sefton didn't just *know* them, he had TAUGHT them! What he had always dreaded had finally come about: he was competing for employment with his own students!

There was only one greater ignominy. Losing to them!

12

Optimist!

Only one greater ignominy before *what?* Did he suppose ignominies were things you could run out of? Did he think he was in sight, at last, of bottom? Sefton Goldberg, of all people, should have known better.

And very soon did.

In the interval, during the last relatively happy moments that Sefton was ever to know on earth, he shook hands and exchanged mutually unflattering anecdotes with his old pupils. Ernest Weekley, now hiding his boy's face behind a man's beard and his natural cowardice and cuckoldry behind a wedding ring and authorship, was someone Sefton had taught briefly at a University somewhere or other (Sefton never taught there long enough to find out) in South Wales — the Old South Wales, not the New. They were both there very briefly: Sefton on an un-tenured temporary Assistant Lectureship which paid about three pounds a week before national insurance, superannuation, graduated pension, tax and union dues were taken out; and Weekley in even briefer self-imposed exile from his stuides at Cambridge, lashed by seriousness and fired by the idea of living in the heart of real organic communities — an idea which, after South Wales, took him to Mykonos and the confectionery trade, before landing him back in East Anglia at the feet of Derek Muten who had initiated it all. Muten had spotted Weekley when he was fresh from school and believed him to be endowed with genius. 'There's nothing more I can teach you,' he had told him after a fortnight's supervision and an unsuccessful bid to get the Faculty Board to award him a degree without putting him through the formalities of an examination. 'You must now learn from life.' When Weekley repeated these words to Sefton Goldberg all that time ago in Wales, Sefton had been sceptical — *he* had not heard Derek Muten string together so many consecutive ideas in three years. Nor did it seem to *him* that Weekley was a genius just because he scratched his head and looked as if he were in mourning for intelligence and truth whenever anyone else ventured to express a thought. He didn't, of course, say as much to Ernest Weekley at the time — as a teacher Sefton knew not to damp the confidence of his students — but he failed his essays whenever he could in conscience do so. Sefton had not liked him then or on the couple of occasions he had run into him since; not least because he had brought back from his travels an exhaustingly vivacious peasant wife with perfect breasts, the habit of wearing his shirts unbuttoned, a bronze medallion for his chest, strong opinions about amphorae and the conviction that although he was no less endowed with precocious genius than ever, he was no longer the swatty under-graduate he'd been.

Sefton hoped that he would be given the opportunity to prove to him that on the contrary the boy was still alive and kicking in the man.

Gunnar McMurphy dated from an even earlier period of Sefton's richly variegated career, was an Australian of Irish-Scandinavian descent, and had been the most attentive listener to the course of lectures entitled, 'Spitting in the eye of Mrs Grundy — Defiance and Sincerity in D.H. Lawrence's later fiction', which Sefton had delivered and made his name with in his first year as head of liberal studies at the Tumbarumba School of Mines and Mineralogy. Gunnar McMurphy had been defiantly, but sincerely, spitting into the eye and indeed into every other vulnerable part of Mrs

Grundy ever since. Even as they shook hands for the first time in a dozen years he hurriedly confided to Sefton that he was only here in Cambridge, looking for a job, because he had been hounded out of any possibility of one back home by the Vice-Chancellor of Oodnadatta University, Sir Alex Sneddon, with whose wife Lobelia he, Gunnar, was at present living and travelling in a white heat of sincerity and defiance. In order to live and travel with Lobelia, it seemed, he had had to give the boot to Hermie whom he had previously rescued from an arid and insincere marriage with the Professor of Animal Behaviour at the same university. Hermie, too, Sefton gathered, was into hounding.

'They all hate us for our veracity,' he just had time to whisper. 'They want to wet on our flame.'

Sefton remembered Gunnar McMurphy well. He used to read out chunks of *Lady Chatterley's Lover* in seminars, his round red face refusing to recognize that there was such a thing as embarrassment in the world, his serious grey eyes fired with solemn purpose, as one by one his fellow students slid below the level of the table. 'Here tha shits an' here tha pisses.' Long before Gunnar McMurphy got to the daisy chain Sefton Goldberg had turned himself inside out like a discarded sock.

Sefton knew that if he found himself isolated next to McMurphy tonight, High Table or no High Table, the conversation would inexorably swing around to Lobelia's labia.

But, 'Ah!' Woolfardisworthy was exclaiming, as another person in need of welcoming and sherry could be heard shuffling in the gravel of the Master's drive. 'Our little party is now complete.' Sefton's head was down, in order not to have to meet McMurphy's manic stare or catch a glimpse of the huge delight that Ernest Weekley took in being Ernest Weekley, and so the first he saw of the new arrival was the legs. They were female and familiar. If he was not mistaken he had seen that orthopaedic walk — not quite a limp, more a kind of niggardliness of gait — and he had mused upon those high laced orphanage shoes, before. By the time he had lifted his head and re-lived the whole of his life three times he knew into whose eyes he was looking and when it was that he had looked into them last, so vivid was his recollection of their wateriness, the way they seemed to float aimlessly behind her lenses, like drowned souls. The Master's introduction, when at last it came — 'Sefton Godsplatt, Dr Helen Burns' — was therefore quite redundant.

Sefton had not laid eyes on Helen Burns since the day the whistling postman had called upon them both, couchant, on the floor of Sefton's office, but he had kept his ears open for stories of her progress, not least because he felt he ought to know the names of all the other academics to whom, on the floors of *their* offices, she was bound to repeat the droll episode. It soon became clear to him that he had nothing to fear. The very scale of her operations nullified gossip; nobody pointed the finger because nobody had clean hands. Helen Burns, like early plagiarism and fear of failure, was the skeleton in the cupboard of every intellectual of renown, the bit of dope that every poet and historian had on every other. And even if something were to be dredged up, a little fish like Sefton Goldberg wouldn't fetch a price. Helen Burns had left Australia (some said because she could no longer bear to see what she was doing to the Governor General's marriage) for Europe, in time to take up with the leaders of the student risings of 1968. Long-time radical groupies who knew her were scandalised. 'She isn't even a socialist,' they complained, remembering all they'd had to read and learn before Rudi and Tariq would look at them. And they were without any clues to understand the appeal of this whey-faced child of the almshouse, whose features were smudged like a wet photograph and who stood with her knees slightly together in the style of a petitioner. What did men of moral purpose and integrity see in her? What did any man see in her?

Sefton didn't know and he had stretched out beside her on the floor of his study. And perhaps the distinguished behaviourists and structuralists and monetarists and unilateralists on whose arms she appeared throughout the seventies didn't know either, but they all deferred to her in footnotes and planned ways of leaving their wives.

The biggest surprise, Sefton decided, once he'd run through them all a few times, was that she was here for the Disraeli Fellowship at all. It shocked him to be in competition with her, but he had to admit that it conferred a bit of dignity on the appointment to have her, with *her* contacts, applying for it. That was the nearest thing to consolation he could find.

And it was in that spirit that he raised his glass of sherry to her at last and proposed a gallant toast, 'May the best man win,' he said, 'or should I say the best *person.*'

'Best *man* is fine,' said Helen Burns. She looked cold and undernourished and neglected; but somewhere faintly victorious as well, as if she knew that at the end of the week her parents were coming to remove her from the home. 'You're all men, as it happens.'

You? You're? Sefton didn't like it. He could hear the distant hooves of the Four Horsemen.

Helen Burns noted his confusion. 'Hang on!' Her Australian accent, which came and went, was back, harsh and twanging. 'You don't think that I'm ...?' She was too amused to finish her sentence; but when the Master strolled over she was able to say, 'I think Mr Goldberg needs disabusing. I think he thinks I'm here for the Fellowship.'

Professor Woolfardisworthy was wonderfully amused and apologetic. 'All my fault,' he confessed with exaggerated solicitude. 'I should have explained to you. Dr Burns is our Director of Studies. She's the one you chaps are going to have to impress.'

The last thing Sefton remembered noticing was the

little ball of cotton wool in Helen Burns' right ear.

In a little panelled antechamber which, though no bigger than a pantry, served as dressing room and green-room and wings to that great stage, High Table, the Master and the Fellows of Holy Christ Hall waited with their guests for the sounds that would tell them when it was time to go on. Sefton wasn't at all surprised to discover just how many clerics could be compressed into one small space — he had been guided round enough stately homes to know what a priest's hole looked like and how little room the word of God took up — but he was surprised to discover just how many of the clerics compressed here he already knew. He exchanged a glance with Mr Collins and nodded at Parson Adams and shook hands perfunctorily with Arthur Dimmesdale. From the centre of a tight circle of Whisky Priests, Father Brown and Father Béron emerged to say hello, and over in the corner, pressed into earnest conversation with Helen Burns, the Senior Tutor, Peter Abelard, was winking Sefton's way. Sefton also noticed — and now that he had nothing left to live or hope for, now that he had broken off all diplomatic relations with his future and his destiny, he was noticing with a fine detachment — that the theatrical atmosphere, the tension of waiting to be called, affected even the most seasoned troupers. They became nervous and irritable. They scratched their faces and screwed their fingers in their ears and yawned a lot. And they roughed themselves up in readiness, too. They made sure that their gowns were on inside out, and they pushed the points of their collars under the knots of their ties, or if they wore clerical collars they slid them around so that the dingiest parts showed. If they had hair they pulled it down over their eyes, if they didn't they put thumb stains of soot on their baldness, so determined were they not to go out there looking like amateurs. Even Woolfardisworthy, who had appeared so elegant a half an hour before, began to take on an inky, careless look, and when the sounding of the dinner gong was followed by the racket of three hundred hungry undergraduates rising from their benches and throwing buns, he was no slower than his fellows to drop into a slouch. Weekley and McMurphy seemed likewise to have understood what was required of them, the one having become, on the instant, a sort of prep-school Zorba, the other a Mellors from a college in the bush. Both succeeded in giving the impression that they had been out all day in the forest, reading books. And Helen Burns could be seen preparing for what was positively her last appearance as a boat-person. Sefton Goldberg, observing this general and apparently mandatory collapse, made a firm decision: after a lifetime of being humiliated by the greater spruceness of everybody else, he was damned if he was going to be humiliated now by the greater spruceness of himself. He tossed his soft curls back from his forehead. He smoothed down the waistcoat of his navy blue Cecil Gee suit and shot out from its sleeves a set of cuffs which were stiffer and whiter and longer than Basher Casofsky's. Miraculously, the waters of perspiration which had flooded his body had receded, leaving his skin as fresh and as odoriferous as morning. His eyes shone. His nose was tiny and turned upwards like a pixie's toes. His brain teemed with apothegms. At the back of his throat Fischer-Dieskau and Pavarotti had finished practising their scales. So that by the time the head waiter had opened the door of the antechamber Sefton Goldberg was ready to emerge like the sun from behind the black clouds of grimy chaplains and clergymen.

'My dear Goldfinger,' Professor Woolfardisworthy whispered as they moved towards High Table, 'will you sit on my left?'

Sit on your left what? was just one of the apothegms Sefton Goldberg rejected, as he felt the admiring stares of three hundred undergraduates on him. He who dines on the left of the devil will not rise on the right of the

213

Lord, was another. What he actually said was, 'Master, I would like nothing more.' But even as he said it Pavarotti was laughing with full-throated menace, and *se vuol ballare* sang Fischer-Dieskau.

Sefton found himself eating with a niceness he did not know he possessed. All those years of watching gentiles toying with their peas and looking under their meat, checking the undersides of their chops — for what? for germs? spies? foreign bodies? — all those years of sitting over his own cleaned plate watching them play slow chess with their vegetables, raising forkfuls no bigger than electrons to their lips at last only to lower them again for further inspection and division — all those years of wondering whether the *goyim* were not in fact keeping themselves alive on something other than food and only pretending to eat in public in order not to arouse the suspicions of the Jews — all those years of staring and marvelling had not passed unprofitably. While Woolfardisworthy slurped his gravy and Friar Tuck and Father Zossima emptied their plates into their beards, Sefton Goldberg examined the ingredients of his meal with the eye of a bored jeweller, wielded his implements as if he were a surgeon. He diced his own carrots. He quartered his peas. He removed the fat from his pork and laid it at the side of his plate, for future research, along with the skin from his potatoes and the stalks from his sprouts and the veins from his lettuce. As the head waiter hovered and both tables, High and low, held their breath, Sefton raised a corpuscle of pig to his lips, looked under it and behind it and around the sides of it, talked over it and through it, pondered and queried and interrogated it, before returning it to his plate in favour of a stain of apple-sauce. And he discovered for the first time the enormous conversational advantage these *goyische* tactics gave one over the poor *schmegegges* whose noses were buried in their bowls. Never before, at a dinner table, had Sefton known the luxury of not having to towel down his lips before he spoke, the suave satisfaction of not having to yell his disagreements over the commotion of his own intestines. Instead, he was able to roll around his vacant mouth and slide through the empty spaces between his teeth phrases of the most tortuous condescension, and on the prongs of a fork that wasn't (on account of its speed through the air) too hot to handle, and wasn't either too heavy to lift, he was able to balance silences of the most awesome gentile judiciousness. If they had bothered to ask him he would even have been able to tell them about the geese — pointing to their flight-path with fingers that bore not a trace of grease or spittle.

While Sefton the born-again *shaygets* was thus wreaking his vengeance and keeping the whole of Holy Christ Hall waiting for its pudding, the Master attempted to introduce a topic of conversation that was general enough to take the mind off starvation while being at the same time literary enough to draw out (without their noticing) the three candidates for the Disraeli Fellowship who weren't, after all, here for their health. He did it lightly, of course, with just a feather-touch of contrivance, so as not to give the impression that anything as gross as an interview was afoot, and he didn't, for the same reason, address his enquiries directly to Ernest Weekley or Gunnar McMurphy or Sefton Hindenburg, but there wasn't one of them who didn't know (even if there *was* one who didn't care) that the time to be clever or honest had come. The particular flower in the garden of conversation upon whose petals Woolfardisworthy gently alighted and into whose trumpet etcetera etcetera, was of the amateur grower's hardy perennial variety: was it any longer fashionable to identify with the characters in literature, as he had once done, was it still permissible to exult in the adventures of the hero and to sigh over the sufferings of the heroine? 'Or have structuralism and feminism put paid to that?' he went on to wonder, elegiacally.

'It's no cause for celebration if they have,' said Ernest Weekley, hungry for bait but fierce in defence of the ordinary Mutenite joys of the ordinary Mutenite reader. 'I don't welcome the professional appropriation of literature. It's perfectly natural that we should become attached to the characters we read about. It's through that attachment that we come to know and feel our humanity.' He employed the words 'we' and 'our' exquisitely, implying an acquaintance with levels of ordinariness that no mere ordinary person — no *ordinary* ordinary person — could ever hope to rival. It wasn't just that he had been to Mykonos and worked for Cadbury's — he had been somewhere for which there were no maps, he had been on some *human* journey, some voyage into *we*-ness, alone but as it were on our behalf. And he had come back more us than we were. 'Of course,' he continued, 'it is silly to suppose that the lives of the characters extend beyond and out of the books in which they appear. We cannot know if Emma will be happy with Mr Knightley. But it is natural that we should ask and wonder. Our interest in what goes on after a book is over is a kind of guarantee of the spaciousness of the author's intelligence. I confess that I often speculate about the future lives of my favourite characters.' He made it sound so thoroughly fair and winning and reasonable that it was impossible to understand why there had ever been any arguments about anything since time began.

Helen Burns, to whom he looked to see if he had caused offence, smiled across at him as who should say, if there is a woman in this room that does not feel the justice of your words then I am glad that I am not she; but she was also letting it be seen that she wasn't going to be easy to impress. Sefton believed he saw her narrowing her eyes like a critic. 'In that case,' she said, inexorable as a juggernaut, 'which character's future do you speculate about most?'

Ernest Weekley scratched his head in imitation of Derek Muten's imitation of the village idiot, and looked around for the hidden detonator in Helen Burns's question. 'I think Elizabeth Bennet's,' he said at last, scanning the room nervously, this time as if he feared his wife, Olympia, was sitting in disguise amongst the undergraduates (which he later marvelled to discover she was). 'I always wonder whether she is ever going to succeed in teaching Darcy how to get a joke. I wonder about Viola in that way, too.'

'I think Viola will do even worse with Darcy than Elizabeth does,' said Sefton Goldberg.

'No, I meant —'

'She's insufficiently self-assertive. That's why she is at best only a near anagram of Olivia — Viola is Olivia with the *I* out. Olivia's *I* is doubled, she has an extra, *me*, she is multi-individuated.' Sefton was enjoying life. When they offer me this job I'll tell them where to put it, he promised himself. 'And that enables her to take more chances. I speak as one who has put his heroine addiction behind him, but I still like a girl who takes her chances.'

'She doesn't take as many as Anna Karenina,' Gunnar McMurphy broke in. He seemed to want to introduce an upset note into the discussion.

'But *she* doesn't have a future for us to speculate about,' said Sefton. He wasn't keen to hear McMurphy on Anna Karenina, he was hoping he might steer him onto Molly Bloom or Connie Chatterley instead. That way there was a chance that he'd treat High Table to one of his fearless recitations. And yes I said yes I will Yes. Or better still, Eh tha's got lovely cunt, Connie. Let the Rev Woolfardisworthy and his starving synod get out of that. 'I thought we were confining ourselves to those who might go anywhere when the book they're in finishes. There's only one way Anna's going. Connie Chatterley now —'

'Anna might have gone in many directions,' Mc-Murphy persisted. He was red-faced, resenting Sefton's lack of feeling, ready to take any slight to Anna Karenina personally, as if she were his sister.

'Yes, but Connie —'

'What destroys her is society — the harpies, the

217

gossip-mongers, that ghoul Karenin.' Sefton admired McMurphy's self-control in keeping Sir Alex Sneddon off that list, but McMurphy was still treating the events of the novel as if they were a family affair. 'If it wasn't for the way she was hounded she would have had a future in the sincerity of her passion for Vronsky.'

At this a little gasp of pain from the Vicar of Wakefield who was sitting on the opposite side of the table to Count Alexei McMurphy. He wasn't a literary expert but he had read the book and surely — 'Surely we cannot simply condone Anna's action in leaving her child and husband.'

Gunnar McMurphy hit the air with his clenched fist. Here was Mrs Grundy again in another of her guises. Sefton watched his old pupil preparing himself for another holy war. If Sefton was going to be able to inveigle him into some serious swearing now was the time. 'I'm inclined to agree with the Vicar myself,' he said, 'but I'm not sure where that leaves me in regard to Molly Bloom and Connie Chatterley.'

McMurphy was promisingly red-faced. Sefton believed he could already hear the rustle of illustrious pudenda. But Ernest Weekley was the fly in the ointment. He was anxious to demonstrate to the fretting country clergyman the higher morality which is art, but he was going to do so with greater clarity and patience than his rivals. 'Tolstoy makes us understand dramatically,' he explained, 'the imperatives of Anna's decision.' He seemed to be anxious, too, to take Anna Karenina away from Gunnar McMurphy, and one of the ways he did this was to pronounce her name and that of her author with a superior show of ethnological know-how — on the principle that linguistic familiarity gave one special rights. 'Whatever our personal views on the sanctity of marriage,' this very slowly for the distressed cleric, 'Tolstoy compels us to acknowledge the intolerable sterility, the impossibility, the *human* impossibility, of Anna's marriage to Karenin.' And for the distressed McMurphy he made Karenin sound as if he had twice as many syllables in his name as Theodorakis and Olympia Weekley put together.

The poor Vicar of Wakefield, though daunted by all these Continental noises, was not prepared to be overwhelmed by all these Continental ideas. 'I still don't see,' he said, 'how that can be any justification for leaving one's child and entering into adulterous relations with a worthless and cynical guards officer.'

That 'adulterous' was coming it a bit thick for some of the speaker's own reverend colleagues let alone for Weekley and McMurphy, but just as it looked as though Gunnar was ready to hurl himself, swearing, through the breach in the wall, Helen Burns decided that the Vicar's 'worthless' and 'cynical' were coming it even thicker for her. The Director of English Studies at Holy Christ Hall didn't voice her objections all at once, but she signalled them with a series of strangled cries and grimaces and muscular spasms. She wound one of her limp curls around her fingers and tried to wrench it out of her scalp, then she pulled a sour face, then she sighed and leaned forward in her chair, then she bit her lip and pulled a sour face again and looked around her, then she caught her breath just as it was about to leave her body forever, and then at last she said, in those tones of tinny domestic exasperation without which, for some women, no conversation would be possible, 'What you need to understand is that there is nothing cheap about Anna. I mean you can't talk about her as if she is a whore or something. It's Karenin that uses and exploits her. He only cares about the look of marriage, what people will say. That's cynicism. Whereas Vronsky, even if he has been amoral, has a vitality which awakens Anna's respect for herself. He isn't just a beautiful animal or something, but he is spontaneous where Karenin was bookish and —' She was becoming more and more exasperated the further she went, but whether it was with her audience, or Karenin, or the limitations of language, or herself, she didn't look as if she knew.

Feeling sorry for her, Sefton Goldberg, that softy in spiv's clothing, bailed her out. He didn't like to see an Australian — even if it was Helen Burns — having difficulties in front of the English. In a similar position he would have done the same for Clive James. 'I'm with Dr Burns on this one,' he said, 'more or less. But I always wonder why *Anna Karenin* is a book that holds so strong a place in us academics' affections, considering that *our* experience of what bored married women get up to is so different from Tolstoy's. And it's not just different, it is the reverse. Who do the Annas that we know run off with? Us! And who are we? Vronsky? Of course not. We are Karenin — bookish, orderly, suspicious of handsome guards officers, dry, vindictive and with sticking-out ears. Vronsky's the one they leave *for* us. The one they come to do degrees to get away from. It's not vitality and spontaneity that bored married ladies are after — vitality and spontaneity are the very qualities they are bored with. Vitality is what takes them to the cricket club when they've an essay on *Anna Karenina* to write; and spontaneity is what gives them a thick ear when they resist. No, what they want is something dark and cerebral and clerkly and donnish — something like us!'

Ernest Weekley had never looked less like any of those things. He was running his hands up and down the front of his shirt, as if on the point of showing Sefton his chest. 'So Tolstoy got it wrong?' he dared Sefton to assert.

'Not so much wrong as lurid. But things were different then. Now she'd go to Girton or a poly, and leave Karenin for Casaubon.'

'Do I understand you to be saying,' the Master of Holy Christ Hall queried, in a rather deliberate manner, as if for the ears of an unseen interview panel, 'that the chief benefit of being an academic, a teacher —?'

Oh well, why not? thought Sefton Goldberg.

'Is that you get to fuck Anna Karenina? Yes,' he said.

He waited for the long silence but there was Gunnar McMurphy with his fists raised in the air and his mouth working. 'And there is no reason to be ashamed to admit it,' he said. His face glowed like a beacon. 'Provided that you fuck her vitally, provided that you fuck a flame into being just as the sun and the earth fuck a flower into being —'

Good on you, thought Sefton Goldberg.

After dinner the Master of Holy Christ Hall led the Fellows and their guests into the Combination Room for wine and further conversation. Sefton found himself sitting next to Helen Burns. Perhaps because he'd agreed with her about Anna Karenina she was being nice to him. Sefton was grateful. He needed some support. There was something dauntingly cathedral about the Combination Room.

An old steward, bent in half, was going round the table pouring port and claret. When he was out of earshot the Master told a moving story about the number of relatives all older and more ailing than himself the steward was supporting off his modest stipend. 'He is a lesson to us all,' the Master concluded, 'in practical humanity.'

'He's practising,' Helen Burns whispered to Sefton.

'What for?'

'For when he's Archbishop of Canterbury.'

'You're joking.'

'No I'm not,' said Dr Burns. 'He's widely tipped as the next one. It's a near certainty.' She had a strange look on her face, as if she'd won a bet herself.

An appalling thought crossed Sefton Goldberg's mind. Surely not. Not even Helen Burns, surely. As if to help him dispel it he reached for the glass on the table before him. Helen Burns laid a restraining hand on his thigh, under the table.

'Don't,' she whispered. 'You mustn't drink yet, there's a little ritual.'

Ritual? Sefton stared at his claret. It was thick and deep red like the blood of you-know-who. 'What kind of ritual?'

'It's nothing. Just a toast.'

'I'm frightened,' Sefton murmured. 'Hold on to me.'

Helen Burns moved her hand from Sefton's thigh to his member and gripped it. Sefton felt that altogether too much had been made of the enigma of her allure.

At the top of the table Professor the Right Reverend Sir Evelyn Woolfardisworthy stirred in his seat and lifted his glass. 'Church and Queen!' he intoned, as if from the pulpit.

Sefton gulped. 'Hold me tighter,' he whispered.

'Only if you say it.'

Sefton raised his glass. 'Church and Queen!' he said, huskily.

13

With the exception of a period of some two or three minutes during which he suffered from the delusion that he was staring at Walter Sickert Fledwhite's double on the opposite platform at Peterborough, Sefton's general condition, on his journey back to Wrottesley, was (all things considered) remarkably sound. He had risen early in his poky room at Holy Christ Hall, disturbed by the rattling chest of some lonely tubercular don, and had foregone a bath, a college breakfast, and a friendly chat about nig-nogs in the porter's lodge, in favour of a quick get-away. He was in that calm state of mind when a man understands the vanities of his ambitions and is satisfied that he has his health, a few basic comforts, and his friends.

Back in his room at the Polytechnic he was only too pleased to perform his usual duties for Nick Lee. He shook out Nick's jacket and found another position for it over his chair. Then he removed his umbrella from the waste-paper basket and took it down to the washroom and held it under the tap. Then he cast an eye over Nick's desk, as he always did, to make sure that no record of Nick's last visit remained — no newspaper announcing the dropping of an atomic bomb on Hiroshima, no one-penny tram ticket or first edition of *Lucky Jim*. But as ever the desk spoke only of a fanatical conscientiousness: essays dated the following week were covered in red ink and students wanting help were referred to critical works so recent that they were still in the hands of the printers.

On his own desk was a pamphlet, indubitably from Fledwhite, on the real meaning of Zionism, and a brief note from Peter Potter reminding him of tomorrow night's party and Cora Peck's lift. Peter also included a map of how to get to his cottage, in case Sefton had forgotten. Sefton knew that Peter knew that Sefton hadn't forgotten; he had simply produced the map and its accompanying instructions in order that he might write 'Turn left under the disused railway bridge' and 'Ignore the double-fronted farmhouse on the corner' and 'After fording the brook remember to test brakes', and so drive Sefton to distraction. Calmly philosophical as Sefton still was, and unshaken in his determination to be relaxed about the present because it was only the broad path to his future, he could not, when it came to Peter Potter, bear free and patient thoughts. It was only when he remembered that Miranda Potter got tipsy easily and flushed when he paid her compliments, thereby reducing Peter to a wrung-out rag of shame and jealousy, that Sefton was able to envisage enjoying himself at the party.

That didn't stop him though, when he ran into Jacqueline on the steps of the Polytechnic, from asking her if she'd like to go to Peter's with him. It had never occurred to Sefton to be seen with Jacqueline in public, but she looked so blooming after her day of lending large-print books to child-molesters in the public library and she towered so spectacularly over Sefton even though he was standing on a higher step, that the invitation popped unbidden from his mouth. Nonetheless, he was not entirely unrelieved when she explained, with a slight colouring of the cheeks which he took for modesty at war with yearning, that she was already going out on Friday night. He respected her discretion; and what was the point anyway, for him, of carting coals to Newcastle? He watched in admiration as Jacqueline clicked away from him in her Italian boots, her matching shoulder-bag slung low on her hips. But his mind was on Miranda Potter.

'No Wally Fledwhite then?'

Cora had invited Sefton into her apartment while she put the finishing touches to her appearance. She was going as a parachutist tonight and she still had some buckles to fasten and some rip-cords to pull. Sefton wasn't heart-broken about there being no Wally; it meant that he and Cora might park the car under the disused railway bridge and test the brakes, perhaps even practise soft landings, together.

'Well actually,' said Cora, adjusting the tilt on her red beret, 'he's been out of town for a couple of days. I said we'd pick him up at the station on our way out. He's due in about eight? Do you mind?'

'Not in the slightest,' Sefton lied. But he felt suddenly queasy. 'Funny,' he said, 'I was out of town myself yesterday and I thought I saw the living double of Walter on Peterborough station.'

'What time was that?'

'I suppose early afternoon.'

'That would have been right, he was on his way to —'

'Don't tell me,' said Sefton. 'Cambridge.'

'That's right. How did you know? He was going for —'

'Don't tell me,' said Sefton, 'A job.'

'Yes. Did he mention it to you? At —'

'No, but don't tell me — Holy Christ Hall.'

Cora was amazed. 'Do you know someone there?'

'Yes, I know a few people,' said Sefton. He wasn't going to give Cora the satisfaction of telling her that he'd just been there himself. That would come out the minute Fledwhite arrived back from Cambridge, asking Cora to guess which common friend of theirs, not so very far from here, had been out on an earlier shift. Until then it could remain a secret. Who knows? — Fledwhite might have had an accident or got lost. Sefton wasn't certain how good homosexuals were at taking care of themselves. He might have accepted a lift from a stranger.

'I hope he gets it,' Cora continued. 'Then he'd be near

me when I move to London. Do you think he might get it?'

Sefton pondered. 'Isn't he a structuralist?' he asked.

Cora gave a little sigh. She knew that Sefton disapproved of structuralists without ever bothering to find out what they did. 'Would that make any difference?'

Sefton recalled Woolfardisworthy's innocent old-fashioned amateur ordinary reader's question: was structuralism interfering with all the innocent old-fashioned amateur ordinary reader's pleasures? Yes, yes, they had all said, not only because they believed it but because they believed they were expected to believe it. Wasn't High Table an old-fashioned amateur reader's Haven? Fools! Down had gone the baited hook and up they had leapt. 'Yes,' said Sefton, 'I guess it would make a difference.'

'Well he's a *post*-structuralist,' said Cora.

Sefton thought about Woolfardisworthy's hard professional handsomeness and Helen Burns' rabid opportunism, her weakness for the latest thing. 'In that case,' he said, 'he's got it all right.' And it didn't cost him too much to say it, so pleased was he that Ernest Weekley had been balked.

Fledwhite was waiting for them outside the station when they drove up, a long woollen scarf around his throat, the sole of his right foot pressed against his left shin, his hands thrust deep into his duffle-coat pockets, his piqued face raised expectantly. He looked posed and stylish, but in the comic mode, as if he were the star of *Carry On Nijinski*. When he saw Cora he ran towards her on points, waving his arms in the air. They embraced like an unfancied doubles pair who had just lifted the women's title at Wimbledon, while Sefton sat at the wheel of his car, a bit left out of things, like the husband of one of the beaten finalists.

And they didn't make very many more efforts to include him once the journey to Peter's got under way.

For himself, personally, Sefton wasn't over-concerned, but on behalf of the principle of the thing he was displeased; they oughtn't to have sat in the back seat together and left him no one to talk to. That was at the very least a breach of automobile etiquette. And he didn't like, either, the way they fiddled and fidgeted with one another, squealing at private jokes and trying to find old sweets in one another's pockets. Sefton wouldn't have minded so much had all this been a prelude to grander and more reckless liberties — he might even have parked his car beneath the disused railway bridge and left them to it for a bit — but it was perfectly clear that Cora Peck's and Wally Fledwhite's interest in one another stopped at a stylized guilelessness. Sefton hated asexuality at the best of times. But especially he hated it when it was artful.

Almost as if he had read Sefton's thoughts, Walter Fledwhite put his hands back into his own pockets and began to boast to Cora about some recent conquest. Sefton kept his eyes firmly on the road in front of him, but the little hairs on the back of his neck rose and quivered. He was unable to discover whether Fledwhite was describing what had happened the previous evening at Cambridge or whether it involved anyone Sefton knew. It might have been Woolfardisworthy or McMurphy or simply some visiting naval rating, for all Sefton could make out. But it wasn't the who that mattered. It was the how. Whoever it was was new to it, that was the point. Fledwhite had initiated him, plucked him fresh from the tree, and taught him everything he knew. And how did he take to it? Cora must have asked, because Fledwhite let out a wild laugh and replied, without shame or remorse, 'Like a duck to water!' Sefton felt his foot slacken on the accelerator. If they'd been near a police station he would have thought about stopping his car. He couldn't recall having ever heard a less pleasing description. Men crowed over women, but never like that. For what Fledwhite's words implied was not simply initiation — it was

227

enrolment! Fledwhite hadn't just had his way, he'd made another convert. Sefton thought again about stopping his car.

But already they were driving up Peter's gravel path. As he pulled up his hand-brake, Sefton realised that whatever else Fledwhite had been knowing about he had not been knowing about Holy Christ Hall. It was impossible to imagine that Woolfardisworthy and Helen Burns and the porter had all been too discreet to mention that someone else from the Polytechnic at Wrottesley had been there the previous night. In which case the discretion was all Fledwhite's. Sefton didn't like it. He didn't want to be beholden to a post-structuralist poofter who had just landed a plum job. But he was determined to be fair; Fledwhite might have disgusting personal habits but he was a good bloke to entrust with a secret.

So was Peter Potter, it seemed, to Sefton's surprise. He welcomed them in his front vegetable garden with sealed lips. He was looking spry and hostly but at the same time intangible and abstract like Rupert Birkin. He wore a blue polo-neck shirt over green trousers. On his feet he wore slippers or moccasins which Miranda had woven out of bean pods and leek leaves. He looked appalled to see Cora Peck and Walter Fledwhite. He seemed to have no recollection that he'd invited Cora as one of the guests of honour, and he shied from Fledwhite as from someone who could read the secrets of his soul. But he joked with them about the journey and Sefton's driving, and took their coats, and brought them beer he brewed himself. When he had the opportunity he took Sefton aside and asked him, 'Well?'

Sefton shrugged.

'No luck?'

Sefton shrugged again.

'Is that for certain, or are you being pessimistic?' Peter wanted to be absolutely sure that he could relax and enjoy his own party.

'It's for certain.'

Peter suddenly looked a lot younger. Less like Rupert Birkin, more like the lad Tom Brangwen. 'We'll keep the champagne corked, then,' he said.

'There's still Cora to celebrate,' Sefton reminded him. 'And that Fledwhite deserves a toast — he's just been given the job I went for.'

Peter put a few years back on again. Sefton was the person he most didn't want to get a good job, but that didn't mean he was pleased when someone else got one. His relation to success was a bit like Sefton's to applause: they both believed there was only so much to go round. So he said, 'I think we might just give that one a miss.'

'Suit yourself,' said Sefton. 'I just thought if you were searching for someone to crack the champagne for —'

'— then here are the very people,' Peter interrupted him, for there indeed, approaching them arm in arm, were Charles Wenlock and Val Peel.

Charles was always a lavish guest. He brought bottles of mead and Beaujolais and local cheeses and chocolates. In the days when he was accompanied by his wife (which were not so long ago) he would also bring Joyce's home-made lemon meringue pies and wonderfully unsubtle cheese-cakes; but now he and Val Peel carried sprays of wild flowers, gathered, there could be absolutely no doubt, from within the environs of their caravan. Sefton could see that Charles Wenlock believed that his life had already improved; it wasn't just the flowers — he was being dressed by someone who preferred him bohemian and who dressed herself, at least for parties, like Tess of the D'Urbervilles. Joyce Wenlock used to come in pale blue slacks under a chiffon blouse, bearing cakes. And she would talk about the weather or the news. Val Peel was bristling with conversation about the theatre and the opera and fabrics and pots. Clearly Charles felt that this was more like what he had always wanted his life to be. But he could expect no sympathetic understanding of what he had done from Peter Potter. Peter didn't believe that people had the right to change their lives when it suited them. He didn't approve of voluptuaries. All his sympathies were with Joyce. He couldn't even bring himself to look at Val Peel. So once he'd swapped their coats and their bottles and their flowers for a couple of glasses of home-brew, he left them to Sefton.

'Well,' said Charles, delighted with the effect he was having (he would have loved to be banned from every decent house in Christendom), 'he isn't being very friendly, is he?'

'You know Peter,' said Sefton. He had to be very careful. The loving pair seemed to be inviting him, a privileged guest, to warm himself at their glow. They wanted an Enobarbus.

'I suppose we must expect a bit of this,' said Charles. And then because Sefton had not realised it was a question he added, 'Mustn't we?'

'People are slow to accept changes,' Sefton ventured. He hoped that kept the question of his own speed of acceptance fairly open. It ought to have been clear to the couple that he too was having trouble meeting Val Peel's eyes. It was only the week before that she'd cried and reported him. And she was still his student as well as being his head of department's Cleopatra. Even if he had been prepared to offer them his blessing he still needed time to get used to her dual role. You couldn't scrawl all over somebody's essay in the morning (not that he had! not that he had!) and offer her peanuts, deferentially, at night. Not without a bit of practice.

But the Wenlocks, or rather Charles and Val, were pressing. They wanted to know where they were with everyone. And they wanted to know now.

Val looked at Charles. 'I think Mr Goldberg is trying to tell us that he too isn't friendly,' she said. She was very sensitive.

Sefton felt Charles Wenlock's searching eyes upon

him. He knew that if he left it much longer Charles' lips would compress and then disappear, as would their friendship. And for what? For Joyce Wenlock whom he would probably never ever see again? For the idea that Charles might have done better, when it was perfectly obvious that Charles believed he was already *doing* better? For the sake of his own integrity — his right not to approve couples if he didn't want to, his right not even to approve couples at all? Feh! 'What's with the Mr Goldberg?' he asked, looking Val Peel full in the face. 'Call me Sefton.'

'Sefton!'
  'Miranda!'
  'How are you?'
  'How are *you*?'
  'Hot.'
She was too. She was hot because the cottage was full of people. She was hot because she was busy being the hostess. She was hot because of the burning properties of her husband's eyes which had not left her since they had seen her wheeling her bicycle a half-a-dozen years before. She was hot because she was always hot. But above all, Sefton liked to think, she was hot because she was talking to him.

'Hot!' He looked around to see if anyone was listening or watching. Only Peter. Good. 'Then perhaps you need a stroll around the garden to cool you down.'

Miranda Potter threw back her head. Then she removed her thicklensed spectacles and wiped her eyes. 'Now that,' she laughed, 'would only make me hotter.' Impossible. Her neck was already furious with blotches. The freckles on her bare legs and shoulders were in a frenzy of irritation.

Sefton had a soft spot for anyone who had so few lines of physical defence. She wasn't what *he* would have chosen for a wife; she was too perpendicular and boyish and dedicated to the household arts. But she had some wickedness left in her still, a little corner of florid vulgarity which Peter Potter had not been able to get at and destroy. Yet.

'I was thinking of a very slow stroll,' Sefton pursued. 'Stopping from time to time to inspect the asparagus and the zucchini Peter has told me so much about.'

'Zucchini? What's zucchini?'

'Courgettes.' From the opposite side of the room where he was pretending to be taking no notice Peter tossed in that answer to his wife's question. He wasn't interested in the conversation or anything, he just happened to overhear her query and he just happened to be able to help her out with it.

'Zucchini? I've never heard them called that before.'

'Never mind what they're called,' said Sefton, and he looked at her hard, down the steep slopes of his fleshy nose. 'Don't you think we ought to see how they're getting along?'

'You won't find any,' said Miranda, in flames. 'They're all in the pan cooking. Which reminds me — I'd better check that they're not boiling over.' And she was gone into the kitchen from which, before it was renovated, the women had looked out to where men moved dominant and creative. And into which her own man now followed her, his blood flowing heavy.

Sefton wandered about the house in search of someone to talk to and something that wasn't home-made to drink. Cora and Fledwhite, who had been separated for the last half-hour — Cora being engaged in girl-talk with Val Peel while Charles Wenlock stood aside, full of pride that he should be with a woman that someone as modern as Cora Peck wanted to exchange dark confidences with, and Fledwhite standing alone in corners, surveying the comforts of the cottage with the eye of a bomber — Cora and Fledwhite were now together again, dancing to Peter's Beatles records. They danced with the abandon of people who wanted to subvert society. Fledwhite's high kicks were aimed at the State's crumbling facade, and Cora's spinning breasts threatened the stability of the family. Under the cover of music they mouthed phrases which might have been the names and addresses of targets, and they shook their shoulders at one another in a manner which was somehow insulting to everybody else, as if they were flicking the pages of private but incriminating diaries. But they were still not as abandoned as Arthur Twinbarrow who didn't want to subvert anything. Unless it was his marriage. Arthur's cowed wife sat with a death-mask grin on her face while her husband threw one of Miranda's neighbours high in the air and low through his legs. White haired and skeletal (through self-sacrifice) and dressed in an old serge suit, he seemed possessed of demonic energy. Sefton hated all forms of dancing and believed that the most dignified attitude the human body could assume was bent in half in a chair with a glass in its hand. But he was especially shocked by Arthur's movements. They struck him as tasteless and eerie. It was as if a polio victim had suddenly leapt from his chair and begun to perform a striptease. Watching him watching, Arthur beckoned him over. Sefton dropped his head like a wallflower, but things were hotting up — Charles and Val were now on the floor and looking dionysiac. Sefton knew his own limits and left them to it.

So he was altogether delighted to discover Nick Lee, flown in from God knows where, pouring himself a drink. Sefton couldn't remember when he'd last seen him.

'Nick! When did you get here?'

Nick was always very casual. 'Hello matey. I've been here about five minutes.'

'Well, where have you been?'

Nick looked puzzled. Everybody knew where he'd been; he'd been in his room at the Polytechnic, hadn't he? Never left it. Oh, except for a quick trip to the States. But he'd seen Sefton since then, hadn't he? 'Haven't I seen you since then?'

'Since when?'

'Since I popped over to New York for a couple of days.'

'No, but tell me about it.' Sefton estimated that he hadn't seen Nick for close to two months, but that wasn't worth calling a bloke a liar for. 'What did you do? Have you had a good time?'

Nick Lee shrugged his shoulders. What could you do in a couple of days, stolen out of a hectic timetable? On the other hand he knew he'd been lucky to have that. 'Yeah, it was nice. Hopefully I'll go again.'

Hopefully was the least of his crimes. He also said feedback when he meant reply, and grass roots when he meant students, and catalyst when he meant cause, and existential when he meant to do with life. And when he wasn't ending his words improperly in -fully he was compounding them ambiguously with -some, as in:-

'So where did you stay? With friends?'

'Yeah, but not the wholesome time. I stayed in a hotel one night.'

'Good?'

'Not bad, but overcrowded. Too fulsome.'

'Ah well,' said Sefton sympathetically. 'You win some, you lose some.'

Nick Lee stared at him for a second or two. Giving Sefton time to notice how healthy he was looking. He was about Sefton's age, but he could have passed for younger. He was thoroughly at home in the world and most of the time he was even happy in it, but his chief interest, apart from food and exercise and international travel, was the literature of alienation and despair. When he did call into the Polytechnic he would lecture his students on the Power of Blackness, shining with good health and using all the wrong words.

'Guess who I met while I was over there?' he challenged Sefton.

Sefton pondered. 'Edgar Allan Poe.'

'No, but close.'

'Melville?'

'No.'

234

'I give in.'

'You haven't said Hawthorne.'

'Hawthorne?'

'No.'

'Tell me.'

'Kurt Vonnegut.'

Sefton was impressed. He'd never read any Kurt Vonnegut, but he was prepared to bet that he had the edge on Ernest Weekley and Cora Peck. 'What was he like?' he asked.

Nick Lee's face lit up. He wasn't envious or vengeful the way Peter Potter was and Sefton used to be. 'A riot,' he said.

Sefton wondered if they'd gone on the town together, drinking all night and discussing the literature of despair until the early hours. It upset him just thinking about it. A riot, eh? Who would ever say that about him? He was suddenly and unaccountably in competition with Vonnegut.

'He's a terrific bloke,' Nick Lee continued. 'He's done everything.'

'And did you talk?'

'We never stopped. We had long fulsome chats. I tried to persuade him to come and lecture at the Poly.'

'And is he coming?' Already Sefton was preparing devastating points to make after Vonnegut's lecture, devising ways of proving to the assembled students that he, Sefton, was as quick as their visitor, and more amusing.

'He might. He said he'd write to me.'

'Who's this that's going to write to you?' Peter Potter and Miranda had come up, being good hosts. And Cora and Fledwhite were arriving, puffing and blowing, also.

Nick Lee was pleased to have a circle to address. 'Kurt Vonnegut.'

'He might be coming to the Poly,' Sefton threw in, in the hope of poisoning all Peter Potter's future peace of mind.

235

'That would be good,' said Miranda.

Peter Potter narrowed his eyes. In their reflection Sefton could see Miranda cycling off with the famous novelist. 'Writers don't always make good teachers,' Peter said.

'Here we go,' said Cora Peck.

Wally Fledwhite was poking holes in the air with his fingers. '*Teachers* don't always make good teachers,' he said.

Cora nodded.

'And they very rarely make good writers,' she said.

Fledwhite nodded.

Peter shrugged his shoulders and showed the palms of his hands. 'Let him come,' he conceded, comically. He didn't care. It didn't matter one way or another to him. He wasn't going to make Vonnegut sweat. 'Let him come.'

'It's not fixed yet,' Nick Lee reminded them.

'Anyway, you like him, Peter,' said Miranda — but gingerly, for she didn't want to give away anything she shouldn't. 'We both enjoyed *Slaughter-house-Five*.' And then, in case they hadn't, she added, 'Didn't we?'

'I like it when married people enjoy the same books,' said Sefton.

Miranda showed him her tongue. It wasn't much, but it was a beginning.

'Yes, we liked it,' Peter agreed. He very much wanted to be light. If Sefton and Cora and Fledwhite could be dead on his carpet, and he could be easy and frothy and light, he would have pretty well everything he wanted. 'We liked it, but I'm not sure what I think about this wang business.'

Sefton was bemused. 'Wang?'

Cora came to his rescue. She was in fact a Vonnegut fan, though she thought he squandered his genius. 'Billy Pilgrim's wang,' she explained.

'Who's Billy Pilgrim?'

'The hero of *Slaughterhouse-Five* —'

'The *anti*-hero,' Nick Lee corrected.

'Well, whatever he is, he's got this tremendous wang.'

'I see,' said Sefton, though he wasn't sure that he approved of novels which proffered this kind of information about their characters. It wasn't necessary for one to know the size of Mr Knightley's wang for example, or Mr Rochester's. But he didn't register his disapproval. After all, this conversation had begun with Peter Potter registering his. He simply said, 'The only Wang I know is the Chinese servant in *Victory*.'

'Different kind of wang,' Fledwhite assured him, with a little squeal. Suddenly he was enjoying the party.

Sefton looked in the direction of Miranda. She would have been enjoying the party too, had she dared.

'So tell us what it is you're not sure about,' Cora Peck demanded. She wanted to catch Peter being moralistic.

'I'm not sure that I'm *not sure* about anything, it's —'

'But that's what you said,' Cora persisted.

'I'm just a bit bothered by these wangs and willies,' said Peter, mystifyingly.

Fledwhite was jumping up and down. 'We're all worried about those,' he laughed.

'Oh, I'm not bothered in *that* way,' Peter Potter assured him.

Cora closed in for the kill. 'Which way *are* you bothered then, Peter?' she asked.

But Sefton did not give Peter time to reply. It was altogether too good an opportunity to miss. 'I'm surprised to hear *you* asking *that*, Cora,' he said. 'Didn't you once mention that you'd made a bit of study of willies and wangs? Surely you discovered then how badly served the English have been, wang-wise. Why else are they so uncomfortable with black men and Jews? I'm assuming,' he continued, looking around him and smiling warmly at Fledwhite, 'that you all know about Jews?'

And it was Fledwhite who took him up on it. 'I know

that they're unusually phallically centred,' he said. He had stopped squealing and jumping about. 'I know that their culture has educated them to attach exaggerated erotogenic significance to the penis.'

Sefton couldn't believe his ears. 'So if the penis had been left to its own devices it would have been erotogenically neutral, like the windpipe?'

'No, that's not what I mean.' Fledwhite was scornful; he had heard all the obvious objections before. 'There are many other erogenic zones which cultures, for their own purposes, choose to ignore or devalue.'

The whole room brooded for a moment over alternative zones, giving Peter the opportunity to get in a word. It was only a query. 'For their own purposes?' he repeated.

Sefton helped him out 'You know the sort of thing, Peter; brutal patriarchal hegemony — all that.'

'There *is* such a thing,' Walter Fledwhite and Cora Peck said together. But Walter said it with more passion. Cora looked the sort of girl who actually liked her father and called him daddy. Patriarchal hegemony was only a phrase for her, a contemporary tic; whereas for Walter Sickert Fledwhite it was life and death.

Sefton thought about Wally's badges and pamphlets and branch meetings and felt suddenly brutal himself. 'So that's it,' he snarled. 'So that's the reason you march and demonstrate and preach and proselytize and leave your bits of propaganda, like little piles of territorial droppings, on people's desks. Because you don't like your old man — I intend the pun, Walter — the planet must quake.' And so saying he swung from the room, propelled by the protuberances his culture had taught him to exaggerate.

He was in a dangerous mood. He prowled the party, drinking more and more of Miranda's daisy wine, looking for trouble. The men — his rivals — were where he like them, their backs up against the walls, looking tired and nervous and gentile, talking quietly; and the women were *how* he liked them — plain and badly dressed and jumpy and mental and ready to pay the highest of tributes to his maleness by trying to scream it down. The thought that he might at any moment make a wild gift of himself to the plainest screamer present, submit to inexpert and badly painted fingers, quaff that old heady brew of scorn and ineptitude and apology and gratitude, caused him to throb to the furthest extremities of his person. He went in search of Miranda or Arthur Twinbarrow's neglected wife; but he only found Cora, squatting in a corner, rooting through Peter's Beatles records, looking for something more modern.

'I'm ready to stop fighting you,' he told her. 'I'm yours to do what you like with. Fledwhite can watch.'

Cora kept her head down and continued her vain search through Peter's records. 'Don't tangle with Wally,' she warned him.

And Sefton would have asked her to explain what she meant had an unexpected visitor not caused a disturbance. Little gasps of surprise were going off by the front-door and in the hall, followed by eerie silences. The whole party had gone mute by the time Sefton became aware that the visitor was Gerald Sidewinder and that the object of his visit was him — Sefton Goldberg!

'I wonder if we might talk?' said Sidewinder. And before Sefton was able to recover from the shock and frame a sentence of his own, he realised that Sidewinder's dead hand was on his shoulder, leading him out into the Potters' vegetable garden and God knows where else.

14

'Well?' They were all curious but Charles Wenlock was especially pressing when Sefton returned, ten minutes later, alone but alive.

'He just dropped out of the sky,' Sefton told them.

'That's not how I'd describe where he comes from,' said Charles Wenlock, 'but what did he say?'

'That *is* what he said. I'm quoting. Verbatim. "He just dropped out of the sky." '

'Who did, Sefton?'

'Kevin Dainty.'

Miranda wanted to know who Kevin Dainty was, and Peter explained to her, in a low voice, that he was the captain of Wrottesley Ramblers, a popular novelist, and figured significantly in Sidewinder's plans.

'Significantly!' Charles Wenlock sneered. 'He's the b****** linch-pin.'

'Not any more,' Sefton assured him. 'He just dropped out of the sky.'

'I think Sefton is speaking in the language of archetype and myth,' Nick Lee cheerfully suggested.

'No I'm not. I'm speaking in the ordinary language of human event. Gerald Sidewinder and Kevin Dainty go hang-gliding together. They were out this morning in Derbyshire. These things happen.'

The light of understanding flickered in Charles Wenlock's eyes. The colour rose in his cheeks. 'Was it from a great height?' he asked.

'High enough,' Sefton affirmed. 'Sidewinder is very distressed. Apparently they were very close friends.'

'So it's all over?' Charles was ready to return to the dance floor and kick up his heels. But he wanted to be certain he'd understood things correctly.

'Well, I suppose there'll have to be an inquest.'

'No, I meant the twinning. I take it it's now shelved.'

Sefton sighed. It wasn't his fault. He'd tried not to get them too excited. 'On the contrary,' he said. 'It's being speeded up. That's why Sidewinder came round. There's to be a joint memorial service tomorrow, at the ground. The Ramblers are playing East Ham — that's Kevin's old club. Sidewinder — and I'm quoting again, Charles — thinks it's a perfect scenario.'

Nobody else did. Cora and Fledwhite sat mumbling to one another on cushions. Arthur Twinbarrow walked out of the room. Val Peel and Miranda stroked the arms of their men.

'So why did Sidewinder come to seek *you* out?' Charles Wenlock wanted to know.

Sefton Goldberg tried not to look shifty. 'Well I'm the novel man, aren't I?'

But Charles Wenlock was remorseless. 'What's that got to do with anything?' he demanded.

Sefton took a deep breath. 'He wants me to make a little speech tomorrow. You know, just say a few words.'

'On behalf of the department?'

'I think the Polytechnic as a whole.'

'About his creative gifts and how much we will miss them?'

'That sort of thing.'

'And have you agreed to do it?'

The room was suddenly very quiet. Even Miranda seemed to be preparing him a reproachful look.

'Well I couldn't very well refuse could I, Charles? The bloke has only this morning dropped out of the sky.' He was certainly not going to repeat to them what Sidewinder had told him about the numbers of mourning fans who would be coming, and the numbers of pressmen and dignitaries and television cameras. He

241

wasn't going to mention that at this very moment he was listening to the applause thundering around the corrugated roofs of the football stands. But he was upset that they'd all turned so surly on him. He didn't want them to think that he'd gone over to Sidewinder. So he let them into a secret. 'One thing I found out that will amuse you,' he told them. 'Sidewinder sees himself as a bit of a poet. He's composed something that he intends to read out tomorrow. Guess what it's called?'

But none of his friends were now talking to him. Only Nick Lee had a shot at an answer and he of course got it right.

'Icarus,' he said.

Neither Cora Peck nor Walter Sickert Fledwhite had a word to say on the journey back. They were both in such bad spirits that they could not even tolerate the proximity of one another. Cora sat in the front and stared fixedly at her own lap; Fledwhite slouched in the back, exaggerating the extent to which Sefton's sharp cornering was throwing him around. His scarf was wound around his ears so that he didn't have to listen to Sefton's whistling. He seemed to have been more put out than anyone by the evening's events. Regarding his closed up face through his driving mirror, Sefton recalled that such an expression, combining superciliousness, squeamishness and fear, was the very one that he and his book-reading friends at Cambridge used to wear whenever a rower or a rugby-player — hearties, as they were called — entered the room. Fledwhite had now decided, after Sidewinder's visit, that he, Sefton Goldberg, was a hearty, and not just an eccentric solitary hearty either, but one in direct touch and contact with hearties everywhere. The charge of conspiracy was unmistakable in the one thing he did say as Sefton let him out at Cora Peck's.

'What puzzles me is how Sidewinder knew where to find you.'

'You'll work it out,' Sefton reassured him, before driving off.

But he never would. For who was going to tell him that Sefton's own curiosity on that score had been painfully satisfied once and for all, during his stroll through the vegetables with Sidewinder, when he saw that there was a passenger in Sidewinder's canary yellow Volvo who wasn't Mrs Sidewinder or even Miss or Ms Sidewinder, but Jacqueline — Jackie Jacqueline — careful not to catch Sefton's eye but otherwise quite comfortable and at home in Sidewinder's front seat, looking at her reflection in the windscreen and sharpening her teeth with her tongue?

It was all exactly what Sefton had ever imagined, only louder. And therefore better. The hymn singing had been going on for an hour, growing in mournfulness and melancholy as the spectators swarmed into the ground. By the time Sefton emerged from the players' tunnel, flanked by Sidewinder and the Director, both wearing dark suits and black arm-bands, the stadium was full and vibrating to the deep bass swell of some unbearable dirge. Sefton had no resistances to sounds of this kind. It seemed to him that the whole populous universe was here, brought into mystic union by the power of song and grief, and the only thing left out was him. The anguish of his isolation added to the solemn grandeur of the music and the solemn grandeur of the music increased the anguish of his isolation.

He was a castaway, bereft of home and hope and friends, washed to the furthest edges of the world, as retentive of the roars around him as a shell.

It was only when he was able to distinguish the individual brute from the angelic abstraction of the crowd that any feeling and purpose returned to his transported limbs. He discerned heavy rounded shapes cut out of leather. He made out faint lines of down on drooping lips, rings and studs in dirty ears, and orange hair. He saw the baffled resentfulness settled, ready for another hundred years, on the faces of the midlanders, and on the southerners the finer lines of foxy cunning and connivance. And then he felt all right again. His notes were still there, yes, in his jacket pocket. And his copy of *Scoring* was still in his right hand, dozens of strips of newspaper sticking out from its pages to mark the spots where Kevin Dainty had either perpetrated the gravest of all civilized crimes and written badly, or performed the greatest of all services to mankind and written well — according to whichever way Sefton decided to play it.

He waited in the middle of the pitch, between Sidewinder and the Director, for 'Abide with Me' to finish. Sidewinder wore a dark striped suit over a striped shirt. The Director had his best pit trousers hitched high above his shining boots. It would have surprised no one had they been tied with string beneath his baggy waistcoat. Sefton wore the white blazer braided with pale blue which he had been awarded for playing darts for Cambridge against Oxford, fifteen years before. It was only a half-blue blazer, darts being — thanks to Oxford and Cambridge snobbery — only a half-blue sport; and it was a bit skimpy now that Sefton was filling out with the assurances of middle-age; but it was the only vaguely athletic garment he possessed (he didn't even own an Adidas bag) and he didn't want to appear out of place. If anyone asked him what the initials C.U.D.C. stood for, embroidered on his breast pocket, he would tell them Cambridge University Decathlon Club. That would show his bond with the deceased athlete, or alternatively that he was not against him because he was against the body.

After 'Abide With Me' the East Ham supporters crooned 'I'm Forever Blowing Bubbles', revealing layers of plausibly misty melancholy in it which Sefton never knew it possessed. Then the local fans, the chief mourners as it were, replied with 'Sailing' and a medley of punk songs unknown to anyone born before 1970. Punk had taken root quickly and easily in Wrottesley.

Its baffled embryonic grumpiness suited the local temper. The Wrottesley young were able to rattle the sullen music through congested noses and they could arrange and rearrange the simple phrases of complaint as if they were spelling blocks, balancing them on the very surface of their lips, which was as near as anyone born in the Midlands was prepared to let language come to him. Their querimony over, they listened, fairly patiently at first, to the reminiscences and tributes. The Club Chairman spoke, and then the Mayor, and then the managers of the two teams — one a London gangster in a complicated raincoat and dark glasses, the other full of northern fussiness and morality, like a haberdasher. Thereafter the populace became a trifle fretful. It was not held irresistibly by the Director's account of what Kevin Dainty's involvement with the Polytechnic had done for Polytechnic recruitment, nor did it seem to care that Kevin Dainty had been a shining example to them all of modular man. Gerald Sidewinder had more presence but his Icarus was a long time falling. The forty thousand fans had listened to enough. They had even sung and mourned enough. They were in the mood for football now. So when Sefton climbed on to the makeshift rostrum and adjusted the height of the microphone and coughed three times and gazed into the television cameras, they were as restive and as hostile as he could have wanted them. Not least because this umpteenth speaker, whoever he was, showed them an extravagantly swooping profile and wore a white blazer braided with pale blue over a white and pale blue cravat.

Jokes and jeers and catcalls greeted him from around the ground. 'Who does he think he is?' the Wrottesley supporters amused themselves with asking and 'Anyone for tennis?' enquired the fans from Ham. 'Wanker!' noticed the home crowd, and 'Nancy boy!' opined the away. 'Off! Off! Off!' they chanted together, and some of them shook their fists at him and some of them gave him V-signs and some of them crooked their little fingers, in parody, he supposed, of the mass detumescence of which he was the cause. All in all he couldn't really have hoped for a more responsive reception. They were going to be as easy to entertain as he'd always suspected. In a moment, once he opened his mouth, they would be silent, laughing only when he made them laugh, cheering only when he told them to cheer. He felt in excellent condition. His heart was pumping blood of the highest quality at just the right speed wherever it was needed. The passages of his throat were clear and smooth and sweet. He was all past and all future, aware of himself yet detached, massively confident but watchful and expectant, like God on the evening of the sixth day.

All that remained was for him to decide whether he had come to praise Kevin Dainty or to bury him. For himself it was all one; only the performance mattered, only the applause. But there were others out there in the crowd whose fears Sefton could assuage, whose hopes it was in his power to dash. From where he stood he could see the members of his department huddled disconsolately, the last remnants of a once proud force, waiting for Sefton to say one thing in favour of Kevin Dainty and thus destroy them for ever. To the left of him stood Gerald Sidewinder, his dreams of a global polytechnic still undimmed by the tragic plummet of his friend, impatient to have it said once and for all that what was popular was good. 'Ladies and gentlemen,' Sefton declaimed, lampooning declamation, but as he rose on his feet he caught sight of Charles Wenlock — Charles Wenlock who was not supposed to be here but who had come in disguise, like a bikey — trapped in a crowd of Wrottesley thugs. They had leather fringes on their jackets and short spiky hair and chains around their shoulders and metallic jewellery in their noses — as did, very nearly, Charles Wenlock. He sat between them in his bizarre borrowed costume, red faced and tight lipped. The little tufts of hair on his cheeks — still visible beneath the visor of his helmet — glistened with perspiration. He looked frightened but also heroic. Despite the massed menace around him, keeping a lonely vigil, Sefton knew then what he had to do. He'd never really had a choice. 'Ladies and gentlemen,' he repeated, as he brought out his annotated copy of *Scoring* and held it before him. He looked hard into the television cameras and hoped they were working. He knew he wouldn't be given another go at this. It was distinctly a once only gesture, like taking a pot-shot at a president. He tried to remember in detail what his father had told him about tearing up a directory. How to ruffle up the pages, when to apply the pressure, where to begin the first rip.

So he didn't see, until he was almost upon him, Walter Sickert Fledwhite, pursued by six policemen, waving his arms in the air, and mouthing incomprehensible insults and allegations. He didn't even know that Fledwhite had been throwing things at him and missing until he became aware that all eyes and all cameras were on Sidewinder, who had gone down, an innocent bystander, under a hail of eggs and tomatoes and zucchini.

Those television stations which did not show the Assistant Director covered in salad and being led from the field, concentrated instead on the balletic movements of his assailant as he eluded a whole police force and delighted the crowd. What no one saw was Sefton Goldberg on the rostrum, wearing a blue and white blazer and holding the two halves of a novel, one in each hand.

Postscript

At an extraordinary meeting of the Fellowships Committee of Holy Christ Hall it was unanimously decided that the reputation of the University had already suffered sufficiently at the hands of structuralists and post- structuralists and even de-structuralists, and could do without the additional disquiet that a self-publicized hooligan was certain to cause. Walter Sickert Fledwhite received a thumb-marked postcard informing him of this decision. He didn't mind. Now that he had brought to his undoubted intellectual excellences a proven practical ability in the field, he was much sought after by international revolutionary organizations and local constituency reform groups alike. At the very least, a rosy future in the Labour Party was assured him.

As next in line, Ernest Weekley was approached by the fellows of Holy Christ Hall and after much consultation with his wife Olympia and the firm promise to her that he would not sit on any of the same committees or find himself alone in the same room as Helen Burns, he accepted the Disraeli Fellowship. Helen Burns herself grew tired of Cambridge life just about the time that Woolfardisworthy failed by a whisker to get that job at Canterbury. Her friends reported that she had suddenly lost all sense of purpose and had gone off to Poland where important things were happening; but whether it was to be the companion of Lech Walesa or General Jaruzelski, not one of them could say for sure. It was presumed that she was waiting for History to help her with her choice.

Naturally her position fell to Ernest Weekley and the Disraeli Fellowship was vacant once again. Weekley's choice was Gunnar McMurphy, but the Master, perhaps fearing for his marriage, put his foot down. 'Well that leaves only Goldberg,' Weekley said. 'Unless we re-advertise.'

'We haven't got the money to re-advertise,' Woolfardisworthy explained. 'And anyway he'd only re-apply.' The thought of receiving another letter of application from Sefton Goldberg was decisive. 'I'll drop him a note this afternoon.'

So Sefton Goldberg became Disraeli Fellow.

But he still hankered after greater fame, and he still had ambitions for his manuscript. Perhaps because of unemployment and recession these were good times for books about failure. Everybody seemed to want to read about channel swimmers who had dozed off in the water and mountaineers who had slipped half-way. A publisher had come to hear what Sefton was working on and asked to see it. Sefton waited, full of hope. But his manuscript was returned to him at last with an apologetic note. It suggested that Sefton had no real feeling for disappointment or deprivation. Perhaps success had spoiled him. If he wanted to know what the bitterness of defeat really felt like he should read the fine new novel that they themselves were publishing, by a lecturer from a polytechnic in the Midlands. They couldn't yet give him a title but they could tell him that the author's name was Peter Potter.

Queen Lucia
E.F. Benson

"We will pay anything for Lucia books."
NOEL COWARD: GERTRUDE LAWRENCE: NANCY MITFORD:
W.H. AUDEN

Queen Lucia is set in the middle-class, garden-party world of the 1920s, a society dominated utterly and ruthlessly by the greatest arch-snob who has ever existed. Lucia and her cohorts – Georgie with his dyed hair, embroidery, and piano duets, Daisy Quantock with her passion for the new and exotic – capture the mood and flavour of a whole period, and the nuances and rivalries of English life are described engrossingly and with a rapier wit.

If the pens of Evelyn Waugh and Jane Austen had mated, Lucia would have been the offspring.

"At long last, here she is again, the splendid creature, the great, the wonderful Lucia."
NANCY MITFORD

"My greatest reading pleasure in 1967 was the discovery of E.F. Benson's 'Lucia' novels . . . I enjoyed them so much that I borrowed (and was tempted to steal) two more of the series: and I confess myself a Lucia addict."
TERENCE DE VERE WHITE

"To describe her as a snob would be to describe Leonardo as a talented man."
MICHAEL MACLIAMMOR

0 552 99075 2 £2.95

BLACK SWAN

Lucia in London
E.F. Benson

"We will pay anything for Lucia books."
NOEL COWARD: GERTRUDE LAWRENCE: NANCY MITFORD:
W.H. AUDEN

Lucia, Queen of provincial society, now launches herself onto the London scene. The crème de la crème of social climbers, Lucia never falters as she dons her real (seed) pearls and prepares to attach the beau monde, wheedling her way into parties where she has not been invited and coaxing the rich and titled to come to tea.

Lucia in London is the second of the famous Lucia books by E.F. Benson. Comic masterpieces, these novels of manners are brought to life by sharp, satirical social observations and are as deliciously funny today as they were when first published in the 1920s.

"He was a master of a certain kind of light fiction, and he can delight even though one knows that his satire is ultimately friendly . . . He is clever and funny, but he writes for his victims."
THE SPECTATOR

"The flow of his comic inspiration never dwindles."
ELIZABETH HARVEY

"Here she is again, the splendid creature, the great, the wonderful Lucia . . . I must say I reopened these magic books after some thirty years with misgivings: I feared that they would have worn badly and seem dated. Not at all; they are as fresh as paint. The characters are real and therefore timeless."
NANCY MITFORD

0 552 99076 0   £2.95

BLACK SWAN

A New History of Torments
Zulfikar Ghose

"A splendid tale of the South American unknown, with
haunting and compulsive narrative drive."
JOHN FOWLES

Erotic, fantastic, sardonic, *A New History of Torments* is a
work of extraordinary imaginative scope by a writer at the
height of his powers – a novel which blends allegory and
thrilling action, illusion and disillusion, passion and suspense
into a rich adventure set in the South American jungle.

"Tremendous power and pace . . ."
SUNDAY TIMES

"Constantly surprising . . . A charming, sustained performance with a shocking but dramatically satisfying ending."
PUBLISHERS WEEKLY

"An exceptional novel."
TIMES LITERARY SUPPLEMENT

"An uncanny mixture of poetry and suspense. A fine novel."
EDNA O'BRIEN

"Marvellously exotic, wonderful adventures – a rare piece of
fiction indeed."
MICHAEL MOORCOCK

0 552 99046 9   £2.50

BLACK SWAN

Going to Meet
the Man
James Baldwin

"Stunning . . . sings with truth."
SATURDAY REVIEW

As a novelist, an essayist, and a playwright, James Baldwin
has proved himself to be a writer of beautiful prose. *Going to
Meet the Man* displays yet another facet of his talent: that of
short story writer. Running through this collection as a theme
is the role of inherited prejudice in shaping man's destiny.
The child in *Rockpile*, who can never be forgiven by his God-
fearing father for his illegitimacy; the child in *Sonny's Blues*,
who learns to understand his father through being told of the
death of an uncle he never knew; and, in a horrifying finale,
the man in *Going to Meet the Man*, whose hatred has its
roots in his boyhood, where his parents and other white
people watch with jubilation the mutilation and lynching of a
Negro 'criminal'.

0 552 99055 8   £2.50

BLACK SWAN

Go Tell It on
the Mountain
James Baldwin

"With vivid imagery, with lavish attention to details, Mr Baldwin has told his feverish story . . . Judicious men in their chairs may explain the sociology of guilt, and so explain Negro religion away. Mr Baldwin will not have it away. In this beautiful, furious novel, there are no such reductions."

THE NEW YORK TIMES

"Masterful . . . Baldwin's penetration is as valid as anything in William James's *Varieties of Religious Experience* and as moving as the interior monologues in Faulkner's *As I Lay Dying*."

SATURDAY REVIEW

"A work of such insight and authoritative realism that it brings into focus an experience of life that outsiders can have been aware of only dimly."

NEW YORK HERALD TIMES

0 552 99043 4 £2.50

BLACK SWAN

Lie Down in Darkness
William Styron

"Remarkable . . . one of the few completely human and mature novels published since the Second World War."
SATURDAY REVIEW OF LITERATURE

Lie Down in Darkness is William Styron's first novel, written when he was 25 years old: the story of a man who helps destroy the person he loves most . . . his daughter.

"It would be a disservice to Styron, and worse than meaningless in these times, to say that he has produced a work of genius. Only the sustained greatness of a richly productive lifetime still deserves that kind of praise. Yet one can say that he has produced a first novel containing some of the elements of greatness, one with which the work of no other young writer of 25 can be compared, and that he has done brilliant justice to the Southern tradition from which his talent derives."
NEW YORK TIMES

0 552 99064 7   £3.95

BLACK SWAN